ALL THE DOGS
OF EUROPE BARKED

ALL THE DOGS

OF EUROPE BARKED

DOGS

BARKED

JAN HOUGHTON LINDSEY

MILL CITY PRESS | MINNEAPOLIS

Mill City Press, Inc.
212 3rd Avenue North, Suite 290
Minneapolis, MN 55401
612.455.2294
www.millcitypublishing.com

This book is a work of historical fiction, but many places, incidents, names, and characters did exist, though not necessarily in the way they are portrayed here. Most of the book is the product of the author's imagination, and all of the characters and their dialogue are used fictitiously. Any resemblance to actual persons, living or dead, places, organizations, locales or events is purely coincidental.

Permission to use the title words and three quatrains from "In Memory of W. B. Yeats," printed in the *Collected Poems of W. H. Auden*, is granted by Random House, Inc.

ISBN-13: 978-1-938690-89-1
LCCN: 2012924083

Cover Design by Ross Patrick
Typeset by Jenni Wheeler

Printed in the United States of America

ACKNOWLEDGMENTS

There are many people who inspired me as I wrote this book, and I would be remiss if I didn't thank them.

First, there were my hundreds of students who eagerly soaked up the story of a gung-ho Nazi teenager who tries to reconcile the facts that his father is a Christian minister who opposes Hitler, his mother is a Jewish convert to Christianity, and he is a half-blood (*Mischling*), who worships Hitler. How he handles these conflicts as he grows into adulthood always left my students begging for more.

Special thanks go to my three daughters, Robin Young, Jenny Patrick, and Heidi Ziecker, who would not let me give up on this book until I got it published.

The book cover is the design of my son-in-law, Ross Patrick.

INTRODUCTION

On December 7, 1941, I was walking down a peaceful country road near Seattle, Washington, when a lady came running out of her house, waving her arms at me and yelling, "Little girl! Little girl! Get home quick! The Japanese have just bombed Pearl Harbor and they're on their way to bomb Seattle."

As a nine-year-old child, I had no idea who the Japanese were, or why they might want to bomb me, and I certainly had no idea where Pearl Harbor was, but the woman's frantic words sent me running for home in terror.

What I did not know then was that there were thousands of children on the other side of the world running in terror that same day, but for many of them, there were no homes left to run to and no safe arms of mothers and fathers waiting to comfort them. The world I had known was suddenly changed that Sunday morning, and so was I.

Years later, when I began teaching US and World History, I was appalled at how few of my students had any real knowledge of the horrors of World War II. So in my spare time I wrote a novel that would make those days come alive for them, and read it aloud in my classes. All these years later, whenever I see my former students, many still tell me it was their favorite book.

All The Dogs Of Europe Barked is much more than a boy's journey into manhood in one of the darkest times of history. Part romance, part historical drama, it will inspire you with the courage and sacrifice of ordinary people in extraordinary circumstances.

Jan Houghton Lindsey

"IN MEMORY OF W. B. YEATS"
by W. H. Auden

In the nightmare of the dark
All the dogs of Europe bark,
And the living nations wait,
Each sequestered in its hate.

Intellectual disgrace
Stares from every human face,
And the seas of pity lie
Locked and frozen in each eye.

In the deserts of the heart
Let the healing fountains start,
In the prison of his days
Teach the free man how to praise.

Europe, 1939

PART ONE

Germany
1938–1943

1

Berlin, 1938

"*Heil Hitler!*"

Paul Falkenhorst glanced up with a frown as his son raced in through the kitchen door, his arm raised in a rigid salute. That greeting always made Paul cringe, but it particularly galled him when it came out of the mouth of his eleven-year-old son, Kristopher. He shot a look of consternation at his wife, but she gave a quick little shake of her head and managed to force the semblance of a smile.

Paul gently pulled the boy's arm down. "You know we don't use that greeting in this house. A simple '*Grüss Gott*' or 'Hello, *Mutti* and *Vati*' will do just fine. Okay?"

Kristopher was breathing hard as he tossed his bookbag on the table. "I'm sorry, Vati. I forgot. Really I did, but I ran all the way home from my troop meeting to tell you and Mutti my wonderful news." A triumphant grin lit up his face. "I've been chosen to represent my *schar* at the Nuremberg Rally in September. Isn't that fantastic?"

Paul and Miriam looked at each other, but when neither of them smiled, Kristopher's face began to cloud. "What's wrong? I thought you'd be happy for me. I beat out all fifty boys in my schar."

Paul reached out and pulled Kristopher onto his lap. "We know how important your *Jungvolk* activities are to you, but Mutti and I have been praying very hard about this rally, and this isn't the way we thought

God would answer our prayers."

Kristopher jumped from his father's lap, glowering. "Why do you have to bring God into everything, Vati? You always do that."

Paul let out a surprised little laugh. "Well, I wouldn't be much of a minister—or father—if I didn't think God was interested in every part of our life. Now would I?"

"My leaders say we don't have to believe in God anymore if we don't want to."

"But *you* still believe in Him, I hope," his mother put in firmly.

Kristopher gave an exasperated sigh. "Of course I do, Mutti, but we're not going there to talk about God. This rally is to honor our beloved *Fuehrer*." His voice took on a slightly superior tone. "He says that God has chosen him to take care of us now."

The look on his parents' faces made it clear he'd gone too far, so he quickly added, "But I don't think he means that we don't need God at *all* . . . just that he's going to *help* God take care of us."

Paul cocked one eye at him. "Well, I'm sure God appreciates any help He can get," he said, "but right now you need to get your homework done because we've got something very special planned for tonight."

Kristopher's glum face brightened a little. "What?"

"Have you forgotten what today is?" his mother asked.

He gave her a questioning look. "What do mean? It's June 20th," he said, then suddenly slapped his forehead. "My gosh! It's my birthday! Why didn't you remind me this morning?"

"Because we're having a surprise party for you tonight, and we knew you'd pester us until we told you all about it," she said.

"Who's coming?"

"Some of your friends from school, and *Oma* and *Opa*," Paul said, then gave him a mysterious little grin. "And Opa has something that you've been wanting for a very long time."

Kristopher started to ask what it was, but Paul raised his palm to him. "That's all you're getting out of me. My lips are sealed."

"Please, Vati! Just a little hint."

Paul gave him a playful swat on the bottom. "You get upstairs and change out of that uniform, then get at your homework, or this party will be going on without its star."

Looking at his son as he scampered up the stairs, Paul had to smile. There were so many times lately when he wanted to wring that boy's neck, but he had to admit that Kristopher was so like he'd been at that age—tall, fair-haired, blue-eyed—and consumed with patriotic fervor. A perfect picture of Hitler's ideal Teutonic youth. No wonder the man wanted to clone millions of young Germans to be just like him.

✝ ✝

Miriam's parents, the Rosenbaums, arrived at the party early in order to hide the bicycle in the parsonage garage. It wasn't new—that would have been impossible to find in Berlin, and no Jew would have been allowed to buy one anyway. Instead, Josef had traded his gold watch to a friend for an old bike the man had stored in his garage. It had been badly abused, but Josef spent weeks straightening out all the dents, patching both tires, repairing the broken chain, sanding off the rust, and painting the whole thing a bright red.

By 7:15, all the children had arrived. Dieter Kraus and Rolf Mueller were in Kristopher's Jungvolk group. Marie von Falkenhorst was Kristopher's cousin, and Hannah von Kemp's father was an important German scientist and a member of Paul's Evangelical Free Church.

Kristopher felt a heady mixture of pride and superiority as he took center stage and bragged about how he'd been the only one from his schar selected to go to the Nuremberg Rally. He was exhilarated by the admiration and excitement that filled the room. Marie and Hannah clearly adored him, and Dieter hung on his every word. Rolf Mueller was the exception, standing apart with a smirk twisting his thin lips. Kristopher dismissed him as just being jealous because he hadn't been chosen to attend the rally.

When the cake had been consumed, and all the presents opened, Grandfather Rosenbaum excused himself for a few moments. The children began chattering excitedly, but stopped abruptly when he stuck his head into the living room, a broad grin lighting his face. "Close your eyes, Kristopher," he called.

Kristopher scrunched his eyes shut, but they popped open when he heard the gasps from the others. There, in the center of the room, stood the most beautiful red bicycle he had ever seen. He yelped with delight.

"Oh, Opa! How did you know that's just what I wanted?" He threw his arms around his grandfather, kissing the old man's down-turned face. "Thank you so much! Where did you get it?"

His grandfather gave him a wink. "Well, that will be my little secret, but it's all yours now, and you must take good care of it. It's very hard to find a bicycle these days."

Rolf Mueller had eyed the bike with envy from the moment it was brought in, and now listened intently to the conversation between Kristopher and his grandfather. "*Herr* Rosenbaum," he said, addressing the elderly man with an imperious tone, "I also would be *very* interested in knowing where you got this bike. I'm sure you know it's against the law for Jews to own one, and since you and Kristopher are both Jews, I feel it's my duty to report this to my father."

Kristopher's face darkened as he started to respond, but his grandfather held up his hand to him. "I'll handle this," he said. He turned to Rolf, his voice kind, but firm. "I traded something very precious of mine to get this for my grandson, who is even more precious to me. I only hope you have a grandfather who would do the same for you. And as for our being Jews, we're not ashamed of that, but Kristopher's mother converted to Christianity before he was even born, and his father is a minister, so as far as all of us are concerned, Kristopher is a Christian."

Rolf let out a caustic little laugh. "Well, we'll see what my father says about that, and we'll see how long Kristopher keeps that bike."

An uneasy atmosphere hung over the rest of the evening, and when the parents came to pick up their children, Paul was especially gracious to Rolf's father, Heinrich Mueller. As chief of the Berlin police, Mueller was not a man to antagonize.

Paul could not sleep that night. Rolf's blatant attack on Josef and Kristopher made him realize that his family was in more danger than he had realized. He needed to talk to his brother right away.

General Kurt von Falkenhorst was one of Germany's top generals, and well respected by Hitler and the High Command. When Paul called him the next day and told him what had happened, he urged Paul to immediately apply for an exemption to the 1935 racial laws for Miriam and Kristopher. Even though these laws already granted legal status to converted Jews who had married gentiles, and to their mixed-blood children, Kurt warned him that the men around Hitler were beginning to interpret these laws in the harshest way possible. Full-blooded Jews were being sent to labor camps on the flimsiest excuses.

Paul hired a high-powered attorney to apply for a reclassification of race for Miriam and Kristopher. It was not easy to get, but with Paul's military record in the Great War, plus a hundred years of von Falkenhorst officers leading German armies, Kurt felt that Miriam and Kristopher should qualify for special consideration.

Family history, and a very generous bribe from Kurt, eventually bought them German Blood Certificates, so they were safe, at least for now. Still, Kurt advised them that no one could predict how long the Nazis could be trusted to honor the certificates. They would need to stay alert, keep a low profile, and do a lot of praying.

But the Rosenbaums were another matter entirely. Josef Rosenbaum was a highly respected university professor, but had been dismissed a year earlier when the university purged all its Jewish professors. And now, with the arrest and deportation of so many Jews in the past few months, the old couple was in a very vulnerable position. It was almost certain that their magnificent old mansion would be confiscated, by someone in the Nazi hierarchy, and they would be sent to a labor camp unless Paul and Miriam could find some way to get them out of Germany, or take them in until they could.

It was times like this when Paul was thankful that he had such godly church deacons to pray with, so he called them together the next evening and laid these burdens before them. After much discussion and prayer, they all agreed it would not be good for Kristopher to attend the Nuremberg Rally, but they wanted more time to come up with a plan for the Rosenbaums' safety.

The next morning, Paul called the Hitler Youth headquarters to let them know that Kristopher would not be attending the five-day rally, but was told—in no uncertain terms—that there would be serious consequences if Kristopher were not allowed to attend. With the question of Miriam's parents still hanging over their heads, Paul could not draw any more unwanted attention to any of them, so he and Miriam reluctantly made the decision to let Kristopher go.

Kristopher immediately joined the other delegates from Berlin in preparing for the September rally. There were intricate marching drills and sports maneuvers to master, new patriotic songs to learn, and solemn oaths to memorize.

In the weeks that followed, Kristopher's time was consumed with these new activities most days after school and all day Saturday and Sunday, prompting Paul's concern that his son was losing touch with his family and church, but Kristopher assured him that these activities included religion, and showed him the prayer they had to memorize:

Dear Adolf Hitler, we believe in Thee. Without Thee we would be alone. Thou hast given us Thy name, Hitler Jugend, the most beloved name that Germany ever possessed. We speak it with reverence, we bear it with faith and loyalty. Thou canst depend upon us, Beloved Leader. Thou and the young millions can never by sundered.

When Paul pointed out that the prayer was addressed to Hitler, not God, Kristopher was unable to see the difference. That's when Paul realized how much his son's thinking had already been perverted by the Nazis.

Two months later, on a crisp September morning, Kristopher boarded his train at the Berlin railroad station—one of 800 trains from all over Germany that were carrying participants to the great 1938 Nazi Party Congress in the medieval city of Nuremberg. The platform was crowded with parents waving small Nazi flags, and women and children throwing flowers at their honored sons. Several bands added to the uproar, but in the midst of the joyful chaos, there were more than a few parents' faces that reflected their apprehension.

Kristopher leaned out the window of the train, trying to get one last look at his parents. He could not locate them in the crowd, but he did see Hannah von Kemp standing near the front, waving a small flag in his direction. Her face lit up as their eyes met, but he merely nodded at her. He had far more important things on his mind than girls.

As the train pulled out of the station, Kristopher settled back in his seat and looked around at the hundreds of other delegates. The train was filled with brown-shirted storm troopers; tall, broad-shouldered SS men in their black and silver uniforms; and hundreds of other uniformed Hitler Youth, all equally awed to be on their way to the great Nazi Party Congress. A delicious shiver went through him to be in such illustrious company.

He had never been away from home for five days, but he was determined not to get homesick. He loved his parents, but it was hard to understand why they were not as enthusiastic as he was about the wonderful things happening in Germany. He guessed that's what happened to people when they were so religious, and he swore to himself that he would never let that happen to him.

He was still angry about the incident that had happened at his birthday party a few months earlier when Rolf had accused him of being a Jew. In his mind there was no connection between his family and what his leaders were telling him about Jews. Although his mother and grandparents were *technically* Jews, they certainly weren't dangerous to

Germany, and they weren't self-serving money-grubbers or communists, nor were they physically or mentally inferior. His grandfather had been a professor at Berlin University for many years, and his father and mother had both graduated from the university with advanced degrees.

None of it made sense to him, but whatever it was that made Jews undesirable to the Nazis, he knew it didn't apply to his family. Still, he hoped that Rolf would keep his big mouth shut. He didn't want the others in his Jungvolk group to get any wrong ideas about him. He wasn't a Jew! He was a Christian!

When the train pulled into the station in Nuremberg late that afternoon, a wildly cheering crowd met it. Within minutes of leaving the train, Kristopher and the other delegates formed into marching units and headed down the main street to the campsite two miles away. All along the parade route, people were packed shoulder-to-shoulder, waving flags, shouting, and throwing flowers. A young girl ran up to Kristopher and handed him a flower, then kissed him on the cheek. He blushed a deep pink, but managed to keep a dignified look on his face. Dozens of bands blared at strategic locations along the way, and Kristopher felt that if that one day was all there was to the festival it would have been worth it just to be a part of such an unforgettable moment in history.

The first three days of the congress were filled with speeches extolling Germany's destiny as a super-race, and denouncing her enemies as bloodsucking leeches that had tried to bleed Germany dry ever since the Great War. The huge delegation of Hitler Youth was present at all the rallies, but Kristopher and his comrades secretly looked forward to the fourth day of the congress when they would have their moment of glory as the Fuehrer spoke to them alone.

The "Day of the Hitler Youth" began early in the morning with the thousands of youthful delegates marching into the stadium in a crisp precision drill. There were Hitler Youth bands, flag bearers, gymnastic and sports maneuvers, singing, and unison chanting. After several hours of performance, the delegates formed long lines the length of the stadium and stood at attention before the grandstand with its two huge stone swastikas rearing majestically under the great German spread-eagle.

An undercurrent of near hysteria gripped the children as they awaited the appearance of Hitler, but the silence was so profound that it was almost as though they were breathing in unison. Kristopher stood directly in front of the grandstand, faint from heat and patriotic fervor.

At last the moment came for which they'd all been waiting. Hitler stepped up to the podium. Smiling broadly as he looked over the waves of adoring faces, he gave a crisp salute, and instantly a deafening "*Sieg Heil*" shook the stadium three times as a sea of rigid arms shot toward him in passionate devotion.

Every eye devoured Hitler as he began to speak. His words were intimate and personal as he told them of his difficult childhood and of how so few of his family and friends had understood his great vision for Germany. His voice rose with growing emotion as he recounted all the evils committed against Germany by the other countries of the world, and then he quietly reminded them that they were Germany's only hope for restoring their Fatherland to the place of greatness and glory that was its rightful destiny.

He kept them mesmerized under a blazing sun for over three hours, but they remained at rigid attention. At the end of his speech, he paused a moment, letting his gaze sweep across the crowd, then dramatically lifted both arms in a victorious gesture and screamed out, "Never forget, my precious children, you will one day rule this world!"

The stadium erupted! Kristopher found himself sobbing and screaming, "Sieg Heil! Sieg Heil! Sieg Heil!" until he was hoarse. The scene was the same all around him, and in that moment he realized he would never be the same.

☩ ☩

When Kristopher returned from Nuremberg, his parents immediately saw the change in him. Gone was their happy, carefree eleven-year-old, and in his place was a rigid fanatic who barely tolerated their views.

"I have to guard every word I say around him or it throws him into a tirade," Miriam told Paul one afternoon as they waited for Kristopher to get home from school.

In a rare display of anger, Paul pounded the kitchen table. "My father would never have allowed me to talk to him the way Kristopher does to us. I'd have gotten a good thrashing, and if these were normal times, I'd thrash that boy till he couldn't sit down for a week!"

"But these aren't normal times," Miriam cautioned, "and God only knows who he'd tell if you laid a hand on him." She dabbed at her eyes with her handkerchief. "I just don't know what to do with him anymore. We can't ignore the awful things he's saying, but we don't dare discipline him for them, either. I feel so helpless."

Paul reached out and took her hands firmly in his. "We're not helpless, *Liebchen*," he said. "We put this child in God's hands when he was born, and that's where he's going to stay, whether he likes it or not!"

✢ ✢

Kristopher's life eventually settled back into its usual routine following his week at Nuremberg. Besides all his Hitler Youth activities, he was studying hard to qualify for entrance into the gymnasium next year. Fewer than ten percent of elementary students were able to qualify, but it was absolutely essential for anyone going on to the university. Luckily, Kristopher had never found schoolwork to be difficult. Besides German, he had a good grasp of English and French, thanks to his mother's insistence that no aristocratic German was really cultured without this language ability.

Although Hitler blamed much of Germany's problems on the aristocracy, Kristopher was secretly proud that the von Falkenhorsts were aristocrats. Everyone knew that Paul, and five generations of von Falkenhorsts, had been decorated military officers. Kristopher loved to hear his father tell of how the Great War had come along in 1916 when he was in the university, and he was commissioned as an officer and spent most of the next two years on the back of a horse in France, until a bullet from a British rifle ended his military career.

During the following year, Paul had been in and out of hospitals trying to save his leg, and it wasn't until 1919 that he was back on his feet, alive, but heartsick at Germany's loss and the loss of his parents to an English bomb.

At that point, the story always lost some of its excitement for Kristopher as his father would go on to tell how he'd seen enough killing and dying in those three years to know that a life in the military was not for him. What was needed now were men who would bring God's message of love and forgiveness to their shattered country, so after he graduated from the university, he'd gone to seminary to become a Christian minister—the first von Falkenhorst in over a hundred years to break with the family's military tradition.

Kristopher had no intention of breaking his family's military tradition, however. He had wanted to be a *Luftwaffe* pilot for as long as he could remember, but that desire could never become a reality until he passed his *Mutprobe*—the test of courage that every German boy must pass to get his dagger with "Blood and Honor" inscribed on the handle. His Mutprobe was set for the following Saturday when he would be required to jump from the Kaiserstrasse Bridge into the rushing water of the Spree River forty feet below.

By Saturday morning, Kristopher's nerves were as raw as the cold October weather. He, like the other forty-nine boys of his schar, stood shivering on the bridge, certain it was the temperature, and not his fear, that was causing his teeth to chatter.

Peering down at the depth below, Kristopher had great difficulty controlling the spasms convulsing his half-naked body, and he turned to the boy next to him with a forced bravado. "It doesn't look too far down to me, Willi. What do you think?"

"Nah, I don't think so, either," the boy stammered, wiping at the tears that kept escaping down his ruddy cheeks.

Just then, the first boy in line went over the railing and plunged downward, his bloodcurdling scream stopping abruptly as he pierced the icy water. When he surfaced with a look of triumph on his face, a cheer went up from the bridge and the group of spectators lining the bank.

"See, I told you there was nothing to it," Kristopher said, turning to Willi.

The shivering boy nodded, but couldn't seem to speak.

The pickup boat hauled the first boy in, and he stood dripping on the deck, a maniacal grin on his face as he waved wildly to those on the bridge.

A small flotilla of boats circled near the pickup boat, proud parents wanting to share in this triumphant moment in their sons' lives. Kristopher glanced at the riverbank and saw his parents huddled together for warmth, their eyes scanning the bridge for the sight of him. He wanted to wave to them, but was afraid the other boys might think him a sissy.

Boy after boy went over the railing. Some screamed as they fell, others pinched their noses and closed their eyes tightly as they hurtled through the air. So far, all who'd jumped had done so successfully and were standing, shivering and wet, on the boat. Kristopher felt his panic growing as it neared his turn. Willi was crying openly now.

Then Willi's name was called. He stood frozen to the spot, incapable of moving. Kristopher tried to shove him toward the railing, but he would not budge. "Come on, Willi," he hissed, "you don't want everyone to think you're a coward, do you?"

Kristopher finally got him to the railing and onto the other side of it, but Willi clung there, grasping the metal rails in a deathlike grip, and would not let go.

"What's going on here?" an angry voice demanded, as the fifteen-year-old *Scharfuehrer* pushed his way through the crowd of boys. His face was livid. "How dare you humiliate our schar with this cowardice?"

The Scharfuehrer tried to pry Willi's hands loose, but he would not let go. Snatching his dagger out of its sheath, the leader stabbed the back of the boy's hand. Willi fell backward, shrieking as he catapulted toward the water below. His body hit the side of the pickup boat, knocking him into the water. When he did not surface immediately, several of the boys on the boat jumped in and began searching for him. Minutes passed before they found him and dragged him on board, bloody and limp.

Kristopher watched the proceedings below in horror, seeing himself in his fallen comrade, and as he looked around, he saw that many of the others on the bridge were now crying openly. Suddenly he heard his name being called. He had never been so terrified in his life. He felt that if he could survive this test of courage, he would never be afraid of anything again.

As he was lifting his leg over the top bar of the railing, he heard an excited voice shouting at him from the riverbank and looked over and saw Hannah von Kemp waving frantically at him. Standing next to her was her father, Dr. Otto von Kemp, and he, too, was waving his encouragement.

Dr. von Kemp was an important scientist involved in the German space program, and definitely someone Kristopher wanted to impress if he ever hoped to get into the Luftwaffe. It was the spur he needed. He quickly pulled the other leg over the railing, raised both arms above his head and jumped.

An eternity passed before he hit the numbing water, and it seemed even longer before he clawed his way to the surface, gasping for air. A shout went up from the bridge and riverbank as his face emerged, a triumphant grin spreading from ear to ear. He had passed his test of courage.

When all the boys had made their jumps, they gathered, wet and shivering, on the riverbank, while their Scharfuehrer presented them with their coveted daggers. Kristopher was ecstatic that, from now on, no one could ever question his allegiance to the Party, and what it might demand of him, especially Rolf.

Hannah von Kemp had brought her father to see her friend's rite of passage, and they approached Kristopher and his family with beaming faces.

"Congratulations," said Dr. von Kemp, heartily shaking Kristopher's cold hand. "This is a proud day for you and Germany. With young men like you, this country's in good hands."

Von Kemp turned to Paul. "Pastor Falkenhorst," he said, reaching out amiably, "how proud you must be of Kristopher today. It's times like this that I'm sorry I don't have any sons."

Paul took his parishioner's outstretched hand. "It was very gracious of you to come today, Doctor. We're honored that you'd take your valuable time to share this experience with us."

"Nonsense! You've given so much to me and my family through your wonderful sermons that this is the least I can do." He gripped Kristopher's shoulder. "This is a very special young man you have here. I'll be interested in watching his progress. I have a feeling he's going to make us all very proud one day."

Hannah nodded shyly, her eyes gleaming with pride.

✠ ✠

During the next week at school, Kristopher and the other boys who had passed their Mutprobe were treated like heroes. The teacher singled him out for the honor of being the standard-bearer at the special inspection parade in front of their *Bannfuehrer*, Fritz Kissinger. After the ceremonies, Kissinger sought Kristopher out and shook his hand vigorously.

"We've had our eye on you, Falkenhorst, and we like what we see," Kissinger announced. He was only eighteen years old, but he handled himself with the confidence of one who knew the power he wielded. "If you continue to impress us with your devotion to the Party, you're destined for an important role in the New Order. Remember, we'll have our eye on you, so don't disappoint us. Heil Hitler!" He spun on his heels, dismissing a stunned Kristopher.

After school, Rolf Mueller approached Kristopher at the bike rack. They had hardly spoken since the night of his birthday party when Rolf had accused him of being a Jew, and Kristopher eyed him suspiciously now, as Rolf pulled him aside from the others.

"I have something I think you'd like to hear about," Rolf said. He lowered his voice and looked around furtively. "There's going to be a raid on some Communist businesses tonight, and my father told me to ask several of my trusted friends if they'd like to join us." A hint of a smile touched his mouth. "Of course, I thought of you right away, knowing your devotion to the Party and all the honors you've had recently. Shall I tell my father you'll come?"

Kristopher was caught off guard. He knew that Communists had to be dealt with firmly, but you could never tell what Rolf and his father might have in mind.

"I'll have to ask my father about it," Kristopher said.

"I wouldn't do that, if I were you," Rolf replied. "He may not feel the same way about Communists that we do."

Kristopher gave him a frown. "He doesn't like them any more than I do."

"Well, that's good, then," Rolf said. "He'll probably be glad to have you join us, but if you're coming, you need to be at my house by seven o'clock."

As Kristopher rode his bike home from school, he began to have some nagging questions about just what he might be getting himself into, but Rolf's father was a policeman, so surely he wouldn't let them do anything that was wrong.

All through dinner, he struggled with whether to tell his father about it, but he had a feeling he wouldn't be allowed to go if he did, so he avoided saying anything until they'd nearly finished eating. When he could put if off no longer, he mentioned that Rolf needed help with a project for the Jungvolk, and wanted him to come over and help him.

Paul glanced up. "After the way he talked to you and Opa at your party, I didn't think you'd want to have anything more to do with him."

"We're not friends," Kristopher said, "but we are in the same Jungvolk group, so I have to work with him on projects whether I like it or not."

Paul thought for a moment, then said, "Well, I suppose it's all right if you're home before curfew."

"I will be," Kristopher said. He grabbed his jacket and got out of there as quickly as he could.

2

Heinrich Mueller had a swarthy, pockmarked face, deepset eyes, and oily black hair, the complete antithesis of what Kristopher had been taught about the fair-haired, blue-eyed Aryan race. Rolf liked to brag about how his father had joined the brown-shirted SA in 1931 and risen in the Party until he got the job as chief of the Berlin police department, but Kristopher knew he'd really been a butcher most of his life, and he felt uncomfortable around such uncouth people. They were just the kind of lower-class Germans that gave the Party a bad name among aristocrats like his parents. Nevertheless, he felt a keen sense of importance in having been asked to participate in the activities tonight.

When he arrived at the Mueller's home, several large flatbed trucks loaded with bricks were parked in front of it. Laughter and loud voices echoed from the house as Rolf let him in. Kristopher was surprised to see it filled with uniformed SS, as well as numerous *Gestapo* agents and several of the boys from his Jungvolk unit. All the adults held beer steins in their hands and were in high spirits. Mueller was just finishing his address to the group.

"All right, men," he bellowed drunkenly, "we all know it's time we taught those dirty Commies that there's no place for them in Germany. If they won't clear out on their own, we'll give 'em a little shove." He stumbled toward the door and the others followed him out, waving their steins in the air and cheering raucously.

When they got to the trucks, a young SS officer boosted Kristopher up onto the back of one of them, spilling beer on him as he did so. Kristopher felt his blood begin to race as the trucks took off, the men singing at the top of their lungs. It was a heady experience being part of such an elite group, and even though he was a little apprehensive about what they might be planning, he was eager for the excitement that awaited them.

As his truck pulled up to the curb on Detmolderstrasse, everyone jumped down. The streets were fairly empty, but here and there a few late shoppers were heading home, their collars pulled up against the cold evening air. Most hurried along as they saw the men with their ax handles and bricks, obviously bent on trouble.

Yellow Stars of David and the word *Juden* painted on the stores made it easy to spot the Jewish businesses. The men began smashing storefront windows and throwing merchandise into the streets. Some stuffed their pockets, setting fire to the rest of the goods. Since it was after closing hours, none of the shops appeared to have shopkeepers in them, so the men went about their destruction without interference.

Kristopher had been dragging bricks from the front of his truck and handing them to the others at the back, so he didn't see that they were only targeting Jewish shops until Rolf came running up to the truck, breathing hard. "I haven't seen you throw any bricks yet," he challenged Kristopher. "You scared of a few old Communists or worried about messing up the shop of one of your relatives?"

Infuriated by Rolf's taunt, Kristopher impulsively grabbed a brick in each hand and jumped from the truck, racing down the street until he found one store that still had an unbroken window. He pulled back his arm and was about to throw a brick when the elderly proprietor hobbled out the front door, frantically waving a cane in the air. Wisps of thin grey hair stuck out in disarray from his pink scalp, and his eyes were wide with terror as he screamed at them.

Seeing Kristopher, he stopped abruptly. "I know you!" he shouted, pointing the cane directly at him. "You're that preacher's son my boy used to go to school with. He used to be your friend. What a horrible boy you are! Go home right now, or I'll tell your father about this."

Panic seized Kristopher. *What if the old man told his father?* Before he had time to think, he threw a brick at the shopkeeper, hitting him on the side of the head. The old man dropped to the ground amid the broken glass, blood pouring from a gash above his ear, plastering the thin hair to his scalp like a bright red pomade. Kristopher stared down at him in horror.

Rolf raced up, followed by several SS men who examined the fallen man. "Good work!" Rolf exclaimed, slapping Kristopher on the back. "You got the first Jew tonight. My father will be delighted to hear this."

Nausea swept over Kristopher. He snapped his head around and gave Rolf a look of pure hate, then suddenly bolted down the street as fast as he could run. He did not stop until he'd run the ten blocks to Rolf's house. He grabbed his bicycle and peddled furiously toward home, hot tears nearly blinding him.

When he reached his house, he could see through the window that his parents were waiting for him at the kitchen table, and he knew he'd be in big trouble if they saw him like this, so he stealthily let himself in the front door and tiptoed up to his room. He undressed as quietly as he could, but as he stepped out of his uniform, his dagger fell out of its sheath and hit the floor with a loud noise.

Kristopher turned toward the door as he heard his parents' footsteps on the stairs. "Oh, no!" he groaned.

He tried to kick his rumpled clothes under his bed as his parents came into the room, but Paul reached down and picked them up. He grimaced as he sniffed at them. "What's going on here? Why do your clothes smell like beer?"

Kristopher stared into his father's angry eyes, hesitated for a moment, then burst into tears and threw himself into his father's arms. Paul held him until his sobbing stopped, then asked him again what had happened. There was no way he could tell his father the truth, so he told him that Rolf had tried to get him to drink some of his father's beer, and when he said he didn't do that sort of thing because he was a Christian, Rolf had thrown the beer at him and said he wasn't a Christian at all—he was just a dirty Jew trying to pass himself off as a Christian.

Miriam turned to Paul in a fury. "I told you that boy would be trouble for Kristopher. I don't ever want him doing anything with Rolf again." She knelt down in front of her son and wiped his tears. "You are a Christian, but you're also part Jewish, and you don't ever need to be ashamed of that. You can be both. Many Germans are."

"Then why does Rolf keep saying I'm not a Christian?" he sniffled.

"He's just saying what he's heard his father say."

Kristopher pulled his pajama bottoms on and sat on the edge of the bed. "How can people tell if you're a Jew? Is there some kind of test?"

"Of course not," Miriam said, "but some people believe you're a Jew if you've got a Jewish mother, and others think it has to do with whether you practice the Jewish religion or not. In my case, Oma and Opa didn't make a big thing out of us being Jews, so I didn't either, and then I fell in love with Vati, and he was a Christian, and I gradually came to believe what he does about Jesus, and now I'm a Christian. I know some people don't think you can be a Christian and a Jew at the same time, but I know you can, because I am. And so are you."

Kristopher began to yawn and Miriam stood up and pulled the covers back for him. "You need to get to sleep now," she said, "but we'll talk about this again. There're going to be a lot of challenges to what you believe in the days ahead, and I want you to have a clear understanding about where you fit into all this. Okay?"

Kristopher let his parents tuck him in and kiss him goodnight, but after they left, his thoughts were too tormented by what he'd done for him to sleep. He'd never lied to them before, and he knew they'd hate him if they found out what he'd done to that old Jew. Especially if the man died. Oh, God! He couldn't think of that. How had he gotten himself into such a mess?

✝ ✝

22

When Kristopher arrived at school the next morning, he knew he'd have to find Rolf immediately and shut him up before he told everyone about what had happened, and someone reported it to his parents.

Walking from the bike rack toward his class, he noticed several groups of students staring at him. He was obviously too late. Rolf had blabbed the whole thing to everybody.

He took his seat in the noisy classroom, and Herr Brewer called for order. Kristopher sat rigid, not knowing what to expect. The teacher tapped smartly on his desk for attention, and Kristopher heard his name being called.

"Falkenhorst! I want you and Mueller up here. Now!"

As he slowly stood, his mind was casting about for an alibi about how and why he'd participated in the night's activities. Keeping his eyes straight ahead, he walked to the front of the room. The teacher put a hand on the shoulder of each of the boys, then turned them toward the class.

"I want you to look at these two boys, here," he said proudly. "They're an example of what the New Order is all about. Last night they risked their lives to help defend our country against the Communist Jews who are trying to take it over. We're so proud to have young men like this in our school. I hope they'll be an inspiration to all of you."

Kristopher was dumbstruck as his classmates thundered their applause, and, at recess, a crowd of admirers surrounded him, asking for all the gory details of last night. The more he told his story, the more of a hero he felt himself to be, until by the end of the day all guilt about the old man he'd hit was gone.

But, as he rode his bike home after school, Kristopher began to worry that his parents might have heard about what had happened, and somehow connect him to it, and as soon as he entered the kitchen, he saw from the look on their faces that they knew.

Paul was furious as he ordered Kristopher to sit down at their kitchen table. "Where were you last night?" he demanded. "And this time I want the truth!"

Kristopher sat at the table and crossed his arms defiantly. "I told you where I was. I was working on a Jungvolk project with Rolf. What more do you want to know?"

Paul shoved a newspaper in front of him. "Read this!"

Kristopher began reading, and as he did so, the smirk on his face slowly vanished. The raid he'd been involved in was part of an organized uprising all over Germany, and over 7,500 Jewish shops had been vandalized, along with several hundred synagogues destroyed. Hundreds of Jewish homes had been burned to the ground, and about 180 Jews had been killed, with dozens more seriously wounded. The article said nothing about this raid being directed toward Communists. Jews had obviously been the target.

His hands trembled slightly as he pushed the paper back to his father. It was one thing to break the windows of a few Communists in your own neighborhood, but quite overwhelming to think of thousands of Jewish shops and synagogues destroyed, and so many people killed. Suddenly he wasn't so proud of his participation in the night's events, and he felt real pangs of guilt about the old man he'd hit with the brick.

"Now, we want the truth about where you were last night," Paul demanded. "*Frau* Epstein was here this morning to tell us that her husband was struck in the head with a brick after some hoodlums had wrecked his tailor shop. He was very seriously hurt, and he said it was *you* who threw the brick at him. Is that true?"

Kristopher looked down, unable to meet his father's accusing gaze.

Paul reached over and jerked the boy's chin up. "Answer me, Kristopher! Was it you?"

Kristopher pulled back from his father's hand. "He isn't dead, is he? Why are you making such a big thing out of it?"

Paul lunged across the table and grabbed his son's neck scarf, nearly lifting him out of the chair. "Because your grandfather was beaten up so badly last night by a bunch of thugs—just like you—that he may never walk again! Isn't that worth making a big 'thing' out of it? Answer me! Isn't it?"

He thought his father was going to choke him. *That couldn't be true! Not dear, sweet Opa!* "Why would anyone beat up Opa? He's not a Communist."

"And neither is Herr Epstein, you little hooligan! Or your grandmother or mother. Is that what you want? All the Jews in Germany beaten up or killed because your leaders say they're Communists?"

Paul let go of Kristopher's scarf and sank back in his chair.

Kristopher rubbed his neck as tears began to trickle down his cheeks. "If they're not Communists, why does everybody say they are?"

"*Everybody* doesn't say they are. It was only when Hitler wanted to get rid of all the Jews that he began calling them Communists because he knew that would turn the Germans against them."

"But, my teacher says that Jews . . ."

Paul cut him off with a slash of his hand. "I don't want to hear one more thing that your teacher says about Jews. You're a lucky young man to have a wonderful mother like you've got, and it's time you realized that."

Kristopher turned to his mother. "I know she's wonderful. I just wish everybody would stop saying there's something wrong with her because she's a Jew."

Miriam reached out and took his hand. "Then you need to remind them that some of the greatest people who ever lived were Jews—people like Mendelssohn and Freud and Einstein and Jesus—so that puts me in very good company."

That night, as Kristopher lay in bed, going over everything that had happened and all the things his parents had said, he came to a definite decision: there was no way he was ever going to let his grandparents or mother be treated like he had treated old Herr Epstein. He would march and drill and plant trees and clear rubble from the streets and go on overnight hikes and work on nearby farms, and milk cows and shovel horse manure from the armory stables—whatever his leaders asked him to do—but he was never again going to harass another Jew.

He would simply make himself so valuable to the Jungvolk that, in spite of this decision, they'd see they couldn't do without him. As he drifted off to sleep, he congratulated himself that he had found the perfect solution to his problem.

3

1938–1939

Christmas, that December of 1938, had not been as festive as many in the past, but despite the shortages, the Falkenhorsts managed to have a small goose on the table and a few presents. When Kristopher was asked to play Joseph in the church's Christmas pageant, he told his father he was too old for that, but when he saw the performance, he'd had to admit that he was a little sorry he hadn't taken part when he saw how beautiful Hannah von Kemp was again, as Mary.

Kristopher didn't have time to think about girls, though. As 1939 unfolded, his days were too filled with all his duties. He and his comrades went all over the city delivering call-up notices to new Army recruits. They combed the countryside on Saturdays, gathering scrap metal for recycling; every Sunday there was a rally or parade; and now that he was twelve and had been promoted to *Jungenschaftsfuehrer* with ten boys under his charge, he had his hands full trying to whip them into shape.

But the activity that excited Kristopher the most was the overnight war games between his schar and the neighboring schars. They usually camped out in the woods on the outskirts of Berlin and one side would be the Germans and the other would be the enemy. They were already being instructed in the use of weapons in their weekly Jungvolk meetings, so it was a thrill to go into battle with real rifles, even though they had no bullets. As a junior leader, Kristopher got to help plan battle strategy, and he was proving himself to be a born military strategist. There were always older leaders from the larger *Gefolgschafts* and *Banns* who observed these games, looking for natural leaders, and Kristopher had been earmarked as just that.

But, busy as he was, he couldn't help noticing that the things being done to Jews were getting worse. A law was passed levying outlandish taxes on all Jews, and a Jewish Community Bureau was set up where Jews were required to register any property and wealth they possessed. They had already been stripped of citizenship rights, including police protection and the right of trial, and their passports had been taken from them. They had been excluded from all public schools as students or teachers, their marketing hours had been limited to the one hour between four and five o'clock when all the good produce was already picked over, and they were forbidden to use public transport. They could no longer attend the theaters or concerts. Their synagogues had been desecrated and their shops vandalized, and now this new law gave Reichsminister Hermann Goering the right to seize any Jewish property without compensation or legal recourse.

Kristopher began to worry about his grandparents' home. He'd grown up playing in the tree house Opa had built for him in the huge oak in his back yard, and the thought of them losing their beautiful old home really worried him.

In August, his fears materialized when the Gestapo confiscated the Rosenbaum's home in the Nikolassee District. They were given one week to show up at the train station for deportation to a labor camp in Poland.

That evening, the Rosenbaums came to the parsonage to see if they could stay there for a few days until they could figure out what to do. Kristopher was outraged that their home had been taken from them. "They can't just take your house without paying for it," he told Opa. "We won't stand for that, will we, Vati?"

Paul shook his head. "There's nothing we can do about it, but we certainly can make a place for them here with us so they won't have to go to a labor camp."

Tears were close to Josef's eyes as he thanked Paul and Miriam for their willingness to put themselves in such danger. He looked over at Rachael with a sad smile. "Mutti's heartbroken to leave all the lovely treasures we've gathered in our travels over the years, but I've told her we don't need those things to make us happy. All we need is each other and the three of you." He gave a hollow little laugh. "I've always told her she's a terrible packrat, anyway."

Rachael tried to smile at his attempt to lighten the moment. "You've been worse than I," she said. "You never met a samovar you couldn't live without."

"Guilty, as charged," he said, then tears popped unbidden into his eyes, and he reached up and wiped at them with the heel of his hand. "What a baby I'm being about all this," he added, flipping his hand out in a dismissive gesture. "Let them have the place and everything in it. Maybe it'll give those uncouth savages a little culture. They certainly need it."

Kristopher threw his arms around Oma and Opa and clung to them, crying.

The parsonage had two bedrooms on the second floor, plus a small study, so Kristopher volunteered to sleep on the sofa in his father's study and give his room to his grandparents.

He and Opa helped Paul build a false wall three feet in from the back wall of his bedroom. They put a small trap door in it down close to the floor, and Miriam wallpapered the new wall and door to match the rest of the room. Obviously it could not be used for any length of time, but it would do in an emergency if the Gestapo came looking for the Rosenbaums, something they all prayed would not happen.

☦ ☦

By September of 1939, the open persecution of Berlin's Jews had become so intense that it was extremely dangerous for a Jew to show himself in public. Since the Rosenbaums had moved in with them, Paul had tried to stay in touch with some of their closest friends, but now he had to stop any further contact with those who were still in their homes. It was simply too dangerous.

One night, early in October, after everyone in the Falkenhorst home had gone to bed, a quiet but persistent knocking on the front door woke the entire household. Thus far, the Rosenbaums had not had to hide, but when the knocking continued, Paul insisted that the old couple get into the hiding place.

He quickly shoved the armoire aside and they crawled into the narrow enclosure, then Paul pushed the armoire back in place. Miriam raced into the study and led Kristopher, half-asleep, into his old room and put him in his bed. She returned to her bed as Paul went down to answer the door. He pulled aside the curtain next to the door and looked out. It was impossible in the dark to tell who was there.

"Who's there?" he called.

"We're friends of the Rosenbaums," a man's voice came back at him.

Paul's heart pounded as he tried to decide what to do. It was very likely these were Gestapo agents posing as worried friends, since these late night calls were their favorite method of trapping people, but if these really were friends of the Rosenbaums, they were obviously Jews in some kind of trouble, and if that was the case, there was no way he could just callously turn them away.

"Dear God, You must protect us," Paul prayed as he opened the door a crack.

There in the darkness stood an elderly man and woman. The man was holding a scuffed leather suitcase in one hand, and a Homburg hat in the other. His clothing was rumpled and dirty, but obviously expensive. The woman's gray hair was partly covered with a brown cloche, and her beige woolen suit looked as though she'd been sleeping in it, but even with that, she had an air of class about her, emphasized by a fur shawl flung jauntily around her shoulders and bright rouge on both cheeks. None of this could disguise her exhaustion, though.

Paul scrutinized them cautiously through the partially open door. "What can I do for you?" he asked.

"I'm Daniel Lieberman, and this is my wife Ruth, and we're so sorry to come at this hour, but we didn't know where else to turn." The man clutched his hat to his chest. "We heard that the Rosenbaums are here with you, and hoped you might be able to give us a place to stay for the night."

The man's desperation seemed sincere to Paul, but he was still not convinced that they were not Gestapo.

"You're mistaken about my wife's parents being here," Paul said, watching closely for their reaction. "We haven't seen nor heard from them for months, but if you'd like to leave me your name, I'll be glad to tell them you were looking for them if we should hear from them."

The shivering old couple looked crestfallen, but it was obvious they understood what the pastor was trying to say. The man turned to the woman beside him. "I think we've made a mistake, Liebchen. The Rosenbaums are obviously not here." He reached out and shook Paul's hand, then placed the limp Homburg back on his head. "Please tell Josef and Rachael that the Liebermans were inquiring after them, and we wish them God's protection in all their trials."

The man took the old woman's arm and turned to leave. As he did so, he nodded toward the bicycle chained to the porch, and turned back to Paul. "I see Josef's grandson got his bicycle. I hope he's enjoying it. I know what pleasure it gave Josef to get it for him."

Paul reached out and grabbed the man's arm. "How did you know my son's grandfather gave him that bicycle?"

The man seemed embarrassed. "Because I'm the one who sold it to him. He traded me a gold watch for it." He paused momentarily. "It really wasn't a fair trade, you know. The bicycle was badly abused, and the watch was much more valuable, but Josef wanted it so badly for your son's birthday, and the watch was all he had to trade for it. I've been ashamed that I took such advantage of him."

This was enough to convince Paul that the Liebermans were genuine, and he quickly ushered them into the house.

Miriam had come to the top of the stairs, fearfully clutching at her robe. "Who is it, Paul?" she called down.

He looked up at her. "It's all right, Miriam. They're friends of your parents who need a place to stay for the night, and I've invited them to stay with us. Come down and meet them."

She came down immediately.

"This is Daniel Lieberman and his wife Ruth. Daniel's the gentleman who sold Kristopher's bicycle to your father."

Miriam embraced them both. "You must be exhausted. Let me fix you something hot to drink."

Ruth Lieberman glanced up at her husband with obvious embarrassment, and he put his arm around her thin shoulders. "We'd be very grateful for a little bite to eat, if it isn't too much bother," he said. "We haven't had anything for several days."

"Oh, dear God!" Miriam exclaimed. "Here, you sit down while I heat up the soup we had for dinner." She started to open the refrigerator, when she suddenly straightened up with a little cry. "Paul! I forgot about Mutti and Vati! Can you get them out, while I warm this food up?"

Paul hurried upstairs and got Kristopher back onto the sofa, then moved the armoire away from the trap door. As the Rosenbaums crawled out, Paul could see they wouldn't be able to take much of this.

He told them about the Liebermans. "Miriam's fixing them something to eat, but we'll bring them up the minute they're through."

When the Liebermans had finished eating, Paul and Miriam helped them up the stairs. Rachael burst into tears when she saw her old friend. Ruth had always been an elegant woman who'd never worn anything but designer clothes from Paris and Milan, and had an extravagant collection of furs and jewels, yet here she stood, clutching this bedraggled fur around her shoulders, her hair flat and greasy, and reduced to begging for charity from strangers. *How could such a thing happen to someone like her?*

"Tell us what happened to you," Rachael said, reaching for Ruth's hand.

Ruth slumped down on the bed, fighting back her tears. "I'll let Daniel tell you. I'm too traumatized to remember everything we've been through."

Daniel patted her shoulder, then turned to Josef. "I know you understand, Josef. The same thing happened to you at the university."

"Siemens fired you?"

Daniel nodded, then chuckled in an attempt at humor. "I'm their top engineer for forty years, and suddenly they notice I'm a Jew? *Oy Vey!*"

"They obviously took your home, too," Josef said.

"Yes, about a month ago. We've been staying with various friends since then. We're trying to get to Munich where we have family and another home, but the Gestapo nearly caught up with us a week ago, and we've been hiding in a boxcar in a railroad siding ever since."

Ruth looked over at Rachael. "We'd heard you were staying with your daughter, and Daniel knew where her church was, so I told him if you'd already left, we'd just hide in the church. But he said, 'No, we're not vagabonds. We'll come to the pastor's door like any civilized person and throw ourselves on his Christian mercy.'" She turned up the palms of both hands toward Rachael. "So here we are, old friend, a little worse for the wear, but we're still alive."

Rachael pulled her into her arms. "And we're going to do all we can to help you stay that way, too," she said. "My daughter doesn't have much room, but you can have our bed for tonight and we'll sleep on the sofa with Kristopher. Is that okay, Miriam?"

"Of course," Miriam responded. "We're certainly not sending you back out to those jackals."

"All we need is a night or two to get some rest and get cleaned up, and we'll be glad to pay anything you want," Daniel said, holding out a handful of diamonds he'd just taken from inside his jacket.

Paul gave him an indignant wave of his hand. "Put those away!" he said. "This home belongs to the Lord, and if you're in need, then you're welcome here, at least until we can find someone who has more room for you. No one in need will ever be turned away from this house or my church."

After everyone had gone to bed, Paul lay awake a long time—thinking and praying—little realizing the price those words to the Liebermans would one day cost him. When he had first entered the ministry, he had told God that he would do anything He wanted him to, but in his wildest dreams he never envisioned that that promise would bring him to this critical moment of decision. But, here it was, and he could not shrink from it. If he didn't do what he knew to be the right thing, regardless of the consequences, then all his preaching had simply been empty, meaningless words.

The next evening, he called his deacons together at his office in the church. He watched each man as he came in and took his place around the oval table. These men were the cream of Berlin's business and cultural community. They were hard-nosed and successful in their work, and earnest and compassionate in their faith. No minister had ever had a Godlier group of men to work with.

Paul stood before them and poured out his heart. "Brothers, we've all seen what was coming with Hitler's treatment of the Jews, and we've talked about our responsibility, as Christians, to them. We've said we'd be willing to do whatever is necessary to give them our help." He paused and looked intently into the face of each man. "Well, that time has come, dear brothers. I have an elderly Jewish couple who came to us last night who need a place to hide for a few days. Is there anyone here who can take them in?"

There was an awkward pause as the men looked back and forth at one another, then a hand cautiously went up. Paul said nothing, just nodded at the man. Then another hand was raised, and then another. Within moments, all the hands were in the air.

It was difficult for Paul to speak, but when he found his voice, he stood unashamedly before them, fighting back his tears. "I'm reminded of the words of our Lord Jesus when He said, *'In as much as you have done it unto the least of these, My brothers, you have done it unto Me.'*"

4

1940–1941

As if nature itself was in rebellion against the madness in Germany, the winter of 1939 and 1940 was the harshest ever on record in Europe. The Rhine and Elbe Rivers were frozen solid for months, as were the many lakes and rivers surrounding Berlin, but not even this hardship could dampen the spirits of the Germans as they rejoiced over Germany's *blitzkrieg* of Poland. The Nazi news media had convinced the citizens that Germany could no longer tolerate the hostile acts of the Poles against the Fatherland, and German armed forces had been forced to neutralize that eastern threat to Germany's security.

There were some Germans, however, who saw the Nazi takeover of Poland as a brazen violation of another country's sovereignty. General Kurt von Falkenhorst was a member of a small group of German military officers and distinguished citizens who believed that Hitler's blatant takeover of Poland would bring the wrath of all Europe, England, and America down on Germany. So it had been no surprise to these men when England and France declared war on Germany following the Polish invasion. General von Falkenhorst found himself having to participate in Germany's offensive against these two great countries, and it galled him. He had spent two years at Oxford following the Great War, and was married to a former English actress, Lady Jeanne Hereford—a beautiful distant cousin of Winston Churchill—and he knew the English were no more interested in war than he was.

Having tasted of such easy pickings as Austria, Czechoslovakia, and Poland without English and French interference, in the spring of 1940 Hitler laid plans to invade Denmark, Norway, Holland, Belgium, Luxembourg, and France.

All the Scandinavian countries had remained neutral in the Great War, and now that Hitler's war machine was grinding its way across Europe toward them, they again proclaimed their neutrality. Consequently, Norway was completely unprepared for the German blitz that hit her shores on April 9, 1940. With British and French help, she held off the German invaders for two months before capitulating to their superior power. Norway had become another statistic in Hitler's blitzkrieg of Europe. The German general who was forced to lead this offensive and receive the Iron Cross First Class for this repugnant victory was General Kurt von Falkenhorst.

✠ ✠

The officer who stood at the parsonage door that glorious June day of 1940 was resplendent in his long black tunic with its silver trim, black jodhpurs tucked neatly into glistening black knee boots. The two lightning bolts on his right collar with the three oak leaves on the left, identified him immediately to Miriam as an SS officer. She had seen him approach the parsonage and quickly gotten her parents into the hiding place, but was breathing hard as she answered the door.

"Heil Hitler," the officer said, his right arm shooting out toward her.

She pulled the door shut behind her and managed a weak salute as she muttered, "Heil Hitler. How can I help you?"

The officer was holding an envelope in his hand. "Is this the home of Reverend Paul Falkenhorst?" he asked.

"Yes, but if you want my husband, he's in his office over in the church."

The man looked disdainfully toward the church. "That won't be necessary. I have an official letter for him, but I can leave it with you."

He handed the envelope to her in his white gloved hand, and her heart pounded even harder as she saw the official seal of Hermann Goering, Minister of War. "I'll just take this over to him right now," she said. "It looks important."

She started to move past him, but he slipped an arm around her waist and pulled her to him. "Nice! Very nice," he said. "What's a beautiful woman like you doing married to a preacher?"

"Take your hands off me!" she exclaimed, jerking back.

"Not even a little kiss for a lonely officer?" he asked plaintively.

"Absolutely not! You should be ashamed of your behavior!"

She pushed past the startled officer and marched across the lawn to the church, praying her legs would not give out under her. Behind her she could hear the SS officer's arrogant laugh.

Paul was at the pulpit in the front of the church and looked up with a smile as Miriam hurried down the aisle toward him. When he saw the look on her face, he left the pulpit and rushed to her. "What is it?"

Paul was furious as she told him of her encounter with the SS officer; furious at the filthy swine who dared to lay a hand on his wife, and furious at his inability to do anything about it. He had been doing his best to keep a low profile since his church had become involved in its rescue of Jews. Over the past ten months they had found homes for dozens of Jews and had entered the names of many more onto the baptismal records of the church, but as much as he'd like to report the officer, he simply could not draw that kind of attention to himself.

Miriam was still shaking when she handed him the letter. "What do you suppose this is, Paul?"

He tore the envelope open and quickly read it, then relief spread across his face. "Thank God! It's only an invitation to a reception at the Reichstag in honor of those officers being awarded the Iron Cross. Kurt is getting his."

Miriam's face tensed. "Do you thnk it's wise for us to go?"

"I don't think we have any choice. We'd draw more attention to ourselves by not going now that we've gotten this special invitation."

"But what about Mutti and Vati?" she said, then let out a little cry.

"Oh no! They're still in the hiding place. I've got to get them out."

"Do you need my help?" Paul called as she raced up the aisle.

"No. I can manage it."

When she got to her parents' room, she shoved the armoire aside and opened the small door. Her father's flushed face peered up at her. "Mutti's fainted," he panted.

Miriam pulled him out, then crawled in and got her arms around her mother, carefully backing out until she'd gotten her through the small opening. She and Joseph got Rachael onto the bed and Joseph undid her blouse while Miriam ran for some water and wet towels. By the time she got back, Rachael had regained consciousness and was looking up at the two of them in confusion.

"Did I faint?" she asked.

"Yes," Joseph replied. "It was just too hot in there." He held her head up and gave her a sip of water.

Miriam knelt beside the bed and began wiping her mother's face and arms with the damp cloths. "You gave us a terrible scare, Mutti."

Rachael reached up and patted her daughter's cheek. "Wipe that worry off your face, Liebchen. I'll be just fine. Was everything all right at the door?"

"Yes," Miriam said. "I took care of it. Everything's fine now."

Rachael gave her daughter a knowing look. "You can't fool your mother," she said. "Everything isn't fine, is it?"

Miriam's eyes teared as she drew her mother's once-graceful hands to her lips and kissed them. "It's so wrong for you and Vati to be treated this way," she said. "Neither one of you has ever done anything but make this world a better place, and this vile treatment is what you get for it. It's so unfair."

Rachael reached up and wiped at a tear that had escaped down Miriam's cheek. "Jews are no strangers to suffering, Liebchen. We aren't the first and we won't be the last."

This was small comfort to Miriam as she put her arms around her mother, and wept.

✛ ✛

All day, the Deutschlandsender had been broadcasting the news through the streets of Berlin that June 22, 1940, was a day to remember. Paris had fallen to the Germans. There was a holiday mood in Berlin as total strangers embraced each other, laughing over the irony of Hitler's demand that the French sign their surrender in the same railroad car at Compiegne where the Germans had been so humiliated at the end of the Great War.

Paul had wrestled with his conscience all day. He was opposed to this war that Hitler had started, but he had to admit that even he felt a certain elation at the defeat of Germany's historical enemy, France. To salve his conscience, he prayed daily that this conquest would finally satisfy Hitler's territorial ambitions, and Germany could settle down and get back to normal.

But what would "normal" be for Germany with the Nazis in control? Could she ever be what she was before Hitler? Not the inflation, unemployment, and despair—Hitler had solved those problems—but the Germany of music and laughter, tradition, pride, and compassion. He wondered sadly if Germany could ever go back to those great virtues with the blood of so many innocent people on her hands.

Miriam had shopped all day looking for a special dress to wear to Kurt's reception at the Reichstag. She could hear the loudspeakers on Kurfurstandamm bombarding the people with war news, interspersed with rousing military music. It was nice seeing people smile for a change, but there was something false about their gaiety; it was too forced, too brittle. Their mouths were smiling, but not their eyes.

Paul and Miriam had never been in the Reichstag. Of course they had passed it hundreds of times—always awed by its grandeur—but in the years since Hitler had taken the reins of Germany, the Reichstag had become a place to be feared and avoided at all costs by any German who wanted to remain inconspicuous.

Miriam's search for a dress had been fruitless, so she decided to wear the navy blue taffeta she'd had for years. Her mother insisted that she wear the double strand of pearls she'd hidden from the Nazis when their house had been taken. "I don't think I'll be wearing them again," she'd said to Miriam, and they both wept, knowing it was probably true.

The night of the award ceremony, Kristopher promised his parents that he would take good care of Oma and Opa. He knew how to get them into the hiding place and get the armoire back in place, so they had nothing to fear. With those assurances, Miriam and Paul reluctantly left for the ceremony.

The glamour and opulence of the high-ceilinged ballroom of the Reichstag, with its colorful frescoes and rich carvings, made them think of the Germany of years gone by. In this room, filled with elegantly gowned women—beautifully coiffured and laden with jewels—and the elite of Germany's manhood in dress uniforms and black evening attire, it was easy to feel that the war was happening to someone else . . . in another time, another world.

A dozen crystal chandeliers scattered tiny explosions of light onto the guests, while an orchestra played Wagnerian melodies from the raised platform at one end of the room. The long tables, arrayed with an extravagant assortment of pastries, cheeses, meats, caviar, and various hors d'oeuvres, was crowned with a giant crystal fountain spewing French champagne into the Waterford goblets of the guests.

Paul slipped up behind Miriam as she lustfully eyed the table. "Don't do it," he whispered. "I can read your mind. You're trying to figure out how to stuff some of this in your purse, aren't you?"

She turned and saw that he was smiling. "This is obscene! We have to pinch every deutchmark just for an occasional piece of meat and cheese, and look at this. It's shameful."

Paul started to respond, then looked up and caught the eye of his brother. "There's Jeanne and Kurt," he said, giving them a wave. He put his hand on Miriam's waist and steered her to where they stood.

"Paul," Kurt said, embracing his brother, then Miriam. "I wasn't sure you two would come. This isn't your 'cup of tea' as Jeanne would say."

"I'm sorry Dad isn't alive to see you honored tonight," Paul said. "I know how proud he'd be of you."

Kurt gave a cautious glance around him. "I'm not so sure. He had some pretty old-fashioned ideas about German honor." He looked as though he would have liked to have said more, but before he could speak, he spotted Heinrich Mueller coming toward them, a fixed smile straining at his thin lips.

"General von Falkenhorst," Mueller said, offering Kurt his hand. "I've been wanting the privilege of meeting you for some time. I'm Gestapo Chief Mueller." He turned to Kurt's wife, Jeanne. "And this must be the famous *Frau* von Falkenhorst," he said, kissing her hand grandly. "Your reputation hasn't done you justice, my dear."

"You're too kind," Jeanne murmured, withdrawing her hand just a bit too abruptly.

Kurt put his hand on Mueller's arm and directed his attention to Paul and Miriam. "You know my brother and his wife, don't you?"

"Why yes," he said. "Our sons have shared some wonderful experiences in the Jungvolk. Isn't that right, Reverend Falkenhorst?"

Paul merely nodded, knowing the man was goading him.

Mueller turned to Miriam. "And Frau Falkenhorst. How nice to see you again. Let's see, when did we last meet?" He pursed his lips as if in deep thought. "Oh, I remember. It was at Kristopher's birthday party several years ago. I believe he had just gotten a bicycle from his grandfather." Mueller's eyes narrowed slightly, but the smile stayed in place. "By the way, how are your parents? Are they well?"

"My wife's parents no longer live in Berlin," Paul injected quickly. "We haven't seen them in over a year. You know how difficult travel is with the war."

"Ah, yes," he said. "This is true, quite true."

Mueller clasped his hands together. "It's so nice to see all of you here together tonight. Germany's strength has always been in her family ties, and the von Falkenhorsts have been an important part of our great history. We look forward to your continued loyalty and service."

41

There began to be movement around the stage, and Mueller looked toward it. "I think it's almost time for the Fuehrer to make his presentations and I need to see to the security," he said. "It's been a pleasure visiting with all of you, and I'm sure we'll be seeing much more of each other."

After Mueller left, Kurt leaned toward Paul. "Did I sense a problem there?"

"I don't think so," Paul said. "He just likes to keep everyone on the defensive."

Kurt gave a derisive snort. "There was a time in Germany when men like that wouldn't be fit for anything but stuffing sausage behind a counter, and now they're running the country."

Jeanne grabbed his arm. "Kurt! Please! Someone's going to hear you."

"I know," he said. "I talk too much, and that can be a fatal disease these days, but my brother and I have always understood each other. Right, Paul?"

Paul smiled and gave him a wink.

Just then the music abruptly stopped and a hush fell across the room. The trumpets began blaring a military fanfare, and all eyes turned to the platform, straining to see Hitler as he ascended the steps to the stage. He was accompanied by his Generals Jodl and Keitel, both members of his general staff; Herman Goering, minister of war; Heinrich Himmler, head of the German police and SS; and Heinrich Mueller, head of the Berlin Gestapo.

It was the first time Paul had ever seen Hitler in person. He was surprised to see that the man's personal appearance did not match the magnetic voice he'd heard so often on the radio. He wasn't a large man; his chin was a little weak, his lips thin and tight, his skin sallow. But the magnetism of his pale, almost hypnotic, gray eyes explained his charisma. This was a man possessed by powerful demons.

Hitler stepped to the podium and raised his hand in an offhanded salute, his head moving from side to side, his pale eyes scrutinizing the faces before him. "Heil Hitler," he shouted.

A thunderous "Heil Hitler" shook the room, then wild applause.

Hitler's whole manner was cocky as he gloated over Germany's great humiliation of France, of the speedy defeat of Norway, Denmark, and the low countries, and of England's cowardice in retreating at Dunkirk. He pounded the podium melodramatically as his voice ran the gambit from anger and contempt to gloating and self-congratulation. He was interrupted continually with unrestrained applause which only spurred him on.

In spite of himself, Paul felt swept along with the delirium as he joined in the mad applause. He was proud to be a German, and pride was something Germany had been short on for too long. He glanced at Miriam and was rebuked to see that she was only making a show of applauding, her eyes brimming with tears.

"Are you all right?" he asked.

She forced a smile. "I was only thinking of how proud Papa has always been to be a German. Of all the things they've taken from him, I think that has crushed him the most."

Paul put his arm around her and gave her a comforting hug.

Hitler had finished speaking, and those generals who were being presented the Iron Cross were called to the stage. Kurt was first. He was a foot taller than Hitler, and Hitler was having difficulty getting the ribbon and cross up around Kurt's neck. Rather than bending to Hitler, Kurt took the ribbon out of his hands and placed it around his own neck.

There was an audible gasp from the crowd as Hitler jerked his hand back.

Kurt stepped to the microphone. "I want to thank my country for this great honor, and assure all of you that I will always be proud to serve you and our great Fatherland."

Everyone looked at Hitler for his response to this obvious snub, but he was whispering something to Himmler next to him.

Jeanne turned to Paul, her face barely composed. "He's gone too far this time. Hitler is furious."

"Kurt must know he's cutting his own throat," Paul said.

"I don't think he does," Jeanne whispered. "He still thinks Hitler can be controlled if enough of the generals stand up to him, and I can't reason with him."

Paul glanced around and saw people looking in their direction. He lowered his voice to the women. "We need to get out of here."

"You two go on," Jeanne said. "I'll wait for Kurt and explain that you had to get back to Kristopher, but please stay in touch. I think we're really going to need each other."

╬ ╬

To a teenaged boy in Germany in 1941, the war was a great adventure. The political realities barely penetrated Kristopher's world. He was too busy with his Jungvolk activities, and Germany was winning the war.

On Kristopher's fourteenth birthday in June, 1941, Hitler invaded Russia along a two thousand-mile front and confidently predicted that Russia would fall within six weeks. The German war machine, in those first weeks, made lightning advances into Russia's breadbasket, the Ukraine, and by the end of August had surrounded Leningrad. By December, German *panzers* were hammering at the gates of Moscow, and German citizens, sitting glued to their radios, really began to believe that their Fuehrer was the greatest military genius since Napoleon. What other leader would be courageous enough to open an offensive on his eastern border while already engaged in one on the west?

On December 13, a group of military leaders, gathered in the small salon of an old estate in the Schoneberg district of Berlin, was debating whether it was courage or insanity that had led Hitler to declare war on America the day before. The most outspoken of these was General Kurt von Falkenhorst.

"That madman has finally done it," Kurt said to the others. "How long does he think it will be before the Americans land troops in Europe? And what's he going to fight them with? He's got three million of our best men tied up on the Russian front."

"Make that two million," Count von Schlabrendorff quipped.

"We've already lost close to a million, and we've only been there six months."

"He's an absolute lunatic!" General Hopner growled. "Against all our advice he insisted on taking Leningrad and the Ukraine before attacking Moscow, and now it's too late to take it before spring. It's buried under fifteen feet of snow and mud. Our men aren't equipped to fight in weather like that."

"It's too bad he didn't take a lesson from his hero, Napoleon," said General Wagner, sarcasm heavy in his voice. "He dismissed me and a half dozen of his other top field commanders because we tried to get him to pull back and cut some of our losses. Can you believe that little 'know-nothing' corporal has taken over the field as Commander in Chief and is personally directing our forces?"

"We've got to admit that he's made some lucky moves in the past," General Hofnagel said, "but declaring war on the United States is his biggest blunder yet. Much as the Americans hate Stalin, you know they'll actively support him, and Hitler must know that, too. He's arrogant, but he can't be completely blind."

"He isn't just arrogant and blind," said General Wagner. "He's seriously deranged."

"We can say whatever we want about him," von Falkenhorst said, "but the point is all of us are caught in the crosshairs with him. If he goes down, so do we." He had now hit at the heart of each man's real concern. "He's got to be stopped, and we've got to negotiate for peace with the Allies while there's still a chance to save Germany and ourselves."

General Wagner stood. "Look, killing him isn't any great problem. There are ways we could take care of that, but as much as we all agree that he has to go, we can't make any move against him until we have the cooperation of his General Staff. They're still supporting him, even though he's treated them all like scumbags, and we'll have complete chaos on our hands unless they agree to go along with us."

Kurt von Falkenhorst had taken out his pipe and was tapping an aromatic tobacco blend into the bowl. He put a match to it and puffed rapidly several times until it lit, then inhaled deeply, slowly exhaling as he punctuated the air with the mouthpiece of his pipe. "At this stage, I wouldn't trust any of those boot-lickers with what we're talking about. We'd find ourselves in front of a firing squad before we could blink an eye."

"He's right," von Schlabrendorff said, looking from man to man. "We're just going to have to sit on this and give Hitler a little more rope until he hangs himself."

"And pray that he doesn't hang us, first," Kurt snorted.

5

Berlin, 1942

Paul Falkenhorst's church began to find itself deluged with desperate Jews. Word of mouth had gotten around to various Jewish quarters that the Evangelical Free Church could provide refuge of some sort to Jews on the run. Since the winter of 1939, when Paul and Miriam had first taken in her parents and then the Liebermans, the church had secretly aided over a hundred Jews in finding refuge in the homes of their church members, but now the flood of Jewish supplicants was more than they could deal with, and Paul was forced to turn many away. It was tantamount to a death sentence.

On the morning of May 1, 1942, as Kristopher was leaving for school, Miriam asked him to stop in at the church and take his father a thermos of coffee. It was a glorious morning. The sweet fragrance of the linden trees filled the air, and Kristopher's spirits were soaring at news of General Rommel's victories in North Africa.

He parked his bike in front of the church and pushed open the heavy, carved oak doors. The church was an old traditional gray stone structure that made no pretensions to be other than what it was—a warm and welcoming house of worship for about three hundred earnest believers. The rows of arched windows on both sides of the sanctuary let in a muted light, but the church's glory was the hundred-year-old stained-glass window above the pulpit that cast its jeweled light down onto the rows of polished oak pews.

Kristopher loved being in the church like this, alone. The faintly musty smell, the coolness in the air, the stillness that shut out the noise and confusion of the world outside its doors. Much more than his father's sermons, these things made him feel close to God.

He ran his hand along the ends of the pews as he made his way down the aisle to his father's office. Just as he was about to step up on the dais at the front, he heard a noise and stopped. It sounded like a muffled cry. He slowly turned around, his eyes scanning the sanctuary, but he saw no one. He stood motionless, listening carefully for a few minutes, but hearing no further sound, he shrugged and turned back to the platform, only to stop abruptly as he heard the sound again. It was definitely someone whimpering. He set the thermos on the floor and cautiously crept back up the aisle, looking down each row as he went. About half way back to the door, he saw something under a pew.

"Who's there?" he demanded.

There was no answer.

He sidled along the row until he reached the spot where someone lay huddled under the bench. Cautiously leaning down, he was startled by a tear-stained face looking up at him in sheer panic. He reached down and pulled at a small arm, only to find to his astonishment that it belonged to a girl about his own age. She was so weak she could not get out from under the pew on her own, so Kristopher pulled her up and set her on the pew where he could get a good look at her. Her frightened face was covered with dried blood, and an ugly bruise colored her right cheek. She clutched the top of her torn dress in an effort to cover her breast.

Clearly shaken, Kristopher peered down at her. "What are you doing in here?" he demanded.

Her dark eyes filled with fresh tears as she brought the back of her hand to her mouth to stifle the sobs. She looked so pathetic that Kristopher's tone softened.

"Look," he said, "I'm not going to hurt you, but you've got to tell me who you are and what you're doing in our church."

The girl finally managed to stammer, "I . . . I was attacked, and I saw the church . . . and I came in to hide."

"Attacked by whom?"

"The Gestapo."

"The Gestapo!" he exclaimed. "Why would the Gestapo attack you?"

She began to cry. "They took my parents, and I was trying to get in the car with them, but one of them grabbed me and dragged me back into our house."

It was then that Kristopher noticed the yellow star on her torn dress. "You're a Jew!" he exclaimed. "Whatever made you come in here? This is a Christian church." When she hesitated, he shook her roughly. "Don't you know you can get us into a lot of trouble by being in here?"

"I was told this church helps Jews."

"What are you talking about? This church has nothing to do with Jews."

Paul had heard the voices from his office and came into the sanctuary. When he saw Kristopher and the girl, he called out, "What's going on, Kristopher?"

"Vati, you'd better come here. Quick! There's a girl here, and she says someone told her this church helps Jews."

Paul hurried to them and bent over her. "You're hurt. Here, let me look at that shoulder." He reached out to touch her, but she shrank back. "I won't hurt you," he said gently.

He carefully pulled her hand back, and when he did so, the torn dress fell away, exposing one of her breasts. It was covered with deep scratches. Kristopher's mouth flew open. He had never seen a girl's breast this close before.

"Who did this to you?" Paul demanded, covering her as best he could.

"She told me it was the Gestapo," Kristopher exclaimed, "and you know they must be looking for her. We've got to get her out of here before someone sees her and reports us."

Paul gave him a stern look. "You go on to school, son. I'll take care of this, but I don't want you saying anything about this to anyone. Do you understand me?"

Kristopher frowned at the curt dismissal, then reluctantly started back toward the center aisle. "I want her gone by the time I get home from school," he shot back over his shoulder.

"Go! Now!" Paul said, pointing toward the church door.

He waited until Kristopher had left, then stepped outside the church doors. Pretending to adjust the small announcement board, he scanned the street for any sign of someone watching the church. Satisfied that there was no one, he hurried back inside to the girl. She had fallen over in the seat and was lying there, moaning softly.

"Here, let me help you stand up. I'm going to take you where we can get some help."

She was too weak to stand, so Paul carried her into his office, laying her on his sofa.

"I'm going next door to get my wife," he told her, "but don't leave this room while I'm gone. Do you understand? It's very important that no one sees you. I'll be back in five minutes."

The girl looked up at him. "Maybe I should go. I don't want to get you in any trouble."

"Nonsense. You can't even stand up. Now, you just rest here for a minute, and I'll be right back."

He hurried next door to the parsonage. Miriam could see instantly that something was wrong. "What is it?" she asked.

Paul told her about the girl, and they quickly gathered together some food and some of Kristopher's clothes and walked casually back to the church office. The girl had fallen asleep on the sofa, and Paul shook her gently. She woke with a start, putting up her hand defensively.

Miriam knelt down beside her and took her hand. "No one's going to hurt you. We just want to take care of those cuts and get you into something clean and warm."

The girl submitted to Miriam's ministrations and was soon bandaged and cleaned up.

"How long has it been since you've eaten?" Miriam asked.

"I don't remember."

Miriam handed her a glass of milk and some bread, and as she ate, Paul introduced himself. "I'm Pastor Falkenhorst, and this is my wife, Frau Falkenhorst. Can you tell us your name?"

"Sarah Klein."

"Do you live near here?"

She nodded. "Maybe you know my father, Dr. Franz Klein?

"Doesn't he own the Klein Medical Building on Wilberstrasse?" Paul asked.

"He used to, but they took it away from him last year."

"I'm sorry to hear that," Paul said. "Has something happened to him?"

Her eyes filled with fresh tears. "The Gestapo took him and my mother away."

"Why didn't they take you?" Miriam asked.

"I tried to get in the car with them, but one of the officers stopped me, and he . . . he . . ."

Paul gripped her shoulders. "Did he molest you?"

She covered her face with her hands and began sobbing. "Yes. He raped me."

"How did you get away from him?" Miriam gasped.

The girl looked up through her tears, her voice barely a whisper. "I shot him."

"You shot him!" Paul exclaimed. "Where did you get a gun?"

"He put his pistol on the table by my bed and I grabbed it and pointed it at him, and it just went off. I was only trying to scare him, but he was all covered with blood, so I ran out the back door as fast as I could."

"What made you come into our church?" Paul asked.

"My father once told me this church helps Jews."

Miriam cradled the girl in her arms and gave Paul a determined look. "We're not sending this child back out to those animals. She's got to stay here until we can find a safe house for her."

Paul nodded. "Looks like Gaston's going to have another visitor."

Gaston Renaud was a robust middle-aged Frenchman whom Paul had inherited with the church. No one knew how long he'd been caretaker at Evangelical Free Church, but he was a man to be reckoned with there, and the furnace room in the church basement was his special domain. So when the deacons had first made the decision to become involved in hiding Jews in the church, they felt they would have to sound Gaston out.

Paul was sure there was nothing to worry about. Gaston's elderly mother had confided to him years earlier that Gaston was the product of a youthful indiscretion with a Jewish boy when she was fifteen. Her French husband adopted him when she married at eighteen. Gaston had never married and still lived with his widowed mother, and he came to look upon this rescue mission as the one great adventure in an otherwise very dull life. No one knew how, but Gaston was able to find many safe houses for Jews with members of the church. He and his mother were never without several fugitives themselves.

Gaston's furnace room was about twenty by thirty feet, a good third of it taken up by the ancient, coal-burning furnace, with a tiny room tucked in behind it where coal was stored.

It had been Gaston's idea to use this coal-bin as a hiding place. He cleaned it out and put a mattress on the floor, and with the door shut, it would be very hard to even know it was there.

Gaston kept an assortment of supplies and a few items of food in a cupboard, and usually ate his noon meals at the small table in the center of the furnace room. It was too dangerous for the Jews who were in the coal-bin to come out to the table, so he took their food in to them. They were allowed to use the toilet in the hall outside the furnace room, but only if they were accompanied by Gaston, Paul, or Miriam.

After Sarah had eaten and regained a little strength, Paul took her from his office down the back steps of the church to the furnace room. He knocked on the door and Gaston's smiling face appeared through the crack.

"Do I have a guest?" he asked.

"Yes," Paul replied, "and this one needs some very special care. She's had a rough time of it."

Gaston got a look at Sarah and whistled through his teeth. "Did you ever know a Frenchman to turn away a beautiful woman?"

Sarah clung to Paul as they entered the warm room. Paul introduced her to Gaston and he explained all the rules to her. "It's going to be a little scary for you in here by yourself at night when no one's around," Gaston said, "but I'll be here during the day and bring you some food and water and take you to the toilet. We'll get you back on your feet in a few days, then find a nice home for you. Okay?"

Sarah nodded, and fell, exhausted, onto the mattress. Paul covered her with a blanket and told her he'd be back a little later. Before he left the furnace room, he told Gaston what had happened to her. "I don't think it's hit her, yet, but she's going to have a rough time of it when it does, so we'll need to keep a close eye on her."

☩ ☩

Kristopher sat at his desk trying to concentrate on the lecture Herr Brewer was giving about the scientific proofs of the genetic inferiority of Jews as evidenced by the shape of their skulls and the size of their noses. He could not keep his attention focused on the subject. His mind kept going back to that soft pink breast he'd just seen.

He was shaken out of his reverie by the teacher's voice. "Isn't that a fact, Falkenhorst?"

Kristopher straightened up in his seat and looked around. "I'm sorry, sir, I . . . I didn't understand the question."

Some of his classmates snickered.

Herr Brewer's blond brows twitched together in a scowl. "The question seemed simple enough to me. I asked if it wasn't a fact that the genetic differences between Jews and gentiles show that Jews are physically inferior."

"I . . . I suppose they are."

"What do you mean, you 'suppose'? I'm telling you that it's a scientific fact that every physical characteristic of a Jew is inferior to that of gentiles. It's a matter of repeated inbreeding."

"If you say so, sir."

The children tittered again.

Herr Brewer shook his head in disgust toward Kristopher, then droned on with the rest of his lecture.

Kristopher tried hard to concentrate on the physical inferiority of the Jews he knew, but that breast kept coming back into focus. There was certainly nothing inferior about that. In fact, it was the most beautiful thing he'd ever seen.

Just then the bell rang, ending the school day. Before Kristopher could get out of his seat, Herr Brewer came up to his desk. "I was not pleased with your performance in class today, Falkenhorst. I'd like you to keep your focus on what we're talking about. Because of your special citizenship classification, people might get the wrong idea about where your sympathies lie. Do I make myself clear?"

Kristopher nodded glumly.

By the time he got to his Jungvolk meeting, he had convinced himself that there wasn't anything so extraordinary about the girl's breast; not that he had anything to compare it with. Anyway, it really wasn't that important after the announcement his Jungvolk leader made. The date had been set for his initiation into the senior Hitler Youth organization, the Hitler *Jugend*, and he had been accepted into the most prestigious branch, the *Flieger* Hitler Youth. This meant he was going to be groomed to become a Luftwaffe pilot, fulfilling his childhood dream.

He could hardly wait to get home and tell his parents. His plan for making himself so valuable to the Party that they would overlook his being half Jewish had worked, and he was ecstatic.

He was in a great mood as he pedaled home, waving to some jack-booted soldiers herding a group of prisoners who were picking up debris from the street. He even decided to forgive his father for the harsh way he had spoken to him in the church that morning. After all, his father was under a lot of pressure with Oma and Opa living with them, and he could understand how, in a weak moment, he might have felt sympathy for the girl and wanted to help her. But he was certainly thankful that his father had promised to get rid of her as soon as possible, especially now, with his initiation coming up in three weeks. He couldn't afford to have anything jeopardize that.

"I'm home," he yelled, as he shoved open the back door.

Miriam jumped at the sound of his voice. "You startled me! Aren't you home early?"

"My leader let us all out early. Oh, Mutti, I have the most wonderful news! Where's Vati?"

"He's still over at the church, but he'll be here in a few minutes."

"I want to get him right now so I can tell you both at the same time." He started for the door.

"Kristopher!" Miriam called, the sharpness in her voice stopping him.

He turned around. "What's wrong?"

"Nothing. It's . . . it's just that your father asked not to be disturbed this afternoon. He's finishing his sermon for Sunday." She took down a plate of freshly baked cookies. "Here, you have some cookies and milk. Vati will be over in just a short while, and then you can tell us your news together."

Kristopher shrugged as the smell of the cookies lured him to the table. His news could wait for a few more minutes.

Paul came in a half hour later. He ruffled Kristopher's hair. "Hi," he said, swiping the last cookie from the plate. "How was your day at school?"

"Oh, Vati, I have the most wonderful news! My initiation into the Hitler Jugend is in three weeks, and I've been chosen for the Flieger division. That means I could actually be flying *Messerschmitts* and *Focke-Wulfs* in three years. Isn't that fantastic? I just hope the war lasts long enough for me to get into the air."

A look of consternation shot between his parents.

"I have to take my baptismal record and my birth certificate to my *Gefolgschaftsfuehrer* tomorrow so I can prove that I'm almost fifteen. I also need to have you write out my genealogy going back four generations on both sides. It's only a formality, though. Everyone has to do it so we can keep the wrong people out of the organization."

"What'll they say when they see that there are Jews in your family?" Miriam asked.

"Oh, I'm not worried about that. They know that you and I have special papers. I keep telling you that the Jews in our family are not the kind that Hitler wants to get rid of. It's the kind of Jews—like that girl in the church this morning—that are giving good Jews a bad name."

Paul looked at him, aghast. "In what possible way could that poor child be giving Jews a bad name?"

"You saw her! She was half-naked! You don't dress like that unless you're looking for trouble."

"Kristopher!" Miriam exclaimed. "That girl had her clothes ripped off her and was raped by a Gestapo agent. She did nothing to provoke it."

Kristopher's voice began to rise defensively. "You don't know if she was raped, or not, Mutti. All you've got is her word for it. She could be a prostitute who got more than she bargained for. I've seen them all over the city trying to get customers. I've even had them come up to me."

Paul drew back his hand, then stopped just short of slapping his son. "I will not allow that kind of talk in front of your mother," he said, his face flushed with anger. "I never thought I'd ever have to say this to my own son, but I'm ashamed of you. You've become a hateful, bigoted child, and it wouldn't surprise me if you turned us in for helping that poor girl. With the way the Nazis have twisted your thinking, it's the kind of despicable thing you'd do."

Kristopher recoiled in astonishment. His father had never spoken to him like this before. "What's the big deal?" he cried. "I didn't say anything wrong. That's what I mean about that girl. She's the cause of this whole thing, and now you're turning on me." He jumped up from the table and stormed toward the door. "At least I know where I stand in my own home." He slammed the door savagely as he went out.

Kristopher grabbed his bicycle and pedaled furiously down the broad, tree-lined avenue. The linden blossoms that had so delighted him that morning now sickened him with their pungency. He cast about in his mind where he could go, and which of his friends he could talk to that would understand the injustice of his parents' accusations, but not one name came to mind. He didn't dare tell any of the boys in his schar about the argument, because if they found out it was over a Jewish prostitute who had come into his father's church looking for help, they'd alert the Gestapo. And if they came snooping around, they might find Oma and Opa, and then he'd be in trouble himself for not reporting them. He was trapped. He couldn't bring himself to go back home, and there was nowhere else to go. Angry tears of self-pity clouded his vision, and his nose was running. He wiped at it with the back of his hand.

He didn't see the piece of broken cement until his bike wheel rammed into it, catapulting him over the handlebars into a mound of jagged bricks and cement piled by the curb. He hit with a sickening thud, his arm twisted awkwardly under him. He tried to move, but the pain in his shoulder was too great. Blood poured down onto his face from a cut on his forehead and dripped onto the front of his uniform. As he felt himself losing consciousness, he could barely make out the man's face peering down at him.

"Don't move," a voice said. "I'm going to try to lay you down flat."

The man gingerly pulled the boy's legs together, but Kristopher screamed as he tried to straighten his arm. "I don't think it's broken," the voice said. "It looks like it's dislocated."

The man looked up and down the street for help, but the few pedestrians he saw quickly moved on. He peered back down at Kristopher. "I'm going to try to pull your arm back into the socket," he said, "but it's going to hurt like hell. Here, grab my arm, tight."

Kristopher gripped the man's arm and gritted his teeth. The man gave a quick jerk and twist on the arm, and it popped back into the socket. Kristopher screamed, then fainted.

The man ripped off Kristopher's neck scarf and tied it around his head to try to stem the blood that was streaming from the cut on his forehead. He stuck his hand in the pocket of Kristopher's shorts and pulled out his wallet. His Jungvolk card gave his address, and the man saw that it was only a couple blocks away. He picked the unconscious boy up and started down the street, struggling under the dead weight.

After a block he dropped to the curb, exhausted, and carefully laid Kristopher on the sidewalk. As he did, Kristopher opened his eyes. "Where am I?" he groaned.

"You had a bad spill on your bike, but I got your arm back in the socket, and the cut on your forehead seems to have stopped bleeding. We're just about to your house, so your parents can look after you."

Kristopher put his hand up and felt his neck scarf around his forehead. His head was splitting, and his shoulder throbbed with pain. He could barely see out of his right eye. All he wanted to do was get home. He sat up, but was too unsteady to get to his feet.

"Here, let me see if I can help you walk the rest of the way," the man said, pulling Kristopher to his feet. He slipped an arm under Kristopher's good shoulder, and they limped down the sidewalk together.

Miriam had been standing at the window and saw them coming up the path to the parsonage. She dashed out the door as they got to the porch. "What happened?"

Kristopher began crying when he saw his mother, and the man helped Miriam get him into the house. "He had a bad spill on his bike a couple blocks down the street," the man said, "and he dislocated his shoulder, but I got it back into the socket. I don't think he's too badly hurt, but you might want to check that cut on his forehead. It's pretty deep."

Miriam took notice of the man for the first time. He was a ruggedly built man about thirty years old. His rough, weathered appearance made it obvious that he was a laborer of some kind. Miriam introduced herself, and as she reached out to shake his hand, she saw that it was calloused and blistered.

"Thank you so much for bringing him home," she said gratefully. "I know my husband will want to meet you, but he's out looking for him right now. He'll be back in a moment. Won't you please sit down and let me fix you a cup of tea?"

The man seemed anxious to go. "No, thank you, *Gnaedige Frau*. I really must go. It wouldn't be safe for you if I was seen here."

Miriam started to protest, but the man held up his hand. Only then did she notice the yellow star on his jacket, and it was smeared with Kristopher's blood.

6

In years to come, June 8, 1942, would be emblazened in Kristopher's mind as the day his world forever changed.

The cut on his forehead had begun to heal, and his shoulder was still stiff and painful, but despite these minor inconveniences, he was eagerly looking forward to his upcoming ceremony.

An uneasy truce existed between his parents and him. He couldn't seem to make them see that he had nothing personal against Jews; he loved his mother and Oma and Opa, and he knew there must be other good Jews like them still in Germany. The Jew who had come to his aid on the street confirmed what he'd been saying all along; there were good Jews and bad ones, and that had obviously been one of the good ones. The very fact that the man was still free to walk the streets showed that he wasn't the kind of Jew the Nazis were after. Anyway, contrary to his parents' opinion of him being a racist, Kristopher *was* grateful to the man for his help, and for the fact that a week after the accident, his bicycle appeared on the steps of the parsonage, completely repaired.

The morning of his initiation ceremony he made sure his uniform was immaculate, every blond hair shellacked into place, and his black leather shoes burnished to a gloss. This was the most important day of his life, the day he was being initiated into the senior Hitler Youth, the Hitler Jugend. The ceremony was set for five o'clock in the school auditorium. Five of his classmates, including Rolf Mueller, were also scheduled to be initiated, and they were all in high spirits at school that day, shoving and poking each other, relishing the envy of the other boys and the frank adulation of the girls.

Hannah von Kemp had already congratulated Kristopher twice and told him she was coming to the ceremony and bringing her father who was in town for a week. He was elated by that news. Dr. von Kemp had been working on the secret weapons that the Fuehrer had promised would end the war, and impressing someone like that could be a great boon in helping him get into the elite flying corps.

By 4:30, most of the seats of the auditorium were filled. The fathers of the boys being initiated stood in a small group congratulating each other, while some of the mothers fussed at the hair and neck scarves of their nervous sons. Miriam glanced around for Kristopher, but he seemed to have disappeared. She was uncomfortable around the other enthusiastic mothers, but made an effort at small talk. Paul spotted Dr. von Kemp coming toward him, beaming broadly.

"Pastor Falkenhorst," von Kemp said, extending his hand to Paul, "it seems we keep meeting at these wonderful tributes to your son. Hannah tells me that Kristopher has made a fine record for himself in the Jungvolk, and I can tell you we're proud that we're going to have him in our aviation program. We need dedicated young men like him."

Paul grasped his outstretched hand. "It's very kind of you to say that, and it's really an honor for you to come when you're as busy as you are. We've missed you at church, but I know your work has kept you out of town a lot. Hopefully, you'll soon be able to get back to Berlin permanently. I'm sure your family misses you."

"Yes, it's been hard on all of us being separated. That's why I've decided to take my family with me when I leave this time. I'd like to get them out of Berlin for a while anyway. The bombings are beginning to get worrisome."

"Do you know where you'll be going?"

Von Kemp nodded. "Yes, but I'm afraid I'm not at liberty to say. We're keeping our home here, though, and I'll be back from time to time, so I'll drop in at the church when I'm here. I need your sermons to help me keep everything that's happening in perspective." He looked toward the back of the auditorium. "Ah, I see the *Fanfarenzug* is lining up to march in. Perhaps we should find our seats." He beckoned to his wife and Hannah, then held his hand out, inviting the Falkenhorsts to lead the way.

Kristopher had belonged to the various Hitler Youth organizations since he was eight, and his proven leadership had brought him fast promotions and numerous merit awards. Consequently, he had attracted considerable attention from the organization's leadership. So, when Kristopher got word just before the ceremony that his Bannfuehrer, Fritz Kissinger, wanted to see him in the principal's office immediately, he could barely contain his eagerness. His mind raced with the possibilities of what his leader might want. He hardly dared to think that he'd been singled out for some special recognition, although it wouldn't surprise him, considering his record in the Jungvolk.

When he entered the principal's office, he was surprised and delighted to see not only Kissinger, but the twenty-two-year-old *Oberbannfuehrer*, Claus Leuning, as well. Kristopher's heart was pounding with anticipation.

"Heil Hitler," Leuning barked, his right arm shooting forward in a crisp salute.

Kristopher returned the salute, hoping he didn't look too eager.

"Sit down," the Oberbannfuehrer said curtly. "Kissinger and I have something serious to discuss with you."

The man was unsmiling and brusque, and Kristopher suddenly began to feel uneasy. He sat nervously on the edge of the hard chair. "What is it?"

Leuning held some sheets of paper in his hands, impatiently rapping their edges on the desktop. His whole manner left no doubt that what he was about to say was going to be unpleasant. Kristopher felt a knot begin to form in the pit of his stomach.

His Bannfuehrer, Kissinger, began to speak. "I'm afraid we've got some bad news for you, Falkenhorst. You won't be participating in the ceremony today. Your promotion into the Hitler Jugend has been denied."

"What?" Kristopher gasped. "That's impossible! All my papers were in order, and I passed my interview with high marks." A sick laugh forced its way up from his throat as he looked from one man to the other. "I know what this is. You're just testing me." He paused. "Aren't you?"

Neither man smiled nor spoke.

"There must be a mistake," Kristopher said.

"It's no mistake," Kissinger said, but it was obvious from his tone that he wasn't happy with the news he was about to deliver to the boy.

"But why?" Kristopher pleaded, fighting to hang on to his dignity. "My record has been outstanding. You both know that."

"There's no question that you've been of some service to the organization in the past," injected the glowering Oberbannfuehrer, "but a special review of your case was requested by *Reichsfuehrer* von Schirach, and he's ruled that the circumstances related to your case make it necessary for you to be expelled from the Hitler Youth."

Kristopher's mind was whirling in sheer panic. Why would the head of the entire Hitler Youth organization make a special review of him, and what possible circumstances could make it necessary for them to kick him out of the Hitler Youth?

Kristopher leaned forward in his chair. "Can't you at least tell me why?"

"We're under no obligation to give you the reasons for this decision," the Oberbannfuehrer said, "but Fritz has been impressed with your performance in the past, and he'd like you to know the charges against you."

The charges against me! thought Kristopher. *My God! They're going to arrest me!*

Kissinger took the papers from the Oberbannfuehrer, and thumbed through them for a moment. "These charges are very serious, but I'm hoping that by telling you what they are, you'll try to learn from this."

He silently read through the lines on the top sheet, then looked up soberly. "The first charge is one of accepting illegal goods from Jews."

"What?" Kristopher blurted. "That's an outright lie! I've never had any improper dealings with Jews."

"Didn't you accept a bicycle from your Jewish grandparents?" Leuning demanded.

Kristopher's mouth flew open. "Yes, but that was years ago and it was a birthday present."

"Ah, yes," he said, "a birthday present. But at the time they gave it to you, you knew that Jews were required to turn in any bicycles they owned, and yet you took it from them without ever reporting that they had failed to turn it in. Isn't that so?"

Kristopher started to protest, but Leuning cut him off abruptly. "We will not argue these charges with you. If you want Kissinger to continue, then you'll remain silent. Is that understood?"

Kristopher nodded numbly.

Kissinger gave the boy a sympathetic look, but continued down the list. "On the night of Kristallnacht, you did not participate in the stoning of Jewish shops until one of your comrades shamed you into doing it, and then, after hitting a Jew with a brick, you panicked and ran, disgracing your Jungvolk comrades."

Kristopher could feel the hackles begin to rise on the back of his neck.

Kissinger went on down the list. "This last charge has to do with your father," Kissinger said. "It's been noted for several years that his sermons have had an anti-Nazi tone, and he places far too much emphasis on Jesus being a Jew. It's insulting that a decorated war hero like him—from one of Germany's most distinguished military families—would display his disloyalty to our Fuehrer in such a vulgar manner, and I find it equally reprehensible that you've never reported him to any authorities for this."

Kristopher had not actually heard his father preach for some time, but he couldn't believe he would be openly supporting Jews in his sermons.

"I see that surprises you," Leuning injected. "Frankly, I'm amazed at that, considering the fact that your grandparents and mother are full-blooded Jews. You must be aware that your father was strongly advised to divorce your mother several years ago, but he flatly refused. Did you think all this would be overlooked indefinitely?"

Kristopher opened his mouth to answer, then thought better of it. What would be the use? Nothing he could say would make any difference to them. They'd already made up their minds.

The Oberbannfuehrer took the papers from Kissinger and put them back into his briefcase. "The overwhelming conclusion from all of this evidence is that you've consistently displayed a contempt for the Fuehrer's policies toward Jews, and have proven yourself unfit to wear the uniform of a Hitler Youth," he said. "It's my duty to inform you that as of today you're dismissed from the organization and stripped of all honors you've received. You're ordered to turn in your uniform and any merit badges you've won, tomorrow. And I might add," Leuning went on in a menacing tone, "even though you and your mother have been granted special citizenship status, that's being reconsidered right now, so I suggest that you watch your steps closely. Do I make myself perfectly clear?"

With that, the two men turned and left the room.

Kristopher sat there, unable to move, unable to fathom what had just happened to him, barely able to breathe. His initial panic and then rage had given way to a numb despair. He had never felt so small, so empty, and so alone in his life. They had twisted everything to make him look disloyal, when all he'd ever wanted to do was serve his beloved Fuehrer and Germany.

What do I do now? he asked himself. *My life is over. No one will have anything to do with me as soon as this gets out.*

He could just picture Rolf's glee when he heard about it. But then, he probably already knew, since Kristopher was sure that Rolf and his father had been the instigators of this whole rotten thing.

He doubled his fists and pounded the table over and over in a helpless rage. He wanted to strike out at someone, anyone. But who? Rolf and his stupid father may have instigated it, but they didn't have enough influence by themselves to get him kicked out. Was it his Oberbannfuehrer, or Reichsfuehrer von Shirach? Or his teacher, Herr Brewer. It couldn't be any of them. They all took their orders from men above them. Not knowing who to blame made it impossible to defend himself and refute the charges.

His eyes fell on a large picture of Hitler hanging over the principal's desk, and he scrutinized every feature of that beloved face. Kristopher could see nothing but love in the pale eyes that looked down at him. It was inconceivable to him that Hitler would ever condone such a miscarriage of justice if he knew about it. What was happening to his beloved country when a loyal German, like himself, could be so unjustly condemned without being able to defend himself?

He sat in a daze, turning everything over and over in his mind, trying to see what he'd done wrong, but each time he came to the same conclusion. He had done nothing wrong. He was simply the victim of the hate and prejudice of bigots like Rolf and his depraved father.

And then it hit him.

Like a jolt of high-voltage power pulsing through his whole body, he saw it. *This is what Vati said would happen. He said they'd turn against him because of his Jewish blood.*

The realization was so overpowering that he could no longer hold back the bitter tears that rushed to his eyes. "Dear God!" he moaned. "How could I have been so blind? I'm just getting back what I've dished out."

The distant sound of the drum and bugle corps beginning its fanfare drifted in from the auditorium, and he looked up forlornly. He wanted to be brave—oh, God, how he wanted to be brave—but at that moment he was a heartbroken fifteen-year-old, and he laid his head on the desk and wept as he never had before.

✠ ✠

Paul never ceased to be amazed at the effort that went into making every Hitler Youth performance an extravaganza, guaranteed to stir the deepest emotions in every child. He watched the glowing faces of the boys as they marched past him down the aisle, heads held high, small bodies erect and defiant, and he shuddered to realize that these children belonged to Hitler—body and soul. Why is it, he pondered, that the church has never been able to capture the hearts of these children the way Hitler has? There must be something we could have done to prevent the handing of an entire generation of children over to a madman.

His thoughts were interrupted as he caught sight of the flag-bearers marching down the aisle behind the Fanfarenzug. Several were so small that they struggled under the weight of the six-foot poles with their large banners of black swastikas on fields of red and white. An honor-guard of about twenty boys followed the flags and made its way to the stage. When they were all in place on the platform, the drums began a long roll and the trumpets blared. Everyone stood as the six honorees began their single-file walk down the center aisle.

Paul and Miriam strained to see Kristopher as the boys filed toward the stage amid the wild applause. As they mounted the steps, the music stopped abruptly, and the Oberbannfuehrer, Claus Leuning, stepped to the podium and clicked his heels together sharply. "Heil Hitler," he shouted.

A thunderous "Heil Hitler" rang back at him.

Paul gripped Miriam's arm. "I don't see Kristopher." He leaned from side to side, trying to get a better look at the stage. "He's not up there!"

He gave Miriam a frightened look. "Something's happened! He'd never miss this unless he's been hurt or something worse." He began to push toward the aisle. "I'm going to see where he is."

Miriam tugged at his arm. "You can't leave in front of all these people," she whispered.

"Oh, yes I can." He turned back to her. "Are you coming with me?"

She gave the von Kemps an apologetic shrug, then gathered her coat and purse and followed Paul as he shoved his way to the aisle. The

Oberbannfuehrer paused in his remarks and glowered in their direction. Every eye was on them as they made their way up the side aisle to the back of the auditorium.

"I'm sorry to put you through that," Paul said, taking her by the arm as they reached the outside door, "but there's no way Kristopher would miss this initiation unless something's terribly wrong. We've got to find him."

They went from room to room in the main school building, calling Kristopher's name, but there was no sign of him. As a last resort, they checked the bike stand and saw that his bicycle was gone. "He must have gone home for some reason," Paul said, taking Miriam's hand. "Let's go."

As they pulled up in their driveway, they saw Kristopher's bike on the front porch. They dashed in, and Miriam raced upstairs and stuck her head in her parents' room to ask them if they'd heard Kristopher come in, when she saw him sitting on the bed with Josef's arm around his shoulder. One look at Kristopher's stricken face told her that something devastating had happened to him. She held out her arms and he came to her, sobbing.

Paul came in just then and took in the scene. "What's happened here?"

"It seems we finally have our boy back," Josef said. "I think he has something he needs to tell you both."

Kristopher sat down on the bed and sobbed out the whole miserable story of what had happened. "I can't believe I was so blind, Vati. Opa's been telling me about all the terrible things that have happened to their friends and about the death camps where they've been sending Jews." He gave his father an accusing look. "Did you know about those places?"

Paul nodded. "Yes, Uncle Kurt told us, and that's why we've hidden Oma and Opa. That's where they were planning to send them."

"But why didn't someone tell me?" he demanded. "You know I wouldn't have gone along with that."

"There's nothing you could've done," Paul replied. "Even some of my fellow ministers have been sent to those camps." He sat down beside Kristopher and took his ravaged face between his hands. "This may be hard for you to accept, but Hitler's behind all of this."

Kristopher pulled back in shock. "I've never heard him say anything about death camps! It must be some of the men around him who've done it. The Fuehrer would never stand for that."

"Oh, son," Paul said. "Don't you know that nothing happens in this country without his orders?"

Kristopher's voice began to rise. "But Hitler says they're just work camps where people go who've lost their homes or their jobs. They don't do anything bad to them. They're just helping them out till the war is over."

Paul and Miriam had tried to hide this horror from him since they'd found out about it from Kurt over a year before, but now that the Hitler Youth no longer had their hooks in Kristopher, it was time for him to have his eyes opened to what kind of monster his beloved Fuehrer really was.

Paul's jaw tightened as he gripped Kristopher by the shoulders and looked him straight in the eye. "Have I ever lied to you?" he asked.

Kristopher shook his head.

"Then I want you to listen very carefully to every word I'm going to say. They are *not* work camps; they're *death* camps. They ship people there from all over Europe—Jews and Christians and Gypsies and homosexuals and disabled people, and anybody else they disapprove of—and as soon as they get them there, they sort out the ones who are strong enough to work, then shoot or gas the rest of them and cremate their bodies."

Paul's eyes bore into Kristopher's horrified face. "You should fall on your knees right now and thank God that they kicked you out of their vile organization before you became just like them," he added.

Kristopher jerked back from his father, and his voice was close to hysteria. "If you knew all this, why haven't you tried to do something about it? How could you just sit back and let it happen?"

"Now wait just a minute," Miriam put in sharply. "Your father has not just been sitting back doing nothing. He's been risking his life, and ours, not only by hiding Oma and Opa, but by hiding many Jews with our church families."

Kristopher's mouth flew open. "Vati! Is that true?"

Paul nodded.

"Then that girl I found in the church was telling the truth when she said our church helps Jews?"

"Yes, she was."

"Why didn't you tell me this before?" he demanded.

"I couldn't. I know you've been struggling for a long time with your feelings about Jews, but I had to wait until you saw for yourself how cruelly they've been treated, and now you've seen it, first hand. Take my word for it. What was done to you today was because of your Jewish blood, and for no other reason."

"But, what about the girl?" he persisted. "What did you do with her?"

Paul gave Miriam a questioning look, and she nodded.

"She's still here," he said.

"Where?"

"In the furnace room in the church," Paul said. "Gaston's been helping us take care of her."

"Gaston's in on this, too?"

Paul nodded. "Yes, and a lot of other people in the church."

Kristopher looked aghast. "But aren't you all afraid you'll get caught?"

"Of course we are, but when God leads you to do something like this, you have to do it, and we're trusting Him to take care of us."

"But what if He doesn't?" Kristopher cried. "What if the Gestapo finds out about it? You know they must be looking for that girl."

"I'm sure they are, but what would you have us do? Turn her out into the street and let them finish her off for good?"

"Of course not, but she's putting all of us in a lot of danger. The Bannfuehrer warned me that they're going to be watching our family very closely."

"They've been watching us for a long time," Miriam said, "but God has protected us so far."

"These people haven't got anyone else to turn to," Paul said. "What would've happened to Oma and Opa if we hadn't hidden them? They'd be ashes right now."

"All of our lives depend on you keeping this a secret," Miriam warned Kristopher. "Can we count on you?"

He looked over at his father, and suddenly saw him in a new light. He wasn't just a stodgy old preacher spouting Biblical platitudes. He was a courageous man who lived what he preached, and Kristopher was suddenly very proud of him.

"You can count on me," he said, "and I want to help, too. Just tell me what to do."

Paul held his arms out to his son, and the boy came to him. "You can start by taking off that damned uniform," Paul said. "I've seen enough of that to last me a lifetime."

"Me, too," Miriam added.

Kristopher looked down at his uniform and the row of merit badges above his heart, and an ache shot through him, then he glanced up with a rueful grimace. "Why not?" he said. "I'm not going to need it anymore. That's for sure."

✠ ✠

That evening at dinner, Kristopher moodily pushed the food around on his plate with his fork. His mind was in a muddle, alternating between cold panic and blistering rage. Miriam saw his conflicted expression and glanced at her watch. "It's time I took some food down to Sarah," she said. "Would you like to go with me? I think it would be good for you to tell her what's happened to you."

He looked up from his nearly untouched plate. "Do you think she'd want to see me? I'm sure I didn't make a very good impression on her in the church."

"You didn't know what she'd been through, but I need to tell you something before we go see her. She was hiding in the church because her parents were taken from their home by the Gestapo, and one of the agents had sexually attacked her."

"Oh my gosh!" he exclaimed.

"But that's not all," Miriam added. "She shot him."

His eyes widened in shock. "She shot the agent? Where did she get a gun?"

"She used his own gun on him."

"Is he dead?"

"She doesn't know. She ran over here and hid in the church."

Kristopher put his hand to his forehead. "No wonder she was scared to death that the Gestapo would find her. Is she going to be okay?"

"We hope so, but she was pretty badly beaten up. I just wanted you to know about this so you can see how terrified she is about being discovered, but I think it'll do her good to hear that you're no longer a threat."

Kristopher found himself nervous about seeing the girl again. She had been in his thoughts more than he wanted since he'd found her, but now that he knew what she'd been through, facing her was going to be embarrassing for him.

He followed his mother out the back door and down the darkened stairs to the church basement. When they got to the furnace room, she unlocked it and they went in.

Miriam laid the food on the table, then squeezed in behind the furnace and tapped on the door to the coal-bin. "I've brought your dinner," Miriam said as she opened the door and shined her flashlight in on the girl. "I don't want you to be alarmed, but I've also brought my son with me. He'd like to apologize for the way he treated you in the church."

Miriam turned to Kristopher. "Get a candle from the cupboard and light it, will you? We'll be out in a minute."

Sarah cautiously followed Miriam into the main room.

Kristopher had just set the candle on the table, and as she moved into the candle's light, he felt his pulse quicken. She was the most beautiful girl he'd ever seen. The bruises on her face were fading, and her long dark hair was plaited into a single braid that hung loosely down her back. Enormous dark eyes, shaded with thick lashes, looked at him warily.

The three of them sat down at the small table in the center of the room. As Sarah ate, Kristopher told her what had happened to him, and how he'd finally had his eyes opened to what a fool he'd been. He asked her to forgive him for the way he'd treated her.

She listened quietly while he spoke, and when he'd finished, tears began to form in her eyes. "I'm sorry for what you've been through," she said, "but at least you still have your family and your home. I don't have anyone anymore. I'm all alone."

Her simple words hit him hard, and he impulsively reached out and put his hand on hers. "We'll take care of you," he said. He turned to his mother. "Won't we, Mutti?"

Miriam nodded. "We'll do the best we can."

✙ ✙

Lying in bed later that night, the reality of all that had happened began to sink in for Kristopher. The realization that he and his family were in great danger was new and frightening. It had never occurred to him that he'd ever have to be afraid of the Gestapo or his Hitler Youth friends, but now that he knew about the church's involvement in hiding Jews, he knew he'd have to watch every step he took. Each time he thought of being sent to one of the camps his father had described, a wave of panic shot through him.

The immediate problem he had to face, however, was going to school the next day. He already knew what to expect. Rolf and his cronies would be all-too-happy to let everyone know he was no longer in the Hitler Youth. And Herr Brewer would probably kick him out of school—or ridicule him like he'd done other Jewish kids when they still went there. He wasn't sure what to expect.

But, since the Hitler Youth now officially considered him to be a Jew, he wasn't going to be apologetic about it. He was the same person he'd always been, and he was proud of who he was. One thing was sure: he wasn't going to be one of those pathetic Jews who just took whatever was handed out to them like those he'd seen standing so forlornly in lines at the train station, or struggling in the work gangs. If the Nazis wanted to give him a hard time, they were going to get more than they bargained for.

No one greeted him as he took his seat in the classroom the next morning. Herr Brewer made more than his usual derogatory remarks about Jews, and, at recess, Rolf and his friends did their best to try to provoke a fight with him, but he shook off their taunts with a sneer and walked back into the classroom.

After school he fully expected Rolf to be waiting for him at the bike rack, but as he rounded the corner of the building, he stopped abruptly. No one was at the bike rack, and his bike was gone! He had started to run back to the classroom when he saw Hannah von Kemp coming toward him, pushing his bike. He ran up to her and wrenched it out of her hands.

"What're you doing with my bike?" he demanded.

Hannah didn't flinch. "Rolf was getting ready to take it, so I took it instead. I was only doing you a favor, so don't get mad at me."

"I can fight my own battles! I'm surprised you're not worried about tainting yourself by even talking to me."

Her indignation caught him off guard as she drew her face up to within inches of his. "You self-centered, pig-headed boy! You're so full of self-pity that you're going to drive off anyone who wants to be your friend. I don't care what anyone is saying about you. You're a hundred times better than any of the stupid boys in this school, and it's because they're so jealous of you that they're saying the things they are."

Hannah's outburst forced a cynical little laugh out of him. "I'm surprised you still want to be friends, with your father being such a big-shot Nazi. I figured he wouldn't want you to have anything more to do with me."

"My father isn't a real Nazi. He had to join the Party or they wouldn't let him work. He's just a scientist who's trying to serve his country, and he thinks it's awful what they've done to you, but there's nothing he can do about it without getting himself in trouble. I hope you understand that."

Kristopher gave a disparaging snort. "I didn't expect him to stick his neck out for me."

"Well, I want you to know that I'll always be your friend. No matter what." Her voice softened. "I just wish we didn't have to move."

Kristopher's brows shot up. "Where are you moving?"

"I don't know, but we're leaving in two weeks. We're keeping our house here, though, because we plan to come back after the war."

Kristopher was surprised at the sudden feeling of loss at the thought of Hannah leaving. He reached out and put his hand awkwardly on her shoulder. "I'm sorry you're moving. You've been a good friend, even though I don't know why."

She drew herself up to her full height and perched her hands on her hips. "Kristopher Falkenhorst," she said, "you are so blind!" With that, she turned and marched off.

He followed her departure with a bewildered look. Was it possible that she had a crush on him? He'd always been so busy with all his Jungvolk activities that the thought of a girl being romantically interested in him had never really crossed his mind. But now that he had so much time on his hands, it might have been nice to have one.

The more he thought about it, the more his thoughts turned to the girl in the church basement. From just talking to her those few moments last night, he realized she really needed a friend. He started to grin. He'd love to be friends with someone as beautiful as her.

He began to pedal faster.

7

1942
Summer

With his eyes closed, leaning back against a gnarled old oak on the bank of the Spree, Kristopher sifted through the tumultuous events of the past weeks. All he'd worked so hard for since he was six years old was gone—even his friends. How quickly they forgot everything he'd done for them.

He shook his head dolefully. His father had told him that the only ones you could really count on when the chips were down were your family and God. He was still having a hard time wondering why God had let the things happen to him that He had, but a smile crossed his face as he thought about Sarah. Something good had come out of all this.

She had been hiding in the church's furnace room for four weeks when they decided they needed that for other refugees, so Gaston had moved her to the cellar of the parsonage until they could determine whether the rape had gotten her pregnant. Paul had already spoken to a doctor in his church who was willing to check her condition if she began to show signs of pregnancy, but they were so busy with their other refugees that they'd put Sarah's care completely into Kristopher's hands, and he eagerly spent every spare minute that he could with her.

School was finally out for the summer, and he was thankful for that. In the past he'd always looked forward to school vacation, filled as it was with his Hitler Youth activities, but, actually, this summer was proving to be one of the most exciting yet. His father had given him the job of contacting people in the church who'd indicated a willingness to take Jews into their homes, and then—if they said they would—secretly escorting the Jews to those homes. He'd come to know every back street, alley, and railroad tunnel in Berlin in his effort to avoid the Gestapo, but it was just the sort of danger a fifteen-year-old boy relished.

One day, on his way home from contacting one of the church members, Kristopher stopped at a spot in the park by the Spree River, one of the few peaceful places left in the chaotic city. From there he could see few signs of the damage the British bombers had wrought on parts of Berlin, and it was easy to pretend that nothing had changed in his world.

He savored the warm sun on his face as he leaned back against an old chestnut tree, listening to the sounds around him. A tugboat passing on the river tooted at him, and he waved at the old captain. He never saw fishermen on the river anymore. In fact, the only civilian men left in Berlin were over sixty or under sixteen, and even they were all involved in the war effort in some way, leaving little time for leisure.

Reluctantly, he forced himself to get up and head back home. As he pedaled his bike across Tiergarten Park, he noticed several women sitting under some ancient oaks, watching their children digging in the dirt of a bomb crater. Coming toward him on the path was a woman pushing the wheelchair of a young soldier with a baby in his lap. When he came abreast of them, he saw that the man's gray army jacket had several campaign ribbons on it, and the squirming baby was snatching at them. As the man reached up to draw the child's hand down, the blanket covering his legs fell to one side, and to Kristopher's complete horror, he saw that there was nothing under the blanket. The man had no legs.

He was so distraught that he nearly veered his bike into a tree. That soldier couldn't be more than a year or two older than he, and his life was over. And for what? There were too many men on the streets of

Berlin like that young soldier for anyone to still believe the propaganda that was coming from the radio and newspapers that Germany was winning the war. Seeing these cruel realities almost made him glad he was no longer in the Hitler Youth, preparing for the "glorious" life of a soldier. There was nothing glorious about spending the rest of your life without legs.

Kristopher was about a half-block from home when he glanced up and saw the black Mercedes parked in front of his house. A surge of panic shot through him. Only one group still drove cars like that. The Gestapo! He ground his bike to a halt, trying to decide what to do. If it was the Gestapo, then it meant they'd found Oma and Opa and Sarah, in which case they would arrest all of his family.

While he sat straddling his bike, Kristopher saw a man in a black trench coat carrying something out the front door of the parsonage. From a distance it was impossible to tell what it was. He made a quick decision. If they were arresting his family, he was going with them. He pedaled furiously toward the house, slammed his bike on the ground, and raced up the steps, nearly colliding with the stocky man on the porch. The man had a typewriter and radio in his arms, and his scowling face registered surprise as he drew back to avoid the collision with Kristopher.

"What's going on here?" Kristopher demanded. "What are you doing with my father's typewriter and our radio?"

The man gave him a dismissive look. "Jews are no longer allowed to own any radios, typewriters, telephones, or any other electrical appliances."

"My father isn't a Jew!"

"Maybe not, but you and your mother are, and the law doesn't allow any of these things in a home with Jews in it."

Kristopher angrily pushed past the man into the house and saw that there was another agent holding his father's camera. "Do you have any film?" the man demanded of Paul.

"Only what's in the camera, but I'd like to keep that roll, please.

Those are pictures of my son's fifteenth birthday. They can't be of any interest to you."

The agent fumbled with the back of the camera and finally succeeded in opening it. He took out the film and maliciously let it unwind. "Is this what you wanted?" he said, tossing the exposed roll to Paul.

Kristopher looked at his father expectantly, but Paul merely gathered the film in his hands and said nothing.

"How dare you!" Kristopher cried out.

"Kristopher!" his father said firmly. "That's enough! They're only doing what they've been ordered to do. Let them finish their business and leave our home."

He couldn't believe his ears. How could his father just stand there and let them take their things without trying to stop them? He started to object, but caught the steely look in his father's eyes and stopped short.

Just then the man who had been out at the car stuck his head in the front door. "I have a bike out here. Can we get it in the trunk of the car?"

Kristopher spun around. "That's my bike! Don't you touch it!"

He started toward the door, but the agent grabbed him by the arm and spun him around. "Just a minute, Jew-boy. We're authorized to take any illegal possessions you Jews own, so get that through your head right now."

Kristopher struggled to break the man's hold on his arm, but Paul quickly jumped forward and grabbed his son in a tight grasp. "Kristopher," he said sharply. "These men are only doing what they've been ordered to. I forbid you to say one more word."

Hot, angry tears sprang to Kristopher's eyes. For the first time in his life, he was ashamed of his father. How could he appease these criminals this way?

"I should arrest your son," the agent said curtly to Paul, "but since you've been so cooperative, I'll let it go this time. However, I think you'd better sit him down and explain these new laws to him, or he's going to find himself in a great deal of trouble."

"Yes, I'll do that," Paul said. His voice was courteous, but not his eyes. They were filled with barely concealed anger as the men departed.

Kristopher ran to the window and watched the two agents drive off. He sucked in a deep breath and leaned his head against the curtain, trying to get control of himself.

Paul came up behind Kristopher and placed his hand on his shoulder. "Son . . . please."

Kristopher whipped around and knocked the hand away. "How could you just let them walk off with all our things? And my bike!" he exploded. "You didn't even try to stop them."

"You don't understand. If I hadn't cooperated with them, they would've torn this house apart looking for things to take, and you know—as well as I do—that we couldn't let them do that. As it was, we just barely got Sarah up to the hiding place with Oma and Opa."

Kristopher stood rigid, his fists clenched. For the first time since he'd come into the house, he noticed his mother. She was seated quietly on the sofa, fingering something in her hands. He looked closer and saw that she was holding a small piece of yellow cloth in the shape of a Star of David with the word "*Jude*" on it.

"Mutti!" he cried. "What're you doing with that?"

She tried to make light of it. "It's just a little decoration I have to wear when I leave the house, but I'm just thankful you don't have to."

Kristopher grabbed the star from her hands and threw it on the floor, viciously grinding his heel into it. "We'll never let her wear it, will we, Vati?"

"I'm afraid she has to when she goes out, or she can be arrested. We can't let that happen."

"But I thought Mutti and I had special citizenship papers. How can they make her wear a star? It's against the law."

Paul's look was bleak. "The law is whatever they decide at any moment, and for some reason, they've decided to harass us."

"Isn't there some way to fight back?" Kristopher asked.

Paul shook his head. "We simply can't afford to draw any more attention to ourselves than we've already done. I have a feeling they're just looking for some excuse to arrest us."

"What about Uncle Kurt? Can't he help?"

"We can't ask him to stick his neck out for us at this point, but if they should arrest us, I know he'll do whatever he can. In the meantime, we've got to give the appearance that we're cooperating."

Paul sat down beside Miriam and slipped his arm around her. "I'm so sorry, Liebchen. What can we do to make this easier for you?"

She patted his knee. "Just don't make a big thing out of it. We'll get through this, and when it's all over, we're going to be a lot stronger. God knows what He's doing, even if we don't."

She bent over and picked up the yellow star from the floor, smoothing out the creases in it. "I'll even wear this with pride," she said, holding it over her heart. "My father always told me that our circumstances can't defeat us, but our reactions to them can, so I choose to think of this as my special 'Star of Bethlehem.'"

She stood up and pulled Paul and Kristopher into her arms. "Enough of these long faces, you two," she said. "God could have chosen any time in history for us to be on this earth, and He's let us be here now, so there must be a reason for it. Now, let's go get Oma and Opa and Sarah out of the hiding place. I'm sure they're frantic with worry."

✝ ✝

When Kristopher brought Sarah's dinner to her a couple of nights after the house had been raided, she was doubled up in pain on her cot, and he knelt down beside her in alarm. "What's wrong, Liebchen?"

"I have terrible cramps, and I'm bleeding."

"Why didn't you tell me sooner?" he exclaimed. "I would've had Vati call the doctor."

"I kept thinking it would get better, but it hasn't."

His eyes took on a wild look. "Do you think you're having a miscarriage?"

"I don't know. I've been having these cramps for several days, and they've gotten worse since last night when I first noticed blood."

81

He pulled her up into his arms, letting her cry against his chest. "I'll talk to Vati right now. He'll know what to do." He took her face between his hands. "Don't worry, Liebchen. I'll take care of this." He brushed the tears from her cheeks, then raced upstairs.

Miriam and Paul were already in bed when Kristopher burst into their room. They both sat up in alarm. "What's wrong?" Paul asked.

"I've just come from Sarah, and she's bleeding and having cramps, and I told her you had a doctor who said he'd help her. Can you call him?"

Paul turned on the bedside lamp and reached for his robe on the back of the chair. "Dr. Schmidt isn't in his office at this hour, and I don't dare use the church phone to call him at home. I'm sure the Gestapo's tapped it," he said, pulling on the robe. "Dear God! It's the worst possible thing to have to deal with at this time."

"It's not her fault!" Kristopher said defensively.

"I know that. I just meant that there's incredible danger in this for all of us." He turned to Miriam. "Will you go down and see what you can do for Sarah?"

Kristopher let out a sigh of relief. "I knew you'd help her. We're all she has."

"I know we are," Miriam said. "I also know you've gotten way too attached to her. Once we get through this, we've got to move her to a safer place. She's too exposed down there in the cellar, and that's putting all of us in danger."

"I'll talk to Gaston, and we'll find a place for her right away," Kristopher promised.

Miriam got an armload of old towels and a basin of warm water, and started for the stairs.

"Can I come with you?" Kristopher asked.

Miriam shook her head. "No, this is going to be very hard for her, and she won't want an audience. After I've cleaned her up, you can go sit with her for a while, but don't stay too long. She needs her strength for what's coming."

When Miriam saw the amount of blood that Sarah was losing, she knew the girl was miscarrying, and—God forgive her—she found herself grateful that things were working out this way. At least it would give Sarah a better chance to survive what she was going to be facing.

8

Hans Schmidt was just a country boy at heart. As a young doctor, his greatest joy had been traveling the backroads of small rural villages at all hours of the day and night, offering help and comfort to the sick. For forty years, he'd done just that, and gladly would have spent his twilight years in the same happy rut if it hadn't been for his wife, Freda, harping that there was no future in the new Germany for a country bumpkin doctor. She was sure that Berlin was the only place where a man's contribution to Germany's great socialist future could be properly noticed and appreciated by Party leaders.

And Hans knew that Freda had every intention of having them both noticed. Forty-three years earlier, when he'd taken her from her beloved Berlin and deposited her in one tiny hamlet after another while he pursued his medical practice, she'd sworn that the day would come when she would get them back to Berlin. Three years ago their life savings had gone into the purchase of a beautiful mansion in the Wannsee District of Berlin that had come on the market quite suddenly when the wealthy Jewish owners had been relocated. Friends of Freda had apprised her of its availability at a bargain price, and she finally coerced Hans back to the big city.

Since then, her life had been one whirlwind after another of Nazi activities. She headed two major Nazi women's groups. One was at the Sisters of Charity Hospital where she coordinated rehabilitation activities for disabled veterans. The other was a committee of women who taught domestic science to girls from ages ten to fourteen in the *Jung Maedel*, the girls' branch of the Hitler Youth.

Yes, life had finally come full circle for Freda Schmidt. That her husband did not share her enthusiasm for the chaotic life in Berlin and the Nazi Party folderol did not seem to phase her one bit. As long as he behaved circumspectly, he could be left to his own dull world of medicine. At sixty-eight, he would gladly have retired to some small country farm and lived the rest of his life contentedly tending his precious roses, but with so many young doctors being called into military service, there was great pressure on the older ones to tend the needs of the homefront, and Hans Schmidt was not a man to shirk his duty.

The one issue on which he had been unwilling to compromise with Freda, however, was the choice of a church in Berlin. She had wanted to join the prestigious Kaiser Wilhelm Church, but Hans had put his foot down firmly. His family had been devout Christians for generations, and Paul Falkenhorst of the Evangelical Free Church was just the kind of Christ-centered minister he was used to.

After three years of sitting under Pastor Falkenhorst's teachings, he realized that he and the pastor also shared similar views of the Nazi excesses, particularly their attitude toward Jews. So the office visit from Pastor Falkenhorst that morning had had a disquieting effect upon him. From what Paul told him, the girl in question was probably not in any physical danger, but was in a serious predicament, and he'd agreed to go to the pastor's home that evening and examine her. If she was in the process of aborting a fetus, it would be a straightforward procedure of assisting her and attending to her medical needs.

As he was putting some supplies into his old black medical bag in preparation for leaving for the pastor's home, a nagging suspicion tugged at his mind. Was it possible this girl was a Jew and that was why Paul did not want to bring her into the office as he'd suggested? Well, it made no difference to him whether she was Jewish or not. His only concern was how to get out of the house with his medical bag without having to make an explanation to Freda.

It was nearly eight o'clock before Freda went upstairs to prepare for bed. Hans waited until he heard her bath water running, then jotted a quick note saying he'd had an emergency call, laid it on the table in the entryway, and quietly went out. His car was parked in the drive in front of the house, and he gingerly opened the door and climbed in. He pulled at the door, but it failed to close all the way, so he gave it another pull. This time it shut, but he winced at the noise it made.

He had just started the engine when Freda's scowling face peered down at him from the upstairs bedroom window. She quickly shoved the window up and yelled at him, "Hans, where are you going at this hour?"

That woman! How in God's name had he been able to put up with her all these years? He shook his head, all too aware of the answer to that question. He lived with the guilt of not having told her before they married that he might be sterile, and she had never let him forget that their childlessness was his fault.

He peered up at her through the open car window. "I've had an emergency call. I left you a note about it on the entry table," he shouted. "I won't be gone long."

"I didn't hear the phone ring," she screeched.

"Oh, for heaven's sake," he muttered to himself, then yelled back up at her, "You must've had the bath water running. Will you please pull your head back in and stop that yelling? I said I wouldn't be gone long."

As he drove off, he glanced back and saw her disapproving face in the window. *Oh, for God's sake*, he thought. *Now she'll be waiting to grill me when I get home, and that's the last thing I need if this girl really is a pregnant Jew hiding in the church parsonage.* He drove cautiously through the darkened streets, trying to concoct a plausible story to tell Freda when he got home.

He pulled up in front of the parsonage and cut his car lights, twisting in the seat to look for any approaching cars. No street lights were on, and all the houses had their blackout curtains pulled. He grabbed his bag and was starting for the house, when a man's voice rang out from the darkened sidewalk a few yards away. Hans froze.

"Hello, there," the voice said with forced pleasantness as the figure of a short, stout man emerged from the darkness. He had a German Shepherd on a leash by his side. "You look like a doctor. Is someone ill at the Falkenhorsts'?"

Hans glanced down at his telltale medical bag. There was no way to avoid the man's question. "Yes," he said. "Frau Falkenhorst is not feeling well. Are you a friend of theirs?"

"I'm Helmut Klinger. I live next door."

Hans recognized the name as a minor Nazi official, but couldn't recall what post he held. He hastily extended his hand to Klinger. "I'm Doctor Schmidt," he said. "It's a lovely night for a walk, isn't it?" He started to reach down and pat the Shepherd's head, but the dog began to growl. He quickly pulled his hand back. "That's quite a dog you have there."

Klinger glanced down at the dog that was now sniffing Hans's pant leg. "Yes, I'm quite proud of him. He's from a litter of *Reichsminister* Goering's shepherd, Isolde. He's championship stock." Klinger yanked on the growling dog's leash, pulling him back by his side.

Hans was becoming uneasy about this encounter and decided to cut it short. "Well, I must get in to Frau Falkenhorst," he said. "Enjoy your walk." He turned and headed for the house, leaving Klinger standing there in the dark staring after him. As Paul let him in, Hans turned and looked back at Klinger, but he was no longer on the sidewalk. He had moved behind the car and was peering down at the license plate.

Dr. Schmidt's account of his meeting with Klinger put them all on edge, but there was no time to talk about it. Paul led the doctor down to where Sarah was lying on her cot and introduced them, then excused himself and went back up to the kitchen.

Miriam and Kristopher were waiting anxiously as Paul came up from the cellar. "Did you tell Dr. Schmidt that Klinger is the Party blockleader of our neighborhood?" Miriam asked.

He shook his head. "No, I thought it best not to say anything at this point. We'll deal with that later if he has to come back."

"But suppose Klinger gets suspicious about Dr. Schmidt being here tonight and starts asking questions? He'd do anything to advance himself with the Party."

"You'll just have to pretend to be in bed with something for the next few days," Paul said. "There's no way the Klingers can prove that Doctor Schmidt was not here to see you, so let's not start worrying unnecessarily. My biggest concern now is what he can do for Sarah." He looked worried. "I haven't told him she's Jewish, but I think he knows."

Twice, Kristopher went to the cellar door and leaned his ear against it. When Doctor Schmidt finally came up from the cellar, his face was grave.

"It's a good thing you called me, pastor. The young lady is definitely in the process of miscarrying, and she has some seriously infected areas on her female parts. She should be in a hospital."

"I think you understand that we can't take her to one."

"I was afraid of that," he said, "but when she does pass the fetus, she should have a thorough pelvic exam to be sure the uterus is cleared, and she needs some attention to those other wounds." He paused thoughtfully. "I don't suppose you'd want to bring her to my office."

"I can't do that, either, Doctor. I hope you understand the danger that would put us all in—including you."

Hans sat down wearily at the table and glanced up at Miriam. "Do you suppose I could have a cup of tea? This has been a long and tiring day, and I still have to face my wife when I get home. I'm afraid she doesn't share our views about our Hebrew friends."

Miriam's glance darted to Paul as she prepared the tea. "You know I'm Jewish, don't you?" Miriam said, handing him a cup of tea.

He looked up gratefully as he took it. "Thank you. Yes, my wife's friends made sure we knew that when I made the decision to join your church. But I hope you both realize that it's of absolutely no importance to me what a person's religious background is. This Nazi obsession with Jews is ridiculous, and to tell you the truth, it's good to be with people that I can say that to freely. I'm awfully tired of having to guard everything I say around my wife's friends." He dipped his head and peered out at Miriam over the rim of his glasses. "I assume our little friend downstairs is also Jewish?"

"She is, and she's been through hell because of it, but it'll be even worse for her if she has to carry this baby."

"I don't think there's anything to worry about there," he said. "She's definitely going to miscarry regardless of what any of us do for her, and—considering her situation—it will probably be a blessing in disguise."

Hans finished his tea and stood up, pulling his big frame from the chair. "Well, Pastor," he said, "she'll probably miscarry tonight or tomorrow, so I can come tomorrow evening and scrape her uterus and give her an antibiotic and a sedative to keep her comfortable for a few days. But if she hasn't miscarried in the next few days, you can contact me as soon as she does, and I'll come by. In the meantime, Frau Falkenhorst, I suggest you stay out of sight for a few days. I'm awfully sorry about that little episode on my way in here, but I have a feeling that your neighbor has more than a neighborly interest in what goes on in this house."

✠ ✠

On the drive home through the darkened city, Hans found himself strangely elated. His decision to flout the Party, even in such a minor way as treating a Jew, was a major victory for him. All his life he had been so predictable, but he had only recently admitted to himself that his life up till now—as his wife had so often reminded him—had been stifling and dull. Now he had the chance to do something for a good cause, and he was glad he could help the poor unfortunate girl. He was even prepared for the cross-examination he knew he'd get from Freda. There were a few things he'd been trying to get the courage to say to her for years, and quite possibly tonight would be the night he would have that chance.

As he pulled up in the driveway of his house, he glanced up and saw the dim traces of light around the blackout curtain in their bedroom window. Freda was waiting up and no doubt primed for him.

She was sitting up in bed with a book as he entered the bedroom, but laid it down on the bedcovers with an exaggerated gesture. When he took no notice of her, she finally emitted a long-suffering sigh. "Well?" she asked.

"'Well,' what?"

"Where have you been for the past two hours? I was worried sick that something might have happened to you, but I guess that makes no difference to you. You could at least have told me where you were going, or called me when you got there."

Hans had taken off his clothes and was hanging them in the closet. He realized that he really didn't want a confrontation tonight, after all. It never got him anywhere, and tonight he felt emotionally drained.

"Freda," he said wearily, "when we lived in the country, I often went out on late-evening calls, and that never bothered you then. People still get sick at night, you know."

She was undaunted. "Yes, Hans, but Berlin is filled with all kinds of unsavory people. Refugees and Jews are flooding the city, making it very dangerous for decent citizens to be out on the streets. If you don't care about yourself, at least you could think of me. What would happen to me if you were waylaid on one of these questionable midnight calls?"

Hans whipped around and fixed his angry gaze on her. "Oh, for God's sake, Freda. These *unsavory people* you're so concerned about are just poor unfortunates who've had their homes bombed out from under them, or confiscated by your precious Nazis. They're no more dangerous than I am. But, if it will make you feel any better, it wasn't one of them who called. It was Pastor Falkenhorst. His wife was ill and needed immediate attention. They had no gas for their car, and, as you are well aware, I'm sure, Frau Falkenhorst is no longer able to use public transportation to come to my office because she's one of the 'unsavory' people you're so worried about." He finished buttoning his pajama top and started into the bathroom.

Freda seemed determined to pursue the issue to its bitter end. "Well, I think it was very nervy of them to ask you to go to their home to treat her," she shouted at his retreating figure. "After all, you're not their regular doctor." As an after-thought, she added, "And it isn't very smart of you to get involved with Jews, even if one is married to your minister. It will reflect badly on both of us if it gets back to any Party officials." She paused, waiting for some response, but all she heard was the sound of running water. "Did you hear me?" she shouted.

Hans came to the bathroom door, wiping his face with a towel. "The whole damn town heard you, Freda."

Her face was drawn into a knot of exasperation. "Well, one of us has to think about our future. If it weren't for me, we'd still be in that miserable little town in Bavaria with you giving your services away for nothing. You should thank me that I'm concerned about what happens to us. Instead, all I get from you is sarcasm."

Hans retreated into the bathroom, toweling his face. It was pointless to argue with her. No matter what they started out talking about, it always ended with how he'd failed her.

He went back into the bedroom, avoiding her glare, and pulled the covers down on his side of the bed. He lay down with his back to her and pulled the covers up around his ears. Her silence permeated the room like heavy perfume, and he could feel her eyes burning into his back as exhaustion overtook him. It was ever thus, he thought, as he drifted into peaceful oblivion.

9

While Paul was at his office in the church the next day, and Miriam was busy upstairs in the parsonage, someone knocked on the front door. Kristopher was in the cellar with Sarah when he heard the knocking. He froze, waiting for someone to get the door. When the knocking persisted, he bolted up the stairs.

"Who's there?" he asked through the closed door.

"It's your neighbor, Frau Klinger."

Oh my God! he thought. *What could she want?* He hesitated for a moment, then opened the door a crack and peeked out.

"I'm sorry, but my father's next door at the church, and Mutti's in bed sick."

"Oh?" Frau Klinger's penciled eyebrows shot up in surprise. "Her illness must have come on very suddenly. I saw her working in her garden yesterday afternoon, and I'm sure I saw her through your kitchen window this morning." She tried to peer past Kristopher into the living room, but he kept the door only slightly ajar.

"I . . . I think she did get up for a few minutes this morning," he stammered, "but the doctor has ordered her to stay in bed for a few days. I'm sorry I can't invite you in, but he said she was to have no visitors."

She nodded, barely able to conceal a smirk. "Will you please tell her I stopped by, and that I'm sorry to hear that she's ill? She has so many responsibilities with the church and you and your father. It must be very hard on her to have to stay in bed."

92

"Yes, it is," Kristopher said. "I'll tell her you dropped by."

He shut the door quickly and leaned against it, trembling. Beads of sweat dotted his upper lip. He dashed upstairs and told his mother.

"She's an evil woman," Miriam said. "You'd better run over to the church and tell Vati. Obviously Klinger is suspicious of what went on here last night, and there's no telling who he's informed about it."

"I don't dare call Doctor Schmidt on the church phone," Paul said when Kristopher told him about Frau Klinger's visit. "I know they're listening to every word I say on it. One of us will have to get over to his office and warn him not to come tonight, but I don't want his office staff to see me there again, so I'll have to ask you to go, son."

He sat down and scratched out a hasty note, then handed it to Kristopher. "Here, take this note to Doctor Schmidt, and make sure you give it *only* to him, then get back here as fast as you can."

☩ ☩

As Kristopher stood waiting for the *U-bahn*, he glanced at the clock on the station wall and saw that it was nearly 5:30. The train was late. He paced back and forth impatiently. When the train finally arrived fifteen minutes later, it was crowded with people going home from work, and he had to stand. It was delayed again at the next station as another crowd of commuters shoved their way on board. By the time he got off at the stop nearest Doctor Schmidt's office, it was five minutes to six, and he knew the office closed at six o'clock. He ran the two blocks to the medical office, but Doctor Schmidt's nurse was just locking the door as he raced up out of breath.

"Is Doctor Schmidt still here?" he panted.

"No, I'm sorry, but he's left for the day. Is there something I can do for you?"

Kristopher looked about in desperation. "I've got to see Doctor Schmidt. Can you tell me where he lives?"

"I'm sorry, but I'm not allowed to give out that information. Are you sure there isn't some way I can help you?"

He was close to tears. "I have an urgent message for him from my father. He's Doctor Schmidt's minister. My mother's really sick and my father said I must get this note to Doctor Schmidt right away. Won't you please give me his address?"

The woman gnawed at her lip, trying to make up her mind. She knew the doctor didn't like seeing patients at home, but she also knew that he was especially close to his church, and the request seemed legitimate enough to her. She took out a pen and piece of paper and wrote the address down. "You'd better be telling me the truth, young man, or Doctor Schmidt's going to be very angry with me."

Kristopher grabbed the paper. "I swear I am. Thank you so much." He turned and bolted down the street.

It took the train twenty minutes to get to the station nearest the Schmidt's, and Kristopher ran the four blocks to their address. He was awe-struck at the grandeur of the stately home and beautifully manicured grounds as he ran up the brick path to the house.

He rang the bell and waited. No one came, so he rang it again several times. When the door finally opened, an elegant, gray-haired woman stood in the door, her brow creased in a frown.

"Yes? What is it you want?" she asked, her voice brittle with annoyance.

"Is Doctor Schmidt in?"

"Yes, but he doesn't see patients at his home."

"I'm not a patient. I have an important message for him from my father."

"And just who is your father, young man?"

"Doctor Falkenhorst from the Evangelical Free Church."

Her annoyance deepened. "My husband was already inconvenienced by being at your home until all hours last night. If you have a message, you can leave it with me, and I'll see that he gets it."

Kristopher shook his head. "I'm sorry, but my father said I was to give the message to Doctor Schmidt in person. He was very specific about that."

Freda Schmidt's face began to redden as the doctor came up behind her.

"What's going on here?" He looked past his wife and saw Kristopher. "You're the pastor's son, aren't you?" He moved his wife aside and stepped out to the porch. "What seems to be wrong? Is your mother worse?"

Kristopher looked hesitantly at the doctor's wife, not knowing whether to give Doctor Schmidt the note in front of her, or not.

He stepped up to the doctor and lowered his voice. "Can I speak to you privately, Doctor? I have an urgent message from my father."

Hans turned to his wife. "Go back inside, Freda. I'll speak to the boy and see what it is he wants. I'm sure it has to do with his mother's condition."

Freda gave him a withering look, then turned and went inside.

Dr. Schmidt lowered his voice. "Now, what is it that's so urgent that it brought you all the way out here? Has your little friend miscarried?"

"Not yet," he said, "but she still has cramps and some bleeding."

"Sometimes it goes on for days like that. Why didn't your father just call and tell me he isn't ready for me yet?"

"The Gestapo took our phone out, and Vati thinks the one in the church has been tapped." He reached into his pocket and pulled out the note and handed it to the Doctor. "He explains it all in here."

"I see," he said. He took his half-glasses out of his pocket and maneuvered them on to the bridge of his nose, then unfolded the note and read it. "Your father feels there might be some trouble with your neighbor if I come to your house again." He started to take the glasses off, then paused thoughtfully, pushing the glasses back up on his nose. He took a pen out of his breast pocket. "Perhaps he's right. I did see him looking at my license plate last night."

He wrote something on the back of the note and handed it back to Kristopher. "Take this to your father. It's the name and phone number of a doctor friend of mine that he can trust. He can contact him when Sarah miscarries, and he'll be able to help her."

He lowered his voice. "And it wouldn't be wise to come here again or for your father to phone me, either here or at the office. My wife is very hostile to Jews, and I'm not sure about all my office help, but this doctor, whose name I've given you, is completely trustworthy and he'll help your little friend."

Hans took a quick glance over his shoulder, then raised his voice for Freda's benefit. "You run along now, young man, but tell your mother to stay off her feet and she should be fine in a day or two."

10

Kristopher ran down the long path to the street, turned left, and started toward the U-bahn. He had walked about two blocks when he noticed a dark Mercedes slowly following him about a half-block behind. He picked up his pace, and the car speeded up. Beginning to panic, he started to run. The subway station was just a block ahead when the car pulled up about fifty feet in front of him, and three men jumped out. They stood blocking his way on the sidewalk. He looked around for some place to run, but a high wall ran the length of the block on his left, and he realized it would be futile to try to cross the street or turn back. He slowed his pace to a walk as the three men approached him. The tallest one, in a black trench coat and a dark felt hat pulled down over his brow, stepped up to Kristopher and asked to see his papers.

He was so frightened that he forgot he didn't have them with him, and began digging in his pants' pockets. After a few seconds he looked up, visibly shaken. "I must've left them at home. I can bring them to you tomorrow."

"Where do you live?" the tall man demanded.

Kristopher told him.

"You're a long way from home, aren't you? It's nearly curfew. What are you doing clear out here?"

A knot of fear began to twist at Kristopher's stomach. He had to tell them something or they might arrest him.

"My mother's ill, and our phone isn't working, so my father sent me to get a prescription from the doctor at his office, but he'd already left for the day, so his nurse sent me here to his house."

The other two men moved in close to Kristopher.

"That sounds like a bunch of bull to me," one of them quipped. "I think we should search him. There are a lot of dangerous people walking the streets of Berlin these days."

"I'm not dangerous," Kristopher stammered. "I'm just running an errand for my father. I haven't done anything wrong."

"That's for us to decide." The tall man motioned to the other two. "Search him."

Kristopher drew back instinctively, but the two men grabbed his arms and pinned them behind him, while the spokesman began going through his pockets.

"What's this?" he asked, pulling the note out of Kristopher's shirt pocket. He unfolded it and read it carefully. "Well," he said, drawing out the word dramatically, "this is very interesting. It looks like our little friend here has been on more than just an errand of mercy. I don't know what this note is all about, but I certainly intend to find out." He nodded his head at the other two. "Get him in the car, and we'll take him to headquarters. I think he'll feel more like talking to us there."

As they rode along in the black Mercedes, all Kristopher could think about was his family and Sarah. There was no way to get word to them about his arrest. The best he could hope for was that they would begin to be suspicious about his being so late and hide Oma and Opa and Sarah.

☩ ☩

The Gestapo headquarters on Burgstrasse was crowded with bedraggled men, women, and children—most of them wearing yellow stars. Kristopher frantically scanned the room, hoping to see someone he could send to warn his parents, but the detainees, huddled together in frightened groups, kept their eyes down as he was shoved through their midst. The three agents led him to a small, windowless room that was furnished with just a long wooden table and six chairs. A shaded bulb hung from the ceiling, lighting the table directly under it. It was just how Kristopher had pictured a Gestapo interrogation room, but he never imagined in his wildest dreams that he would ever see one, let alone be interrogated in it.

For two hours he sat alone in the room, his mind in chaos. Had they gone to arrest his family? What about Doctor Schmidt? Had they arrested him? And the doctor whose name was on the note? Would they bring him in, too? When the door finally opened, he was jarred to see Heinrich Mueller.

"Well, well, well," Mueller chortled. "Kristopher Falkenhorst. I thought it would be only a matter of time before you'd be in here. We've had our eye on you and your family for some time and knew you were up to something. We figured we'd just let you all go until you hung yourselves, and it looks like you may have done it now."

He pulled a chair out and sat down across from Kristopher, removing his leather gloves with a dramatic air. "Now, I think you'd better tell me what kind of mischief you've been up to. It'll make it a whole lot easier for you and your parents."

Kristopher glared across at him. "I don't know what you're talking about. I was only taking a note to our doctor because the Gestapo took our phone out—as I'm sure you know."

"And the note?" Mueller asked, holding it up. "Why did your father tell Doctor Schmidt it was 'unsafe' to come to your house tonight? Why would it be unsafe?"

"I don't know," Kristopher said. "All I did was deliver the note."

"Kristopher," Mueller admonished in a patronizing tone. "You can do better than that. We know Doctor Schmidt was at your home last night, but we want to know why. There may be a perfectly legitimate reason for his visit, so just tell us."

"I already told you. My mother is sick."

"Your mother isn't sick," Mueller snapped. "Her neighbor saw her working in her garden yesterday morning."

Kristopher began to perspire. "She got worse as the day went on," he said.

Just then an agent came in and whispered something to Mueller. He nodded and turned back to Kristopher with a sneer. "Well! Well! Well!" he said, punctuating each word. "My men just came from your home, and it seems like there are a *lot* of sick people there. Did you really think you could put this over on us?"

Kristopher's face blanched. *They've found my grandparents and Sarah.* The door opened again, and two Gestapo agents shoved his parents into the room. Kristopher tried to run to his mother, but one of the men jerked him back.

"Keep your hands off him!" Miriam cried, grabbing for Kristopher.

The agent pushed her back roughly. "That's enough out of you. If you try to interfere with what's going on here, you'll find yourself in handcuffs. Is that clear?"

Mueller chuckled. "Well, Reverend Falkenhorst, I can't say I'm surprised to see you and your family here. We've suspected for some time that you've been up to something. What I am surprised at is that you, a Christian minister, would deliberately violate the laws of our Reich. Doesn't the Bible teach that men are supposed to obey the laws of their land?"

"When those laws violate God's laws, then a man is not obligated to blindly obey them," said Paul.

"Then you admit that you've been giving illegal shelter to Jews?"

"I don't ask what a person's religion is if he seeks my help."

Mueller squinted at him accusingly. "Are you saying that the old couple and the girl in your home aren't Jews?"

"I'm saying that it makes no difference to me if they are. The girl came to us after you'd arrested her parents and one of your men had savagely raped her. Of course we took her in without asking whether she was Jewish or not. Any good German would have done the same."

Mueller's face darkened. "Don't lecture me about what a 'good

German' would do. A good German obeys the laws, and the law says that the residences of all Jews must be registered with the authorities. No one is authorized to live at your address but you and your wife and son." A sneer spread across his thin lips. "I presume the old couple are your wife's Jewish parents?"

Paul hesitated a moment. "Yes, they are," he said quietly.

"I thought so. We've been looking for them since the summer of 1939 when they were selected for relocation to one of our work camps."

"You mean extermination camps, don't you?" Kristopher blurted out.

The agent standing near him reached out and slapped him across the mouth, and Kristopher let out a cry. "You keep your mouth shut unless you're asked a question," the agent snarled.

Miriam grabbed at the man. "You bully! He's only a child."

The Gestapo agent twisted her arm behind her until she screamed out in pain. "You don't seem to learn, do you?" he said, shoving her toward Paul. "You keep her under control, Reverend, or I'll gag and handcuff her. Do you understand me?"

Mueller watched this outburst with amused detachment. "I think you can see that this is not a game we're playing. You people are in serious trouble."

He turned to one of the agents as he picked up his gloves from the table. "It's late, and I'd like to get home. I have a lot more questions I want to ask these people, but it'll have to wait until tomorrow. Show them to one of our 'guest rooms' for the night."

He shoved his chair back and got up. As he started out the door, he turned back to Paul. "Oh, and, Reverend, don't get any ideas about your brother being able to help you out of this. The Fuehrer isn't too happy with him right now, and I doubt that General von Falkenhorst will want to stick his neck out over something as serious as this. He may be a fool, but I don't think even he's that big a one."

Mueller left and the two agents herded the Falkenhorsts down to a small room in the basement of the Gestapo headquarters. A single bulb hung from the cciling in the barc room, and there were bars on the one high window. The family was shoved in, and the door locked behind them.

As soon as the door had closed, Kristopher grabbed his father. "What did they do to Oma and Opa and Sarah?"

"We don't know, but when you were so long in coming back, we put all three of them in the hiding place, but those animals were tearing our place apart, so I'm sure they found them after they dragged us out."

Kristopher let out a pitiful wail. "Do you think they hurt them?"

"I don't know," Paul said, "but tomorrow when Gaston comes to the church and sees what's happened, he'll let Uncle Kurt know immediately, and regardless of what Mueller said, Kurt will be able to do something to help us. But in the meantime, we just have to trust God to protect us."

Kristopher angrily wiped at his tears. "God doesn't have any control over the Gestapo. We know what they do to people who cross them. Look at Sarah and her family."

Paul took Kristopher by the shoulders and looked firmly into his eyes. "Yes, they're ruthless and powerful, but we have a God who does miracles, so I'm not giving up on Him. Those goons out there are *not* going to decide our destiny. That's in God's hands."

11

The three of them spent a miserable night huddled together on the hard cold floor. They were awakened around six o'clock and herded upstairs to the interrogation room. A burly agent took them, one by one, to the toilet, and when they were all back in the room, another agent brought them some hard Kaiser rolls and strong black coffee.

About eight o'clock, Gestapo Chief Mueller came in, a broad smile on his face. "Ah, good morning," he beamed. "I trust you had a good night. I apologize for the lack of beds, but we don't want our guests to get too comfortable here. They might want to stay on." He winked at the agent standing by the door. "Now," he said, pulling out a chair and sitting down across the table from them, "let's talk about your friend, Doctor Schmidt, and the cozy little coal bin in the basement of your church."

Kristopher's hand flew to his mouth.

Mueller regarded him with amusement. "Oh yes, we know about the room with the mattress. Would you like to tell me about it, Kristopher?"

"Let him alone," Paul said. "I'll tell you what you want to know."

Mueller turned to Paul, his brows raised in mock surprise. "Well, that's even better. It'll make this whole situation much more pleasant if we can cut out the lies and get right to the truth. Now, what about the room in the church basement? Have you been hiding Jews there?"

Paul weighed his words carefully. "Many homes have been lost in the bombings, and my church has taken in people who need a place to stay for a few nights. We don't ask anyone what their religion is, so it's quite possible that some of them were Jews."

Mueller's eyes narrowed. "So you've just been good little Samaritans, is that it? We both know it's much more than that. You've had a regular Jewish underground going on in your church, haven't you?"

"I took my wife's parents in because you confiscated their home and they had nowhere to go, and we kept the young Jewish girl with us while she recuperated from the rape and beating by one of your agents. So if you want to punish someone for showing kindness to those in desperate need, it's me you want. Not my family or my church."

"Do you really expect me to believe that you were in this alone?"

"I didn't say I was in it alone. I said I was solely responsible for it happening. I'm the pastor of the church and I decide what happens there. It's me you want, not my family or my church members."

Mueller turned as the door opened. The agent who came in whispered something to him, and Mueller nodded. "Bring him in," he said.

He turned back to Paul. "We have a friend of yours out there, your Doctor Schmidt. We'll be very interested in hearing his version of the interesting note we found on your son."

The door opened again, and two Gestapo agents led Hans Schmidt in. His normally ruddy face had paled, and his compassionate hazel eyes were fixed in a glazed stare. *Dear God*, thought Paul. *What have they done to him?*

As Hans caught sight of the Falkenhorsts, he seemed to snap out of his trance, even managing a wan smile. Paul smiled back encouragingly as one of the agents shoved Hans' bulky frame into a chair.

Hans searched Paul's face for some clue as to what he might have told Mueller.

Mueller shook his finger reprovingly at Paul. "No hints, now, Reverend. Let's hear Doctor Schmidt's story about what's going on between you two, and we'll see how his matches yours."

Hans sat quietly for a moment, his head bowed as if in prayer, then he straightened up, and his voice was suddenly strong and clear. "I'm sure Pastor Falkenhorst has already told you that I went to his home to treat Frau Falkenhorst. She was too ill to come to my office. It's really not at all unusual for me to see patients in their home. You can check with my wife and she'll verify that."

"Oh, you can be sure we'll check with her," Mueller said, "but what interests me is the note you and the pastor sent each other. Would you care to explain why Reverend Falkenhorst felt it was unsafe for you to come to his home to see his wife again, since you'd already been there to see her the night before?"

Hans looked at Paul. "I can't speak for Pastor Falkenhorst, but I respect him enough to know that he must have had a good reason for asking me not to come last night as I'd planned. Consequently, when his son brought the note from him, I merely made arrangements for him to contact me at a later time through a friend."

Mueller pounced on that. "Why didn't you want him to contact you in person?"

"Because my wife was against me treating Frau Falkenhorst, who is—as I'm sure you're aware—a Jew." He looked at Miriam kindly. "I did not want to provoke my wife any further by having the Falkenhorsts call my office or home."

Hans looked at Paul, who nodded his head almost imperceptibly.

Mueller's face reddened. "You're both lying, but don't worry, we'll get the truth out of you."

Just then, the door opened again and the three agents in the room clicked their heels together in attention as an SS colonel entered the room, followed by an elderly woman in a high state of agitation. Mueller turned to see what was going on, and jumped out of his chair with a salute as the officer approached the table.

"What's going on in here?" the officer demanded. "This woman has informed me that you've arrested her husband. Is this true?"

Mueller was obviously cowed by the vehemence of the officer's question. "We have reason to believe Doctor Schmidt is involved with aiding fugitive Jews, Herr *Standartenfuehrer*."

"That's highly unlikely," he snapped. "Frau Schmidt is one of our most active Party members, and Doctor Schmidt is a close personal friend of the Fuehrer's physician. I think that should vouch for his loyalty. I want him released immediately."

Mueller started to protest, but thought better of it. The Falkenhorsts were the ones he was after, and he had enough evidence on them without Schmidt's involvement. He smiled deferentially at the officer. "Of course, Herr Standartenfuehrer, if you're willing to accept the responsibility for his release." Mueller turned to Schmidt. "I'm sorry for any inconvenience we've caused you, Herr Doctor, but I'm sure you understand the need to investigate illegal activities by Jews, and those who aid them."

Freda Schmidt could contain herself no longer. She glared down at Paul. "You should be ashamed of yourself, Reverend Falkenhorst. You, a Christian minister! It's bad enough that someone from an aristocratic family like yours married a Jew in the first place, but now you're trying to corrupt innocent people like my husband. I told him it would mean trouble for him if he got involved in your church, but he's always been too soft-hearted for his own good." She gave Hans an exasperated look. "I hope this has taught you a lesson, Hans. People aren't always what they seem."

Hans gave a rueful nod. "I wish I'd learned that lesson years ago, Freda."

"Well, I think our business here is concluded," the SS colonel said. "You and your wife are free to go, Doctor Schmidt. I'm sure Gestapo Chief Mueller would like to get on with his work."

Freda started for the door with the officer, but Hans hesitated a moment, then leaned across the table and put his hand on Paul's, his eyes suddenly moist. "God bless you, Pastor. You will always be the greatest inspiration in my life." He turned abruptly and followed his wife out the door.

The interrogation of the Falkenhorsts went on for most of that day, but that night they were transferred to a regular cell on the second floor of the Gestapo headquarters. Paul was still hopeful that his brother would be able to get them out, but as the next five days passed—and they heard nothing from Kurt—the waiting became unbearable. They had not been allowed to contact anyone, and as far as they knew, no one had tried to contact them.

Each day, Gestapo Chief Mueller interrogated Paul for several hours, but he refused to give him any names of church members, and Mueller was becoming more threatening. Paul and Miriam had had no word of the fate of the Rosenbaums and Sarah, and were filled with foreboding. Paul could not understand why someone in the church had not contacted his brother by now. Surely Gaston would have done his best to alert him, unless something had happened to Gaston. Paul was trying his best to remain optimistic, but with each passing day, he was becoming more convinced that they were in great danger. He could see the toll it was taking on Miriam and Kristopher.

On the seventh day of their captivity, as they were finishing their meager evening meal, they heard loud, angry voices outside the room. When the door opened, they let out cries of relief as General Kurt von Falkenhorst strode into the room, followed by two angry Gestapo agents. The men planted themselves on either side of the open door and crossed their arms in a gesture that indicated they intended to remain there.

General von Falkenhorst was in a rage. He turned to the two agents and pointed to the door. "Get out of here, immediately! I want to see my brother and his family alone."

Neither man moved.

"Did you hear me?" Kurt boomed as he started toward them. "I said, get out!"

The two agents looked at each other uncertainly. They had been given strict orders that no one was to see the Falkenhorsts, but the general had barged into headquarters demanding to see his brother, and since Gestapo Chief Mueller was not there at the time, no one seemed willing to take the responsibility of standing up to the general, especially after he threatened to call *Reichsminister* Himmler. To mitigate the situation, the agents decided to stay in the room while the general visited his brother, but now that was clearly impossible, so they backed out of the room and stationed themselves outside the doorway, but left the door open. Kurt stormed over and slammed the door.

Paul and his family had been standing there, half terrified and half mesmerized at the drama unfolding in front of them. Now that they were alone, all three ran to Kurt and threw their arms around him. Between the laughing and crying and barrage of questions, Kurt finally managed to get a word in. "I'll only have a few minutes before they get Mueller over here, so let's sit down, and I want you to tell me what's happened, and I'll tell you what I've found out."

They pulled the chairs together in a huddle. Paul began telling him about their arrest and the charges against them.

"Are the charges true?" Kurt asked.

Paul looked at his brother and nodded. "I'm sorry if that disappoints you, but somehow I feel you'd have done the same thing if you'd been in our place. I wanted to tell you about it sooner, but I felt it would be safer for you not to know. It would've been just another thing for you to worry about, and I knew you were already grappling with some very heavy concerns of your own. I hope you'll forgive me for getting you involved in this. I'm sure you've had to stick your neck out just coming here."

"Don't worry about me. It's you three I'm worried about. I'm so sorry I didn't know about this sooner, but I've been in Norway for the past month and just got back to Berlin today. The janitor from your church had contacted Jeanne and she's been frantic with worry, not daring to try to contact either you or me. She did go over to your house and the church, but the Gestapo has sealed both of them. As far as I was able to find out, Miriam, your parents and the girl were taken to the Grosse Hamburger Strasse. That's the collection center for Jews who are to be deported. Where they're being sent, or if they're even still there, I don't know, but I'll find out. In the meantime, I'm going to see Himmler in the morning and plead with him to let you out. I can't promise anything. He's an absolute fanatic about Jews, but when I tell him about Miriam and Kristopher having citizenship papers—which he himself signed—he may release you."

Kurt leaned over and clasped Paul's hands. "In any case, my dear brother, you're going to have to hang on a little longer. There's some things about to happen that I can't tell you about, but if it comes out as I'm praying it will, this whole nightmare the country's been living through will come at an end."

Paul was clearly frightened as he searched his brother's face, then threw his arms around his shoulders and held him in a long embrace. "I love you, little brother," he whispered. "Be careful."

"I love you, too," Kurt said softly, "and whatever happens, I want you to know that you'll always be my hero."

The door burst open as the two men were embracing, and Mueller stormed in, out of breath. "What's the meaning of this, General?" he demanded. "I left specific orders that this family was to have no visitors."

"And they've had none, to my knowledge," Kurt replied. He drew himself up to his six-feet-four-inches and stared down at Mueller disdainfully. "I'm part of the family." He turned to Miriam and Kristopher and hugged them, then strode out the door.

Mueller whipped on Paul, fuming. "I suppose you're feeling very smug, aren't you? Well, don't get any ideas that your brother can get you out of this. I've already spoken to Reichsminister Himmler, and he's urged me to proceed full speed in the prosecution of this case. He intends that your conviction be a lesson to any other radical aristocrats who might be tempted to coddle Jews."

Mueller started toward the door, then turned, a sadistic grin lighting his face. "Oh, and by the way, I thought you might be interested in knowing that the Jews we took from your home left this morning for one of our relocation centers in Poland. It's called 'Auschwitz.'"

One week from the day that General Kurt von Falkenhorst visited his brother, he was charged with complicity in an unsuccessful attempt to assassinate Hitler and was executed by a Nazi firing squad. The following day, Paul and Miriam Falkenhorst and their fifteen-year-old son Kristopher were sent by cattle car to a labor camp in the Hartz Mountains of southern Germany where Hitler's V-1 and V-2 rockets were being assembled under the watchful eye of German scientist Dr. Otto von Kemp.

PART TWO

The Central Works
Southern Bavaria
1942–1945

12

1942
Autumn

The hardest thing for Hannah von Kemp about leaving Berlin was not knowing if she'd ever see Kristopher again. That thought brought her to tears as she gazed out through the weathered lattice of the summerhouse to the valley below. Ruins of an ancient castle stood silhouetted on the hill beyond the valley, somehow making her feel lonelier.

This secluded retreat, hidden among the tall pines and stately oaks that covered the estate her parents had rented, was her refuge from the depressive atmosphere of the nearby labor camps that furnished workers for the Central Works. She had never been inside one of those grim compounds, but it was impossible not to see the bedraggled workers walking each day to the tunnels that dotted the mountainsides where the rockets were being assembled.

Her father had tried to explain to her that it wasn't as though all these workers were prisoners; many of them were Germans or other nationalities who could not find work in the larger cities and had chosen to work in these war-related facilities. They received a small wage and were occasionally permitted to go, with guards, to the villages near the camps. Others were political prisoners, and had less freedom of movement, but were treated decently as long as they performed the jobs assigned to them. But he admitted that the living conditions of all the workers left much to be desired as the war progressed.

"The war will soon be over," her father would tell her, "and then these people will be grateful that they had some meaningful work to do while their friends back home were starving."

This seemed incongruous to Hannah when she saw how gaunt and undernourished the workers were in their striped gray-and-white uniforms, with blue twill caps pulled down to cover the despair in their faces.

Her father had made it clear that he wasn't responsible for the condition of the workers. His job was to see that the rocket facilities in the tunnels of the Central Works were built as quickly and efficiently as possible and, once they were ready, to oversee the actual rocket production. He told her that it was up to the SS to see to the camps and workers.

Autumn was especially beautiful in this part of southern Germany. The foliage was the rich color of an artist's palette. Small animals romped uninhibited through the woods of the estate, and had it not been for her loneliness, Hannah would have loved this mountain retreat.

It was very much like their summer home in the mountains near Oberammergau. But in the five months they had been at the Central Works, she had made no friends. The children in her new school were too provincial to appreciate someone of her family's status.

There were children her age in the various camps, and she often watched them from the upper window of the estate as they trudged back and forth to the village or to work with their parents, but her father had forbidden her ever to speak to any of them. At fifteen, she missed the parties, dances, concerts, and friendships of her beloved Berlin. But, most of all, she missed Kristopher.

A persistent breeze moaned through the tops of the pines, swirling stray oak leaves and needles from the dense pile that covered the forest floor. Hannah lay back on the summerhouse's faded blue chaise, daydreaming. A flock of wild geese rose from the meadow far below, calling to each other in a cacophony of shrill honking, then flew in formation out across the valley like so many tiny Focke-Wulf fighter planes. It made her think of Kristopher again; of how he'd longed to be a pilot; of how shattered and bitter he'd been when that dream was stripped from him. Always her thoughts came back to Kristopher.

✠ ✠

At thirty-nine, Otto von Kemp was an expert on rocket propulsion fuels and had worked closely with General Walter Dornberger, Werner von Braun, and other top scientists in the development of rocket technology. He had little patience with Hitler's goal of European conquest, but his pride in Germany's scientific superiority had kept him working away at his various projects despite the direction some of them were taking. Like von Braun, his great passion was space exploration, and he dreamed of seeing machines that could travel supersonically through space in his lifetime.

In the 1930s, Germany was well ahead of any other nation in space research, and in this regard, the gathering signs of war had been a mixed blessing to Germany's scientific community. Hitler's insistence that Germany develop aerial weapons capable of raining destruction on England across the channel had pushed their rocket experiments well ahead of schedule.

In the early days of his work, von Kemp had accepted the militant function of rocketry as a necessary part of the greater goal of space exploration, but as Hitler relentlessly pushed for the exclusive development of his "vengeance weapons"—the V-1 and V-2 rockets— von Kemp had become increasingly alarmed at the ramifications of such lethal instruments in the hands of someone as mentally unstable as Hitler.

He had agonized over his own part in this insane venture, but his whole life's work and career were at stake. Even if he'd wanted to resign from the program, no sane person would. More than one colleague had disappeared after imprudently expressing similar concerns.

Von Kemp struggled with his conscience for months, and finally

115

came to the reluctant conclusion that in order to live with himself, he had to inform England of the exact nature of this threat against her. So, on November 9, 1939, with great inner conflict, he anonymously sent to the British Embassy in Oslo, Norway, a three-inch-thick packet of handwritten notes describing the weapons he and his colleagues were developing. The simple cover note read: "From a well-wishing German scientist."

Satisfied that he had discharged his responsibility to his many English friends, he continued with his research at Peenemunde, Germany's secret northern coastal facility where the "vengeance weapons" were being developed.

Unfortunately, Peenemunde kept him away from his family for long stretches of time, so when the Russian threat to that facility made it necessary to look for a new location for assembling the V-2s, he'd been delighted for the chance to move his family to the quaint little cotton-mill village of Bleicherode near Nordhausen in southern Bavaria.

Once there, he directed the construction of the rocket facilities in the Central Works, a vast underground rocket factory. The work was taxing, but rewarding, as he saw the miles of old salt and gypsum mines and natural caves in Mount Kohnstein daily expanding into a grid of cavernous galleries capable of holding all the equipment necessary for rocket assembly.

To von Kemp's relief, the SS volunteered to take responsibility for procuring the workers and running the various labor camps. Their offer was far from altruistic: they stood to make a lot of money from German industrialists who were supplying the machinery and component parts for the rockets, as well as charging for each worker brought in.

The Nazis operated various kinds of camps all over Germany and the occupied countries. Some were extermination camps whose main function was to eliminate Jews, homosexuals, gypsies, political and religious opponents, Russian POWs, and the handicapped. Other camps provided laborers—both paid and forced—for farm work and repairing railroads, bridges, and factories that had been bombed. A few camps housed a select group of prisoners capable of more skilled technical work.

Juno was such a "skilled labor" camp. The inmates there were mostly craftsmen, or intellectuals capable of learning the skills needed to assemble the rockets and the Junker aircraft engines that were also manufactured in the tunnels. These "guest workers" were not as subject to the cruelties and deprivations of the other camps that serviced the Central Works, and some of the conscripted workers even received wages or could earn credits to use in the camp canteen.

As camps go, Juno was a small compound with six barracks forming a U shape and surrounded by an electrified wire fence. Each barrack was designed to house sixty workers in rows of double-tiered bunk beds, but there were usually more than that crammed into a barrack.

One building contained the camp commandant's quarters on one side, and a canteen next to it where toothpaste, soap, socks, candies, etc., were available on occasion. Juno's inmates were all issued passes identifying them as "guest workers," so they had more freedom in coming and going without official escort.

But a prison camp was a prison camp, and von Kemp knew that most of these workers had been sent to the camps against their wills. Knowing he wasn't responsible for the condition of the workers did relieve him somewhat whenever he had to go into one of the camps, but there was only so much one man could do. His hands were full just preparing the tunnels for the production of the rockets. After all, this wasn't his war! He was only a scientist doing his duty to his country, and the moral considerations of that duty were on Hitler's head, not his. He had done what he could with his secret letters to the British.

13

Camp Juno, 1943

At nearly sixteen, Kristopher was put in charge of the children in Camp Juno. Their main responsibility was to hand-polish the delicate fittings for the engines and gyroscopes of the rockets, but they were also required to keep the grounds and barracks of the compound clean, and to empty the latrine buckets.

The months of December through March during the winter of 1942 and 1943 were particularly bitter in the Hartz Mountains, with record snowfall that piled high around the buildings in the compound. Kristopher organized the children into teams and made a game out of who could shovel snow the fastest. The first team to complete their shoveling would get to make a snowman. It was the highlight of the children's day as they rolled the snow into clumsy balls, then stacked and decorated them with bits of glass, cloth, and stones.

One day in early March, 1943, Hannah accompanied her father on a visit to the commandant's headquarters at Juno. As the guard opened the gate to the electrified barbed-wire fence that surrounded the camp, he tapped on the frosty window of von Kemps's black Mercedes as it drew to a stop. Von Kemp rolled the window down partially and showed him his papers. The guard leaned down and glanced across at Hannah.

"If you'll pardon my saying so, sir, I don't think your daughter should get out of the car. There's a bunch of camp kids playing out there in the snow, and I can't say how they'd react if they saw a pretty little thing like her walking around the camp."

"I appreciate your advice," said von Kemp.

As they drove slowly to the commandant's headquarters, Hannah caught sight of the children and the snowman they were working on. "Oh look, Vati! Isn't that the cutest thing?"

Von Kemp peered out through the windshield at the pathetic group of children laughing and running around in the snow. The resilience of these children never ceased to amaze him. Half-starved and ill-clothed, they still managed to enjoy the few childish pleasures left to them.

"It sure looks like they're having a good time, doesn't it?" he replied.

He glanced over at Hannah, her face pressed against the window looking longingly out at the children, and a twinge of guilt jabbed at him. There was such a contrast between the smiling children and his own daughter who rarely laughed anymore. He knew it had been very hard for her since they'd left Berlin nine months earlier. She'd made few friends in her new school, and he blamed himself. It wasn't that the townspeople were anti-Nazi; it's that they feared the bombings that were sure to take place as soon as the location of these rocket facilities got into Allied hands.

Von Kemp pulled up in front of the commandant's headquarters. "Would you like to come in?"

She gave him a hopeful look. "If it's all right with you, I'd rather stay here and watch them build the snowman. I promise I won't get out."

"I think it'll be all right. Just keep the doors locked and put this blanket over your legs. I'm sure it's below freezing out there. I won't be gone long." He got out and dashed up the slippery steps into the headquarters.

Hannah rolled her window down halfway and looked out at the children who were no more than thirty feet away. Oh, how she'd love to be out there throwing snowballs with them and working on that snowman. The tall boy, who seemed to be in charge, stopped his work on the snowman and stared at her car. Embarrassed, and more than a little afraid, she quickly rolled the window up. The children gradually ignored her and went back to their playing, but she noticed that their leader kept glancing her way, and it frightened her. She checked to be sure that she'd locked the door.

The windows of the car began to steam up, so she wiped a little circle on the window with her glove. To her horror, she saw that the tall boy was standing right next to her window. She shrank down into the seat, but not before she got a quick look at him. Even with the dirty rag tied around his head and face, his eyes looked just like Kristopher Falkenhorst's.

It took her a few moments to get the courage to rise up from the seat and peek out the window again, but when she did, he was gone, and so were all the other children.

Hannah sat shivering, more from fear than the cold. That couldn't have been Kristopher! There was no way he could be in Juno. She pulled the blanket up around her in an effort to stop the shivering. Several times she cautiously peeked out the window to see if he had come back, but there was no one in sight.

By the time von Kemp returned to the car a half hour later, Hannah had convinced herself that she'd been mistaken. Her obsession with Kristopher was making her see things.

On the way back to their home, Hannah was unusually quiet. Her father reached over and patted her on the knee. "Is something bothering you, Liebchen?"

She hesitated a moment, not wanting to reveal how much she missed her old life in Berlin. "It's nothing," she said. "One of those boys playing in the snow looked a lot like Kristopher Falkenhorst and it made me realize how much I miss all my friends in Berlin."

He glanced over at her. "I know you do," he said, "that's why Mutti and I have been talking about your spending this summer with *Tante* Ellen in Berlin. How would you like that?"

Hannah's face lit up. "Oh, that would be wonderful!" she cried, then quickly reached over and touched his arm. "I'm sorry, Vati. I didn't mean to sound like I'm anxious to get away from you and Mutti, but it would be so nice to get to see all my old friends again. Do you really think I can go?"

"Our only reservation has been whether the bombings will get any worse there, so why don't we just wait and see how things are by summer. Okay?"

✠ ✠

During the next few weeks, Hannah tried to curb her impatience for the promised visit to Berlin by throwing herself into her Jung Maedel activities, though her local chapter was small and did not require her rigid participation. She had been knitting on the same pair of wool stockings for several months, and had only finished two sets of ear-warmers and one long scarf, but her heart wasn't in it. She had written a few letters to lonely servicemen at the front, and occasionally read her copies of *Marie Luise* magazine, but even the patriotric stories she used to enjoy didn't hold much interest for her anymore. She was simply too lonely so far from her friends in Berlin, and especially from Kristopher.

April had arrived with its warm winds and intermittent sun, and most of the snow had melted, leaving the earth full of promise for a glorious summer. Hannah began going to the summerhouse again, and everywhere she looked, crocuses and trilliums poked their heads out of the moist earth in search of the sun. It was as though everything was starting to come alive again, including herself. She could hardly wait for school to be out so she could get back to Berlin and Kristopher. She had long since given up the notion that the boy she'd seen at the camp was him. It simply wasn't possible that the Falkenhorsts could be in a place like Juno, not with Reverend Falkenhorst being such an important man. Anyway, she didn't need an imaginary Kristopher. She would be seeing the real one in only two months, and she could hardly contain herself.

One night during Lent, von Kemp mentioned at the dinner table an idea he had been toying with for some time. He'd become concerned about the sullen attitude of many of the workers and the effect it was having on their productivity, and he thought of possibly allowing them to have an Easter service. He decided to see if there was a minister in one of the camps who might be able and willing to do the job.

During the next few days, von Kemp bounced his idea off some of the camp directors, and by and large they all thought it was a good idea. Anything to calm the workers down. There were four main camps within a five-mile radius of the Central Works, plus several camps in the tunnels themselves that housed the bulk of the workers: approximately 20,000 in all. Von Kemp was convinced there must be a minister somewhere among these, so he suggested that each camp commandant check his records and do some asking around with the workers. He wanted to make the final selection himself so he could make sure the man chosen would not try to use the occasion as a personal platform to rail against his German employers.

A week before Easter, von Kemp gathered the lists of names from the various commandants and saw that there were only eight clergymen. His eyes ran down the list: Zelinski, Polish, Roman Catholic; Vergun, Czechoslovakian, Roman Catholic; Haufman, German, Lutheran.

Von Kemp's brow raised in surprise. What was a German minister doing in one of these camps? He must be a communist, he reasoned.

His eyes continued down the list: Nedich, Yugoslavian, Roman Catholic; Petrovsky, Russian, Russian Orthodox; Falkenhorst, German, Evangelical.

Von Kemp's eyes had already moved on to the next name when it registered on him what he had just read. *Falkenhorst? That can't be Paul Falkenhorst from my church. That's impossible! What would he be doing here?*

He glanced at his watch and saw that it was lunchtime. There was no way to check this out until all the workers were back in their compounds that evening, so he stuffed the list into his pocket and drove back to his home for lunch. There was a gnawing uneasiness in the pit of his stomach as he sat down at the table.

"You seem worried, Otto," his wife, Eva, said, as she set his lunch in front of him.

"I am." He reached into his shirt pocket and drew out the list. "I ran across some very disturbing information this morning." He laid the paper in front of her. "You know my plan for having an Easter service. Well, these are the ministers the commandants came up with, and there's a 'Paul Falkenhorst' on the list. You don't suppose there's any chance that's *our* Paul Falkenhorst, do you?"

Hannah grabbed the list, her face suddenly ashen. "Vati, that *must* be Pastor Falkenhorst. Remember? I told you I saw a boy at the camp that day I went with you who looked just like Kristopher, but you told me it couldn't be him." Her voice began to rise. "You've got to find out if the Falkenhorsts are here. It would be so awful if they are! You've got to do something!"

She was on the verge of hysteria, and von Kemp reached over and patted her hand. "Calm down! If they're here, you can be sure I'll find them. This name was on the list from Juno, and I plan to go over there this evening to see if it's really Pastor Falkenhorst." He frowned toward his daughter. "I can't imagine why Paul and his family would be here. Anyway, there's nothing I can do about it right now, so let's just finish our lunch, and we'll wait until I go over there tonight."

That evening, von Kemp found himself apprehensive as he pulled up in front of the commandant's quarters at Juno. Paul Falkenhorst was one of the finest men he'd ever known, and he shuddered to think that such a man could be sent to a place like this. What could the Nazis be thinking if they were now arresting some of Germany's elite families and forcing them into what amounted to slave labor? Well, he intended to get to the bottom of this, and—if it was Paul—to use what influence he had to get him released. That's the least he could do for a man who had given so much to him and his family through the years.

As he mounted the steps of the commandant's quarters, he found himself praying that the man was *not* Paul Falkenhorst. It would certainly make matters easier for him if he could avoid a confrontation with whoever had sent him there.

The commandant looked up from his desk and smiled as he recognized von Kemp. He leaned across the desk and stretched out his hand. "Otto. Good to see you. What brings you here at this hour?"

Von Kemp sat down across from him. "It's about our search for a minister to conduct the Easter services. I see you have a German minister here, a Falkenhorst. Can you give me any information about him? Where he's from, and why was he sent here?"

The commandant rolled his chair back and pulled out a drawer in a metal filing cabinet behind him. He flipped through his files until he got the one he was looking for. "Let's see—Falkenhorst." He thumbed through a number of sheets. "It's hard to keep up with all these people. There's been so many deaths over the months, and sometimes my clerk doesn't stay on top of the paperwork." He found what he was looking for and pulled out a file marked "Falkenhorst, Paul." "This looks like what we're after."

He read quietly for a moment, shaking his head as he read. "Hmm," he said, raising his eyebrows, "it looks like Falkenhorst got himself into quite a mess. It says here that he was a ringleader in hiding Jews in his church in Berlin and giving them false identity papers. That would've been bad enough, but they suspect that he was involved with his brother, General Kurt von Falkenhorst, in an attempt to assassinate the Fuehrer. It looks like he and his family are going to be here quite a while." He shoved the folder over for von Kemp's inspection. "I don't think this is the man you want for your Easter services. No telling what kind of stuff he might spew if he got up in front of a crowd."

Von Kemp frowned as he read down the list of charges against Paul and his family. "This is bad, very bad," he murmured, shaking his head.

He didn't know whether to believe what he read or not, but the charges had been signed by Himmler personally, and that didn't look good to von Kemp. What could have possessed Paul Falkenhorst to jeopardize all their lives by getting involved in such activities? He'd heard that General von Falkenhorst had been executed for his attempt on Hitler's life, but what Paul could have had to do with that was beyond his understanding. It certainly didn't sound like the man he knew, yet it was definitely Paul Falkenhorst there in the camp.

Von Kemp shoved the file back at the commandant. "I'd like to talk to this man. Can you have someone show me to his barracks?"

"Are you sure you want to go into one of those? I can always have him brought up here."

"No, I know this man, and I'd like to see what the conditions are where he and his family are staying."

"Suit yourself, but if I were you, I wouldn't go into one of those barracks alone. Take my *kapo* in with you."

The man assigned to show him the way to the barracks was about twenty years old, but looked more like forty. He was a Polish inmate serving as a guard. The kapos were hated by the other workers who saw them as opportunists who would betray anyone to save their own lives. He carried a German Luger and looked like he would enjoy using it.

The sun had gone down behind Mount Kohnstein and the air was chilly for April. Von Kemp pulled the collar up around his neck as they walked across the grounds of the compound. When they got to Falkenhorst's barracks, he asked the kapo to wait outside. The man started to protest, but von Kemp silenced him.

"I'm perfectly capable of taking care of myself with these workers. You do what I say. That's an order!"

The kapo shrugged and leaned insolently up against the outside of the barracks.

As von Kemp stepped into the dark barracks, he was surprised to see that there was no electricity, the only light being the floodlights outside filtering in through the dirty windows. It took him a few moments to adjust to the dark, but when he could see clearly, he grimaced at what he saw. The room was lined along both walls with two-tiered wooden bunk beds, leaving only a narrow aisle for people to pass or stand. Most of the beds had at least two people in them, and a number of dirty, emaciated workers stood in the narrow aisle glaring at him. He quickly estimated that there must have been at least a hundred people in a space that was designed to hold only fifty or sixty.

A gaunt man approached him. His hair was greasy and unkempt, his fatigues hanging loosely on his body. Von Kemp braced for hostility, but was surprised by his gracious manner.

"May I help you, sir?" the man asked.

"I hope so. I've come to see Reverend Paul Falkenhorst. Could you point him out to me, please?"

The man pointed down the aisle to the last bunk. "He and his wife are in the bottom bunk at the end there."

Von Kemp thanked him and began to make his way down the crowded aisle. The smell of sweat and human waste was strong. Coughing and moaning punctuated the foul air and von Kemp took out his handkerchief and discretely held it up to his nose.

When he'd finally pushed his way to the end of the row, he leaned over and peered down at the couple in the bottom bunk, a thin blanket barely covering the two of them. Two wan faces stared back at him, and he recognized Paul Falkenhorst and his wife.

He reached down and tapped Paul on the shoulder. "Pastor Falkenhorst? It's Otto von Kemp. From your church in Berlin."

Paul managed a weak smile, and reached up a hand to him. "Yes, I recognize you," he said. "I'm sorry we're not able to greet you properly, but neither of us is feeling too well. What are you doing here, Doctor?"

"I just found out you and your family were in Juno, and I was shocked. I can't believe such a thing could happen to you, and I'm very distressed to see you like this. Have you had any medical attention?"

"We're not sick enough for the infirmary," Paul said. "Most of the people who go there don't come back, so we're just trying to get back on our feet by ourselves. I . . . I think we're both a little better now that the weather's warming up."

Miriam tried to sit up, but deep coughs rumbled up from her chest, and she fell back on the bed. "Please don't take us to the infirmary," she managed to say. "We're much better off here."

"Nonsense! You both need medical help immediately. Now, you just lie back down and try to rest. Someone will fetch you in the morning, and I'll be in to see you both in the infirmary. Is Kristopher here with you?"

Paul pointed to the bunk above him. "Yes. Up there."

Von Kemp straightened up and found himself staring into Kristopher's hostile face.

"Kristopher! It's Hannah's father, Doctor von Kemp," he said.

"I know who you are. What do want with my parents? Haven't you Nazis done enough to them already?"

Von Kemp was stunned by the boy's hostility, but he kept his temper. "I just found out all of you were here, and I've come to see if I can help in some way."

"Can you get us out of here?"

"I'm not sure about that, but I can see that your parents get some medical attention. As for getting you out of here, that's not a decision I can make, but I'll certainly do what I can."

"I didn't think you'd dirty your hands with us," Kristopher said, then lay back down and turned his back on von Kemp.

"You seem to blame me in some way for your being here," von Kemp said, "but I knew nothing about it until today. Please believe me."

He waited a moment for a response, but none came, so he leaned down and said goodbye to Paul and Miriam and walked out, depressed and angry; not angry at the boy, but angry with a system that could turn a special child like that into a bitter, caustic rebel, and reduce a great man like Paul Falkenhorst into a shell of a man. He got into his car and slammed his fists against the steering wheel. "Damn these Nazis! Damn that madman, Hitler! Damn them all to hell where they belong!"

14

Paul found himself getting stronger since he'd been brought to the infirmary a week before. True to his word, von Kemp had visited them every day, and when he told Paul about the success of the Easter service, Paul's spirits brightened considerably. The past nine months had been a long nightmare for him, but now, as he felt the strength flow back into his body, he was ashamed of how he'd let his family down by not showing more trust in God.

He was certain that God had led Doctor von Kemp to them, but was very worried about whether it would be in time to save Miriam. Her tuberculosis was in an advanced stage, and she was too weak to leave the infirmary when he did. Von Kemp assured him that he would see that she continued receiving care until she was able to return to the barracks. Paul reluctantly left her there, knowing he had to get back to Kristopher.

It was a week before Paul could get permission for him and Kristopher to visit Miriam. She tried hard to be cheerful and optimistic for them, but Paul could see that she was failing fast.

As they walked back to the camp after their visit, Paul could barely hold back his tears as he tried to prepare Kristopher for his mother's death.

The boy's jaw tightened. "I'm holding von Kemp personally responsible if she dies."

Paul turned to him, aghast. "Why?" he exclaimed. "He had nothing to do with us being sent here, and he's doing everything he can to try to get us released."

"Then why hasn't he if he's such a great friend of yours?"

"Because Himmler told him to keep his nose out of this if he knew what was good for him."

"And you believe that?" Kristopher scoffed.

"Yes, I do, so please don't be so hostile to him. He's the only hope we've got." Paul could hold back his tears no longer, and they began to stream down his cheeks. "I don't want to lose your mother," he sobbed. "I don't see how I could go on without her."

Kristopher had never seen his father cry like that before, and his own lips began to quiver. "You'll still have me, Vati."

Paul saw that his words had hurt Kristopher, and he pulled his son to him. "Of course I will," he said, patting his back, "but your mother has been the other half of my life for eighteen years, and I'll only be half a person without her."

His father's simple words seemed to drain some of the anger out of Kristopher. "Isn't there anything they can do to save her?" he asked.

"They're doing all they can," he replied, "but if she doesn't make it, at least we know we'll see her again in heaven. That's some comfort."

"I don't know if there's a heaven or not," Kristopher said, "but I know for sure there's a hell, because we're in it."

☩ ☩

So much had required von Kemp's attention that a week had passed since he'd visited Miriam in the infirmary, and he was feeling guilty about his promise to Paul to look in on her regularly. He consoled himself that she was far better off there than in the disease-ridden barracks. At least she had some chance to get well in the infirmary.

Sometimes he asked himself why he'd gone to all the trouble he had for the Falkenhorsts, but in his heart he knew. Besides the fact that Paul Falkenhorst had ministered to his family so faithfully through the years, it was his small way of trying to set right the SS's treatment of the workers. The coldblooded disregard for their welfare was repugnant to him, but he was in no position to try to change the system. The best he could do was to hang on to his own values and not let all this corrupt him. He blamed it all on the greed of Himmler and the SS. They had schemed and connived to take over all the camps, and they were getting plenty of money from the armament manufacturers to build adequate housing and pay these people decent wages as they'd been promised. Instead, they pocketed the bulk of the money and gave the workers barely enough to get an occasional extra bit of food in the villages or canteen when it was available, which wasn't often.

He was also genuinely distressed that his efforts to get the Falkenhorsts released had failed. Their case had drawn the personal attention of Himmler, and von Kemp had been informed—in no uncertain terms—that the Falkenhorsts would not to be released, and if he valued his position there, he'd mind his own business. Von Kemp had enough of his own secrets that he was more than willing to take that advice.

Hannah approached her father as he was about to leave that evening. "Vati, I've been wondering if there isn't something we can do to keep Kristopher from ending up in the tunnels. Can't you assign him to work here on the grounds like the other workers you've used? You know he's just going to rot away if he has to go into those tunnels. Please!" she pleaded.

Hannah was von Kemp's weakness. As his only child, he had always indulged her, but as he looked at her now, he realized she was no longer a child. She had grown into a beautiful young woman of sixteen, with a graceful, mature body—and he wasn't at all sure that he wanted a virile young hot-head like Kristopher around her. But he wasn't going to tell her that. She was lonely enough, and he knew how fond she was of the boy.

"Let me think about it," he said.

Hannah wouldn't drop the subject. "I won't go to Tante Ellen's this summer if you let him work here," she said.

He raised his brow at her. "Are you trying to bribe me, young lady?"

"I'll do what I have to to keep him out of the tunnels."

"Well, let me talk it over with his mother tonight. I haven't seen her for a week, and I was just on my way to the infirmary now." He started toward the door, then turned and gave her a mischievous grin. "By the way, Liebchen, Mutti and I have already decided it's too dangerous to send you to Berlin this summer." He winked at her and went out.

+ +

The infirmary was a depressing place. It was far too small and understaffed to handle the hundreds who daily needed medical help. The overcrowded wards were filled with workers suffering from typhus, tuberculosis, pneumonia, malnutrition, overwork, and a variety of physical injuries. As von Kemp walked through the ward to Miriam's bed, the moans and cries made him think of what Paul had told him that first night in the barracks—about people not coming back once they went to the infirmary. It was nonsense, of course. Even though they were grossly overworked, this was a dedicated staff of nurses and doctors, and he was certain they did their best, even under these difficult conditions.

He came to Miriam's bed and was mildly surprised to see that she had been moved. He motioned to the nurse on that ward. "Where is Frau Falkenhorst who was in this bed?"

The nurse checked her clipboard, then looked up at him. "She died yesterday."

Von Kemp let out a groan. "Has her husband been notified yet?"

"I think the head nurse was planning to notify her camp commandant tomorrow. Would you like me to call her?"

He paused for a moment, then shook his head. "No, I'll speak to her on the way out. Thank you very much."

He stopped at the office and told the head nurse he'd notify Paul Falkenhorst himself, then left for Juno. The sun had set, and the gray murky shadows matched his mood as he drove down the isolated road to the camp. How many more good people, like Miriam Falkenhorst, would have to die before this disregard for human life came to an end?

Arriving at the camp, he went to the commandant's office, explained to him about Miriam's death, and asked to see Paul. "I'd like to be the one to tell him when he gets here," von Kemp said.

The man shrugged. "Fine, but I don't know why you're going to all this trouble over the death of one inmate. We've had hundreds die here in Juno."

Von Kemp looked at the man coldly. "These people are special."

The door opened and Paul was led in by a kapo. He looked worried when he saw von Kemp. "What is it, Doctor? Is it Miriam?"

Von Kemp nodded. "I'm afraid it is, Paul. I'm so sorry, but she died yesterday and I wanted to be the one to tell you." He reached out and touched Paul's arm. "The doctors did everything they could, but she was just too weak by the time they got her."

Paul covered his face with his hands, unable to staunch his sobs. After a few moments he looked up at von Kemp. "She was one of the most marvelous women God ever made. I don't know how I can go on without her."

Von Kemp put his arm around Paul's shoulders. "Come on, old friend. I'll walk back to your barracks with you."

The kapo started to follow them out, but von Kemp's look stopped him. "I'll walk him back by myself," he said.

The full moon, illuminating the broad quadrangle of hard-packed dirt, cast an eerie beauty on the rows of barracks surrounding its three sides, masking the reality of what this place was. In the pale light, it might have been a family summer camp. The strident chirping of crickets mingled with Paul's quiet sobs as the two men made their way to the barracks.

Von Kemp kept his arm around Paul's shoulders as they walked. "I really can't tell you how sorry I am about Miriam. I hope you know how much I hate what's happened to your family, but the SS has it in for you because of your brother."

Paul looked up at him. "I don't blame you. You've been more than kind to us. I don't blame anyone but myself for our being here. I knew what I risked when I made some of the choices I did. I just prayed that my loved ones wouldn't have to suffer like this." He turned his head as tears welled up again.

"There's nothing more I can do for Miriam," von Kemp said, "but I can have Kristopher assigned to work on the grounds of my estate, and that'll keep him out of the tunnels. He'd still have to stay here at nights, but I'd see to it that his work wasn't too hard, and at least make sure he got extra food. Do you think I could trust him not to run off? I know he's very bitter toward me, though I don't know why."

A surge of hope lit Paul's face. "You'd do this for my son?"

"It's a very small way to try to repay you for what you've suffered," von Kemp said. "Besides, Kristopher is just the kind of boy we'll need to put this country back together after this mess is over. What do you think? Is he too bitter for me to give him the kind of freedom he'd have working without a whole lot of supervision?"

"He's very bitter, but I'll talk with him. I'm sure I can convince him not to abuse your kindness." He reached out and touched von Kemp's arm. "I can't thank you enough for doing this. It helps a little with the pain of losing Miriam."

15

The Central Works, 1943

Once school was out for the summer, Hannah spent most of her spare time in the summerhouse. She kept her favorite books there, as well as her easel and paints. With no social life, in the past year she had amassed quite a collection of paintings—landscapes, the castle across the valley, flowers and birds, and the summerhouse, itself—all of which she had leaned against the bench inside the summerhouse. She gave them a critical appraisal, wishing she could show them to Kristopher, but he had been avoiding her ever since he came to work on the estate a month ago.

"It must be nice having nothing to do but paint all day while the world is going to hell all around you," Kristopher said, coming up behind her.

Hannah whipped around and her hand flew up to her heart. "Kristopher! You scared me to death."

"You shouldn't be so jumpy. I'm not really dangerous, you know."

"Of *course* you're not dangerous. I'm just so surprised to see you. You've hardly said a word to me since you came to work here."

He stepped into the summerhouse and looked around at her paintings, then picked one up and gave it a cursory glance. "Well, it wouldn't do for an inmate to get too friendly with his warden's daughter, now would it?"

"Please don't say things like that! You know you've always been one of my best friends."

He set the painting down. "Is that why your father warned me to stay away from you?"

"No! He didn't! Did he? Oh, that makes me so mad!"

"Oh, he was quite clear about it. If I so much as look at you crosswise, I'll be on my way to the tunnels."

"He's just worried because he knows how much I care about you," Hannah said.

Kristopher gave a shake of his head. "Don't waste any emotion on me. We're on two different sides now." He turned to leave, but she grabbed his arm.

"Don't go yet," she begged. "We've hardly talked."

He looked down at her hand, and then at her. "What's there to talk about? We don't have anything in common anymore."

Her cheeks colored slightly. "I . . . I just wanted to tell you how much I've missed you, and . . . that I can help you while you're here. I can get extra food for you and your father."

"Your father would never allow that."

"He doesn't have to know. I usually eat my lunch out here, and I'll just bring something extra every day."

Kristopher's expression softened slightly. "I don't know why you're willing to go to all that trouble."

"You really don't know, do you?"

"No."

She perched both hands on her hips. "You are still so blind, Kristopher Falkenhorst!"

"Wait a minute!" he said. "You told me that once before, back in Berlin. What do you mean by that?"

"Think about it. Why would a girl risk so much for someone, unless that someone was very special to her?"

Kristopher stepped back from her and gave a quick shake of his head. "You don't want to get mixed up with me, Hannah. There's no future in it for either of us."

She swallowed to hold back her tears. "It's too late for that. I've loved you for as long as I can remember." She quickly thrust up her hand to ward off the sarcastic retort she knew he'd make. "I'm not asking you to love me back. I know that's too much to ask. I just want you to know how I feel and that you can always count on that, no matter how bad things get."

His response was curt. "Don't waste your love on me," he said. "I don't have any to give back."

It was obvious from the despair on her face that his rejection had devastated her, so he added, "I don't mean to hurt your feelings, Hannah, but you need to find yourself some nice Aryan boy your father would approve of."

"I don't want anyone else. You're the only one I've ever wanted."

"You wouldn't want me if you really knew me. Everything inside me is dead."

Without thinking, she reached up and pulled his face to hers. "My love can bring you back to life, if you'll give it a chance," she whispered.

He jerked back in surprise, then, as her body began to press into his, he leaned down and began kissing her mouth. As his passion mounted, his hand sought her breast, but she caught it and held him back.

"No. Not there," she murmured. "I'm not ready for that yet," but a wave of hope shot through her.

He was breathing hard as he let go of her. "Don't read too much into this," he managed to say. "It can't lead anywhere."

Before she could respond, he turned and walked off through the trees.

She desperately wanted him to stay, but could see he had not been prepared for what had just happened between them. He'd obviously discovered he wasn't dead inside after all, and it would take him some time to decide how to handle it.

Hannah stood and watched him disappear through the trees. Her heart was bursting with hope as she ran up the path to the mansion.

16

Camp Juno, 1943–1944

As the summer of 1943 turned to autumn, the tide of the war turned more and more against Germany. Hannah kept Kristopher apprised of what she overheard from her father and his friends. The Allies had begun pounding German cities with tons of bombs. On July 4, Germany's second largest city, Hamburg, was virtually destroyed by British fire-bombs. For nine days, fires swept the city, destroying over ten square miles and killing nearly 60,000 people.

When news of the devastating raid against the secret rocket base at Peenemunde on August 17 reached von Kemp, he was thankful that he was not among the scientists who were still there. The rocket program had been set back by at least six months by the bombing, and it was obvious that the bulk of the production work would now have to be transferred to the Central Works. This meant he would have to double the work shifts to get it finished in time. He hated to do it, knowing the workers were already pushed far beyond their limits, but his neck was on the line. The SS was bringing in fresh laborers daily from some of the eastern camps to replace those lost in Dora, Juno, and the other camps nearby where the death rate had been very high in the past months as an outbreak of typhus had wiped out hundreds of the weaker inmates.

Von Kemp had lived in fear of his family, or him, coming down with the highly infectious disease, so he had spent as little time as possible around the workers. Reluctantly, he had stopped Kristopher and the other workers from coming to the estate until the danger of the epidemic had subsided.

✠ ✠

Hannah was worried sick about Kristopher. She hadn't seen him for almost two months, and she had no way of knowing whether he had come down with typhus or not. She begged her father to try to get some information about him, but he told her he had no intention of going into the camp to look for him. "When his commandant tells me this epidemic is over, then I'll check on him," he said. In the meantime, we can all be thankful that I told him to keep away from you, so there's no danger of your having been infected."

Hannah's face flushed as she thought back on the times that she and Kristopher had secretly met in the summerhouse and spent those furtive moments in each other's arms. They had not progressed beyond kissing and fondling, but despite the risk of contracting typhus from him, she would gladly be in his arms right now.

It wasn't until October that the typhus epidemic was over, and Hannah begged her father to take her to Juno to check on Kristopher. Once there, the commandant sent for Paul.

When Hannah caught sight of Pastor Falkenhorst making his way across the grounds to the commandant's quarters, she was shocked. She had not seen him since before his arrest, and the man who came shuffling through the door bore little resemblance to the tall virile man she had known in Berlin. He was very gaunt, and his hair had thinned and turned white. No wonder Kristopher had been so fearful about his father's condition.

When Kristopher wasn't with him, Hannah was suddenly frantic. "Has something happened to Kristopher?" she blurted.

Von Kemp gave the commandant a questioning look.

"He's still alive, as far as I know," the man said. "Did you want to see him?"

138

Von Kemp shook his head. "No. We just wanted to make sure that both he and his father had come through the epidemic in one piece."

Paul let out a ragged cough, and von Kemp patted him on the back. "Did either of you get typhus?" he asked.

"I had a touch of it, but, thank God, Kristopher didn't," Paul replied. He looked up at von Kemp gratefully. "I know it was because of all that fresh air and extra food he got while he worked for you. I never did thank you properly for giving him the job. I hope he wasn't a disappointment to you."

"Not at all. In fact, I'd like to have him back now that the epidemic is over. I'll make the arrangements with the commandant."

Paul's face brightened perceptibly. "That's a blessing. He's all I've got left."

Von Kemp slipped his arm around his daughter's shoulders. "Hannah and I will take good care of him for you, won't we, Hannah?"

Her face was radiant. "Oh yes, Vati! We'll take very good care of him. You can count on that!"

✝ ✝

Kristopher had been back at the estate for about a month when the snows came early that winter of 1943, making any work on the grounds impossible. Hannah was desolate when her father told her he no longer needed Kristopher until the spring. She begged him to find something else for him to do on the estate, but von Kemp had become extremely alarmed at Hannah's infatuation with the boy, and this was the perfect opportunity to put a halt to it.

"I'll see to it that he's given an easy job in one of the plants," he told her, "and perhaps he can come to see you on occasion. But I hope it isn't necessary for me to warn you again about developing serious feelings for him. He's going to be here a long time."

When he saw the distress on her face, he added, "I'm not blind to your feelings, Liebchen. Sixteen is a perfectly natural age for you to begin thinking about boys, but I'm sure there are plenty of nice ones in your school who'd be interested in a beautiful girl like you if you gave them half a chance."

"I'm not interested in any of the stupid boys in my school. They're a bunch of jerks!"

She was so upset that von Kemp decided to let the subject go. He realized now that it had been a mistake to have Kristopher back at the estate after the typhus epidemic. He'd been thinking of the boy's good, but hadn't reckoned on Hannah's deep attachment to him. Well, all girls had their crushes, but they grew out of them, and he was certain Hannah would, too.

He put the whole thing in the back of his mind as the alarming events of the spring of 1944 unfolded. The Allies had begun a saturation bombing of Germany's cities, with Berlin coming under a siege that lasted for four and a half months.

Hitler sought to pacify his people with the promise that he was developing powerful secret weapons that would soon put Germany back in control, and the development of those had become his obsession, even over that of such conventional weapons as tanks and bombers. The pleas of his generals had failed to upset his view of his own military genius, and he would fly into a rage if anyone dared to challenge his tactical leadership. He was suspicious of everyone around him.

Von Kemp was especially on edge about this. His secret collaboration with the Allies was so potentially damaging to him that even a hint of its existence would cost him and his family their lives. For this reason, he decided that if he wanted to throw off any suspicion of his loyalties, he had to accelerate the production schedule of the V-1s and V-2s. Unfortunately, this would mean working the prisoners until they dropped. Hitler wanted the rockets ready to blast England by June, and only a superhuman effort was going to make that possible.

The step-up in production had an antagonizing effect on the workers. There were numerous acts of sabotage on the production line. Kristopher, himself, had been involved in some of that—loosening screws on the rockets, leaving out vital parts of the gyroscopes and engines, pissing on the electrical components, and faking welds. The SS hanged those they caught, hoping this would deter further subversion, but it had just the opposite effect. The workers simply became more subtle in what they did, knowing that the effects of their sabotage would only be discovered in the actual firing of the rockets, which was still months away.

As the snow melted and the warm spring rains began to bring new life to the foliage surrounding the Central Works, the prisoners began to hope that their long ordeal was coming to an end as they watched American planes fly over their camps on the way to bomb the heartland of Germany. During the winter, their favorite pastime had been watching dogfights between the American and German planes in the air above the Central Works, but lately the Americans had flown to and from their destinations with little interference by the Luftwaffe.

Maybe—just maybe—the end was near.

✛ ✛

By June 6, 1944, every German citizen knew the end was near as word of the Allied landing at the beaches of Normandy spread like wildfire throughout the beleaguered cities of Germany. An armada of more than 4,000 ships—the greatest fleet the world had ever known—had deposited nearly 200,000 Allied soldiers on the coast of France. Thousands of tons of bombs from an accompanying air armada of 3,000 planes peppered German cities already digging out of previous bombings. The devastation to Germany's industrial centers was overwhelming. Vital bridges were knocked out, railroad lines obliterated, communications disrupted throughout the country, and thousands of citizens lay bleeding and dying amid the rubble. The country went into a paralyzing shock.

Germany was knocked down, but not out. On June 13, the first V-1 rocket struck London. Carrying a one-ton warhead, this 25-foot aerial torpedo—with its stubby fins and internal guidance mechanism—lifted off a launching pad on the French coast with a blast of steam from its jet engine, and climbed, screeching, into the air above the English Channel toward the heart of London. Ten more followed that day and, by the end of June, two thousand of the flying "buzz bombs" had been launched toward England. Initial reports from German spies in England reported that the British were in terror over this long-awaited threat, but as the weeks went by, it became known that less than twenty-five percent of the V-1s were actually reaching their targets. Many of them exploded on the launching pads, or veered off course to land harmlessly in the English Channel or countryside.

But the Germans still had their trump card: the V-2. Standing forty-six feet tall, with four arrow-like fins on its tail, weighing three tons, and capable of carrying more than a ton of explosives, it looked like a giant, wingless, artillery shell. It was guided by an automatic pilot and had an electronic brain that shut off the rocket engine at the proper height, causing it to dive on its target. It was launched straight up like a skyrocket—to the unprecedented height of sixty miles—then traveled faster than the speed of sound and, within four minutes, could hit any target within two hundred miles with deadly accuracy. There was nothing in military history to compare with it.

What the V-1 had not been able to do, Hitler was certain the V-2 would. Otto von Kemp prayed that it wouldn't.

☩ ☩

The Germans were just recovering from the shock of the Allied landing at Normandy, when another attempt was made on Hitler's life by some of his top generals at his Wolf's Lair in East Prussia. In the ensuing weeks, thousands of suspected plotters were rounded up and killed, including many who had no knowledge of the assassination plot, but had in some way offended Hitler in the past. No German leader was above suspicion, and many of them, seeing the handwriting on the wall, began to make plans to disappear. Von Kemp was one of those.

The von Kemps had had a summer home near Oberammergau for many years. It was tucked in the mountains near the site of the famous

142

Passion Play, and it had been their dream to retire there in that tranquil setting when Otto finally completed his years of work. It looked now like there would be no retirement. Convinced that Germany was going to lose the war, he knew there'd be no peace for him there, considering the role he'd played in the development of Germany's rocket program. The Allies would not allow him to simply fade into oblivion in his mountain retreat. He'd heard that some of his former colleagues had already been recruited by the Americans and British to go to work in their space programs. Considering the secret information he'd been feeding the Allies throughout the war, they'd obviously want him. He prayed he could hook up with the Americans or British before the Russians got hold of him.

It was all too depressing to think about. He'd just have to take things one step at a time and do his best to survive until the war came to an end. He couldn't leave his post before then, anyway, or he'd have the SS on his tail.

Nobody in Germany was speaking openly about a German defeat, but privately few believed that Germany still had any chance of winning the war. The greatest terror Germans had was not the thought of the war ending—most prayed for that daily, even though it might mean Germany's defeat—it was the realization of what would happen to the Germans who fell into the hands of the Russians. For years, the Ministry of Propaganda had painted a picture of the Russians as being cold-blooded barbarians who gleefully slaughtered and raped women and children. Stories from soldiers returning from the Russian front had corroborated that image, adding to the general hysteria about a Russian victory.

Von Kemp was determined that no matter what happened to Germany, he would not let the Russians get their hands on him and his family. He sat Hannah and his wife, Eva, down one evening and told them of his fears. He pulled no punches. Germany had lost the war and they needed to begin making plans to get to their place at Oberammergau when the time came.

17

Camp Juno, 1944

The blast rocked Kristopher's bunk back and forth and threw him and his father onto the floor, toppling the bunk over onto them. He fought to disentangle himself from the debris and broken glass.

The room was lit with a brilliant orange glow as another shock rattled the building, and an acrid smoke drifted in through the broken windows, filling the air with a toxic haze, nearly choking him. The screams and moans of those around him, mixed with the sound of one explosion after another, were deafening. He finally managed to pick himself up and crawl over to his father, who was lying under the bed frame.

He clawed the frame off him. "Vati! Vati! Are you okay?" he cried.

Paul's face was covered with blood, and he put his hand on his chest. "I'm having a hard time breathing." He looked up at Kristopher. "What about you?"

"I'm okay." He slipped his arms under his father's shoulders and started dragging him toward the door, shoving aside hysterical people tangled in the mess. He finally stumbled out into the open area in front of the barracks and laid his father on the hard ground.

The compound was a madhouse. People were running back and forth screaming, the continuing concussion of bombs driving them into still greater frenzy. The earsplitting rumble of anti-aircraft guns shook the ground with each blast. Kristopher looked over at their barracks and saw flames leaping from the windows and roof. He knew from the screams that there were still people inside, but no one could go into that inferno after them. He sat, holding his bleeding father, and wept like a baby for those still inside.

☩ ☩

Two barracks in Juno were completely destroyed the night of the bombing, requiring that many of the surviving workers sleep on the floors of the remaining barracks. Paul and Kristopher were among that group. Forty-eight people from Juno had perished, so they felt lucky just to be alive. The Central Works itself went virtually unscathed, located as it was inside the mountain. Numerous rail lines and bridges leading into the tunnels were destroyed, but none of the missiles were touched. Within two weeks, the rails had been repaired and temporary bridges put in place by the corps of engineers.

Paul Falkenhorst had a mild concussion and several broken ribs. He was allowed a few days to recover in the barracks along with others who had been injured, but when a week had passed, the guards herded those who could still walk back to the tunnels. Every hand was needed now that the V-2s were ready to be sent to their launching pads on the French and Belgian coasts.

Something died in Kristopher the night of the bombing. For the first time since coming to the camp, he realized their situation was hopeless. There was no way out for his father and him. If the Germans didn't kill them, American bombs would. They were doomed to die, and now—as he watched his father gallantly struggling to go on each day—he realized how he had added to his father's burden with all his bitterness, and he had to set things right between them before it was too late.

"Vati," he said one night after they pulled their thin blankets over them on the floor of the cramped barracks, "Do you feel strong enough to talk for a little bit?"

Paul turned over, wincing with pain. "Of course," he said. "What is it?"

"I just wanted you to know how bad I feel for being such a disappointment to you. I know I haven't turned out to be the good Christian son you wanted me to be, but I just can't understand why God would let all this happen to us when all we tried to do was help people."

Paul reached out and squeezed his son's arm. "You're not a disappointment to me. You're all I could ever have wanted in a son, but I can see why you might think God has forsaken us."

"Don't you wonder whether he has?"

It was the first time since they'd gotten to the camp that Kristopher had shown any interest in spiritual things, and Paul found himself searching for just the right words to encourage the boy's fledgling faith.

"It's never easy to understand why God does what he does," he told Kristopher, "but I've walked with him long enough to know that I can trust whatever he does."

Kristopher's face darkened. "Even letting us end up in this hellhole and taking Mutti away from us?"

Tears suddenly appeared in the corner of Paul's eyes, and he wiped at them. "This was no place for Mutti," he said. "As much as we both miss her, we know she's better off where she is, and we'll see her again. We know that. And as for us still being stuck here, God will get us out when he's ready, and not before."

"Well, I'd never treat someone I loved the way he's treated us," Kristopher said.

"There are different ways to show your love for someone," Paul said. "Do you remember when you were about four years old and you had that old toy doggie with all the stuffing falling out of it, and you dragged that thing around behind you, and slept with it, and never let it out of your sight, and one day I asked you to give it to me so I could throw it in the furnace? Remember? You cried and cried and told me what a 'bad daddy' I was, but you finally gave it to me. Then, do you remember what happened?"

Kristopher gave a reluctant nod. "You and Mutti gave me my first real puppy."

"And you loved him more than anything you ever had," Paul said, "but you had to be willing to trust us when we told you we were going to throw that old toy in the furnace. Didn't you?"

Kristopher nodded again.

"And that's the way it is with God," Paul said. "If we know he loves us, we'll trust him, no matter what he lets us go through."

Tears began to blur Kristopher's eyes. "I don't see how you can still believe that, with all that's happened to us."

Paul reached out and brushed at the boy's tears. "I just wish I'd taken more time when you were growing up to help you understand how much God loves you, but he'll show you that himself. Just don't give up on him. Give him a chance."

Three weeks later, Kristopher's trust in God was put to its ultimate test as he watched his father being loaded into a boxcar headed toward the camp called Auschwitz. Prisoners judged too weak to work were being exchanged for fresh workers from the east.

Standing on the platform as the sick and beleaguered workers were pushed and prodded into the cattle cars, was the new Central Works director, SS General Hans Kammler. Next to him stood a grim-faced Otto von Kemp.

18

The Central Works
1944–1945

The winter of 1944 marked the beginning of the end for Germany. Having liberated France and the Low Countries, Allied planes pounded German cities from her western border all the way to Berlin. The country was in shambles—physically and emotionally—as every available man, woman, and child was forced into trying to save the country. Fourteen and fifteen-year-olds manned anti-aircraft guns, while women, children, and old men dug anti-tank traps and trenches around the cities. The war was on the doorstep of those who still had doorsteps.

From September on, the V-2s bombarded England in the hope that she would be cowed into surrendering, but what they delivered was too little and too late.

Desperate, and against the advice of all his generals, Hitler made one last fatal move before his empire collapsed around him. He pulled his strongest divisions from the Russian front and concentrated them along a fifty-mile line opposite Luxembourg and Belgium for one final, all-out offensive against the western Allies. On December 16th, the Battle of the Bulge began. For forty-four days, the offensive went back and forth on frozen ground, through Christmas and New Year's, until by the end of January the Germans had run out of men and fuel.

Thousands of wounded, embittered German soldiers dragged themselves back to Germany on foot, or bicycle, or any other conveyance they could commandeer, to cities, homes, and families that were no longer there, while in the east the Russians were knocking on the borders of Germany with little to deter them.

None of this had escaped the attention of Otto von Kemp. That Germany had lost the war was a conclusion he had come to six months earlier. The only question in his mind was how soon could he get himself and his family out of the Central Works? For months, he had been making plans to get them to safety in their home in Oberammergau, but it was a delicate situation that required that he wait until just the right moment before disappearing. One thing he knew for sure from a captured Allied document known only to the German High Command: Germany was to be split into three sectors, and the Central Works was in the sector being given to the Russians. He was definitely going to be gone before the Central Works was captured. Nothing could compel him to risk falling into the Russians' hands.

From the increasing fortifications and efforts at camouflaging the Central Works, the prisoners also realized that Germany's days were numbered. Each had only one prayer: that he or she could hold on until they were liberated.

The exception was Kristopher Falkenhorst. He had two prayers: one was that he could survive until the Allies got there; and the other was that he could get his hands on Otto von Kemp before they did. It was no longer hate that propelled him; in his mind it was simple justice. He was going to save the Allies the trouble of bringing von Kemp to trial. He had already been tried and found guilty by a seventeen-year-old orphan. All that was left was the carrying out of the sentence with any instrument he could lay his hands on.

☩ ☩

In early March, 1945, Kristopher received an unexpected shock. Hannah von Kemp appeared at the commandant's office in Juno with a letter signed by her father, requesting Kristopher's release for the evening to his custody. He was sending his daughter to pick him up.

It had been months since Kristopher had last seen Hannah, and he couldn't believe his eyes when the commandant sent for him. She had wound her long blond hair into a seductive upsweep around her head. Her cheeks were dabbed with rouge, and her mouth was a provocative slash of iridescent red. Looking at her in her high heels and a tight dress that showed off her dazzling curves, he could hardly believe this was the same young girl he had once held in his arms. This was a beautiful, sensuous woman—a little overdone, perhaps—but from the look in the eyes of the commandant and guard, it was having the effect she was after. None of them could take their eyes off her.

"Hello, Kristopher," she said. "How've you been?"

The question startled a surprised little laugh out of him. "How do think I've been in this hellhole? What're you doing here?"

Hannah glanced over at the commandant behind his desk, then back at Kristopher. "My father sent me to see if you'd like to spend the evening with our family. He's always been very grateful for the wonderful work you did for him on our estate, and he thought it would be a nice way to thank you." She motioned toward the paper in the commandant's hand. "He sent the commandant a note requesting it, so it's all cleared if you'd like to come."

Kristopher looked over toward the desk, and the officer waved the sheet toward him. "I don't know why, but von Kemp wants your company for the evening. There's no accounting for people's tastes, I guess. Anyway, if you decide to go, I want you back here within three hours." He turned to Hannah. "And I want you to let your father know that I'm holding him completely responsible for this Jew. Is that understood?"

Hannah gave him an enchanting smile. "Of course. That's no problem. Kristopher used to be in our home all the time when he was working there. My father has a great deal of confidence in him."

Kristopher couldn't believe what he was hearing—von Kemp

wanted him in their home? Something was fishy. Was he really behind this, or was this some hair-brained scheme of Hannah's? But, what did he have to lose? He shrugged noncommittally. "Why not? I don't have any other social engagements tonight."

Hannah thanked the commandant for his trouble, and she and Kristopher went out and got in von Kemp's car.

"I didn't know you could drive," he said as he got in the passenger's side.

"I've been teaching myself," she explained, fumbling with the gearshift. After several attempts she finally found first gear. She looked up sheepishly. "Sorry. I guess I need a little more practice."

They took off, lurching erratically across the compound. The guard jumped back as the car nearly clipped the gate. When they were on the outside, Kristopher finally turned to her. "Okay. What's this all about? Why are you decked out like this?"

Hannah kept her eyes straight ahead, but a grin tugged at the corners of her mouth. "I wanted to see you, and I couldn't think of any other way to do it."

"You mean your father didn't write that note?"

"My father isn't even here. Do you think I'd be driving his car if he was?"

Kristopher's brows shot up. "You took it without asking?"

"I'm only borrowing it."

"What about your mother? Does she know you took it?"

"She's with Vati."

"Then who's taking care of you?"

"The maid," she said nonchalantly.

Kristopher shook his head in disbelief. "I can't believe you'd pull a stunt like this. What if your parents find out?"

"They won't. The maid's having her boyfriend in to spend the night, so she's hardly in a position to tell on me."

Kristopher's face broke into a slow grin. "You're really something, you know that?" He reached over and ran a finger across the rouge on her cheek. "What's all this for?"

She smiled coyly. "I wasn't sure I could get the commandant to buy my story if he thought I was just some kid, so I decided to dress up a bit."

He gave a rueful snort. "Yes, you certainly did."

A triumphant grin spread across her face.

"Keep your eyes on the road!" he yelled, grabbing for the wheel. "The last thing we need is for you to wreck your father's car." He leaned back and looked at her. "By the way, how did you get his signature on that note?"

"I copied it from some of his papers. Pretty good job, if I do say so myself."

"Let's hope the commandant doesn't check with him."

"You worry too much," she said, turning in at the estate. Kristopher's fingers gripped the edge of the seat as the car barely missed the wrought-iron gate.

Hannah pulled the car up to the house and slammed on the brakes, throwing him into the dashboard. "Sorry," she laughed. "I guess I really do need a little more practice."

"You need more than a little," he said. "Give me those keys. I'll drive us back when my three hours are up."

"When did you learn to drive?" she asked.

"I haven't," he said, "but I can't be any worse than you."

She handed him the keys with a laugh, and they got out. "What now?" he asked.

"I've got a surprise for you in the summerhouse."

He frowned. "I don't like surprises. I've had too many bad ones lately."

She grinned at him. "You'll like this one. Come on."

It was growing dark as they followed the familiar path through the trees, and Kristopher had to admit a sad nostalgia as the summerhouse came into view. Hannah had set candles all around the benches, and she lit them now. He was amused to see a bottle of red wine and two crystal goblets sitting on the table next to a bouquet of white lilies.

He nodded toward the bottle as she poured them both a glass. "I suppose you swiped this from your father."

"He won't miss it. He's got a cellarfull at the house."

"Who'd he steal that from?"

Her mouth pulled down into a little pout. "He didn't steal it from anybody. It was a gift from somebody in France."

"Yeah, I'll just *bet* it was a gift."

"Don't be so negative. I went to a lot of trouble to make this a special night for us."

"What's the occasion, if I may ask?"

"It's a going-away party."

He was instantly alert. "Who's going away?"

"Both of us are. Vati says Germany can't last more than a month, so the Allies will liberate you, and we'll be leaving, too."

"Where are you going?"

"I don't know. My parents are gone now, making arrangements. Vati doesn't want to be here if the Russians get here before the Americans."

Kristopher felt a rage begin to rise up in him. "I hope the Russians *do* get him. They'll give him what he deserves."

Hannah's joyful look suddenly faded. "Don't say that. I've told you a hundred times that he was only doing his job."

Kristopher angrily set his glass down, sloshing some of the wine onto the table. "Oh, come off it, Hannah! You don't really believe that anymore, do you?" He spit his words out. "Your father's *job* cost me my mother and father."

Hannah refused to be baited by his anger. "I'm not going to fight with you on our last night together. I know we'll never agree about the things my father has done, but I went to a lot of trouble to make this nice for us, so please don't spoil it by getting mad."

"What do you want me to do?" he asked. "Stand here and talk about the wonderful future we can look forward to?"

Her mouth quivered, but she refused to cry. "No. I want you to hold me in your arms like you used to do here." Her voice dropped to a whisper. "I want you to make love to me."

He gaped at her in amazement. "You want me to make love to you when you know how much I despise your father?"

She reached up and put her hand over his mouth. "I don't want to hear one more word about my father. That's all behind us now. All I know is, I love you, and I want to belong to you completely—even if it's only for a few hours."

Before he realized what was happening, she began unbuttoning her dress, her hands trembling as she fumbled with the tiny pearl buttons. She flung it off and stood before him completely naked.

He was suddenly aware of a sharp surge in his groin, and he looked around to see who might be watching. He'd be a dead man if someone told von Kemp about this. He'd never believe that Hannah had instigated this whole thing. Then suddenly the thought struck him: what a perfect way to finally get back at von Kemp. Deflower his little virgin. His precious Aryan daughter raped by a Jew.

As he wrestled with these thoughts, he continued staring at her nakedness, and every part of his body screamed out for her. He tried to clear his head, but a wave of desire so intense he was powerless to resist it swept over him. He pulled her to him, crushing her lips with his, then pushed her down onto the chaise and tugged at his pants. When he got them off, he looked down at her trusting face, tears seeping from under her closed lids, and his anger began to dissipate. This girl had never harmed him in any way; in fact, she had remained loyal to him when everyone else had turned against him, and she had proved that loyalty again and again.

Then Sarah's precious face suddenly came before him, and he knew he could never do to Hannah what that Gestapo animal had done to Sarah.

He stepped back and shook his head. "No! I can't do this."

Hannah sat up in alarm. "Why?"

"Your father would kill me if he ever found out."

"He won't find out. I promise!"

"But what if you get pregnant?"

"I won't get pregnant. It's not that time of the month for me." Her mouth began to quiver. "You just don't want me, do you?"

As she sat there with her body and soul bared to him, his voice was suddenly husky. "Of course I want you. It's just that . . . I've never done this with anyone before, and . . . I don't want to make a fool of myself by doing something . . . stupid."

She let out a relieved little laugh and held out her arms to him. "Come here, you," she said. "I think the two of us can figure out what to do."

19

Camp Juno
Spring, 1945

The last week in March, the prisoners were exhilarated at the sound of heavy cannons in the distance, knowing the Allies were near. The SS began frantic preparations to defend the camps and the rocket facilities. Prisoners were forced to dig anti-tank trenches, and anti-aircraft guns were put in place at intervals. Gallons of white paint were brought in, and the inmates in the camps were ordered to paint their barracks, inside and out. Heavy blankets were issued to each person and their tattered uniforms were replaced with newer ones. For the first time since Kristopher had arrived at Juno, huge supplies of food were dropped off at the camp, and the prisoners were ordered to eat their fill. Boxes of medicine and cigarettes were distributed, along with shampoo and cosmetics and lotions for the women.

None of the inmates were fooled by this sudden spurt of compassion. The SS was buying insurance for itself—but whatever the motivation, the prisoners greedily made use of their good fortune.

On April 5th, an inspection team, headed by von Kemp, toured Juno. Kristopher watched as they made their way through the grounds and barracks, nodding their worried approval as they saw the improved conditions of the camp and the inmates' appearances. Every now and then, von Kemp looked up nervously as the sound of another blast in the distance warned of the nearness of the Allies.

Kristopher could only pray that a bomb would land right on von Kemp. He had already come to the conclusion that there was no way he could personally get his hands on the man. He was going to have to be content to let the Americans or Russians deal with him, whoever got there first. He hadn't heard from Hannah since their night in the summerhouse two weeks earlier, and hoped that von Kemp had already gotten her and her mother out of the area. As beautiful as Hannah was, he didn't want her falling into the hands of the Russians or the sex-starved American troops.

Few people slept the night after the inspection as the guns in the distance grew louder and louder. At the first rays of dawn, a grinding, rumbling noise brought everyone out of the barracks. In the half-light, Kristopher saw tanks approaching on the road leading to his camp. He was straining to see if they were American, Russian, or German, when suddenly, a shell burst in the air above him, and he hit the ground, covering his head with his hands. He wasn't sure whether it was the Germans or the Allies, but whoever it was, he wasn't going to just lie there and let them kill him.

He jumped up and ran toward the gate, and to his astonishment, saw it was open and unguarded. He looked in the guard shack and saw a rifle leaning against the wall. He grabbed it and ran from the compound in the direction of the woods. He was panting as he reached the cover of the trees and sat down to catch his breath. The firing behind him continued, and he began to scramble up the steep hill, certain they were right behind him—whoever "they" were.

Kristopher had been climbing through the trees for about thirty minutes when what he saw in a small clearing in front of him caused him to flatten himself in some bushes. Six German tanks were lined up with their cannons aimed in the direction of Juno. His heart pounded wildly as he slid back down the steep slope for about fifty yards and lay breathless against the hill, trying to decide what to do. He was trapped between the Germans in the camp and those above him. He looked at the rifle he was carrying to see if he knew how to use it. Thank God! It was just like the ones they had practiced with in the Hitler Youth, and it had a full clip of ammunition. If they came after him, at least he wouldn't be completely defenseless.

The firing below had stopped, but he could see the smoke from the compound rising above the level of the trees. There was no way he could go back there.

Then it suddenly came to him. Hannah would hide him if she was still there. He knew the estate was not too far off to the right. He started traversing the steep slope, glancing back over his shoulder every few seconds. The sun was up, and it was easier to make his way through the dense trees and underbrush.

It took him a good hour to reach the top of the canyon on the edge of the estate. Cautiously, he worked his way through the trees until he could see the summerhouse. There were no sounds coming from the direction of the mansion, but he could hear the occasional pounding of large guns off in the distance.

He staggered into the summerhouse and threw himself down onto the chaise. Memories of his last night there with Hannah added to the uncertainty and fear he was feeling. Were the von Kemps still here? Who had bombed Juno? Were the Americans anywhere near? Where could he go to be safe?

He remembered that Hannah used to leave him letters under the chaise pad, and tossed the pad off it. His pulse quickened as he saw one of her blue envelopes with its scalloped trim on the flap. He tore it open.

My Dearest Kristopher,
When you read this, I'll be gone, and I don't know where. The thought of never seeing you again is breaking my heart, but I give you my solemn promise that I'll spend the rest of my life looking for you, and I beg you to look for me. You're a part of me now, and always will be.
Your Hannah

He lay back on the chaise, exhausted and beaten. It was all over. Hannah was gone, his parents were dead, von Kemp had gotten away with his crimes, and he had no place to go to be safe. What more could go wrong? He fought the weariness that engulfed him, but finally gave way to an exhausted sleep.

✠ ✠

He awoke abruptly at the feel of a gun muzzle under his chin. Terrified, he tried to sit up, but the tall American soldier standing over him kept him pinned to the chaise with the barrel of a rifle.

"What . . . what's going on?" Kristopher stammered. "Who are you?"

"English, Kraut. *Sprechen Sie englisch?*"

"*Ja* . . . Yes," Kristopher answered, stumbling over the language he had learned in school but seldom used. "Who are you?"

"I'll ask the questions," the soldier growled. "What's your name, and what're you doin' out here all by yourself with this rifle?"

Kristopher frantically tried to interpret the words, then saw another shorter soldier examining the rifle he'd taken from the camp. "Ich bin Kristopher Falkenhorst von Juno," he managed to get out.

"What're you doin' out here, then, and where'd you get this rifle?" He pointed at the rifle. "Rifle! Kraut, and no lies."

Kristopher's eyes were wide with terror as the soldier jabbed the end of his rifle against his throat. "Guard house at Juno," he stammered.

The soldier lifted the end of his rifle from Kristopher's throat, and he sat up, rubbing the spot where it had been.

"Let's get you back there and see if anyone knows you. You'd better pray you're tellin' us the truth."

"Germans are killing prisoners there!" Kristopher cried in alarm.

"Nobody's gonna kill any more prisoners. We've cleaned out all the Krauts around here."

"Tanks on the hill?" Kristopher exclaimed, pointing frantically in the direction he'd just come from.

The soldier looked at his buddy. "You know anything about tanks on a hill?"

"Nope!"

The tall soldier turned back to Kristopher. "I dunno what you're tryin' to pull, but why don't you take us to these tanks you saw. If you're lyin', I'll blow your head off." He turned to his friend. "Come on, let's get this Kraut in the Jeep and have him show us where he saw those tanks."

They drove off in the direction Kristopher showed them. On the road, they passed a convoy of American trucks and tanks rumbling along, headed for the Central Works. Some GIs gave a thumbs up from the back of a truck as the driver sped past them.

When they got to where Kristopher had first entered the woods, he pointed up the hill. "There," he said. "Six tanks."

The man pulled the Jeep off the road and said something to the other soldier, who jumped out and flagged down one of the trucks that was passing. It turned off and pulled up beside the Jeep. He climbed up on the running board and spoke to the driver, then ran around behind the truck, motioning the soldiers out.

Kristopher watched in wonder as the men scrambled down from the back and trotted over to the Jeep, rifles slung over their soiled uniforms, their weary unshaved faces grim. The tall soldier explained what Kristopher had told him, then led them off up the hill. Kristopher was taken over to the truck and deposited with its driver.

He sat there beside the man for nearly an hour, terrified that the German tanks might have left, and the soldiers would think he'd been lying, and shoot him. Suddenly they heard violent explosions from up on the hill, and the sound of gunshots echoing down through the trees. Kristopher looked up through the windshield of the truck, desperately trying to see.

A short while later, the GIs came sliding down the hill and dashed out into the open from the trees, broad grins covering their tired faces. The tall soldier ran over to the truck, breathing hard. "Well, Kraut boy, it looks like you were tellin' the truth. We got 'em all and didn't lose a man. You're a hero. You know that?" He opened the truck door and motioned Kristopher out. "Come on, boy," he said, "let's go find your family."

Kristopher looked at him bleakly. "I have no family."

20

April, 1945

The darkened BMW sedan made its way along the desolate country road, veering erratically around potholes and bomb craters in the pitch-black night. There were no lights in the homes that dotted the isolated back road. There was no sign of any kind of life outside the car that was carrying Otto von Kemp and his family away from imminent capture at the Central Works. He peered anxiously through the windshield, sweat beading on his forehead despite the chill April evening. "What I wouldn't give to be able to turn these headlights on," he said to his wife.

"You don't dare," Eva cautioned. "There must be soldiers all over this area."

"I just wish I knew whether it's the Americans or the Russians," he said.

Eva glanced into the backseat at their sleeping daughter, and her brow wrinkled. "I'm worried sick about Hannah. I don't know what she's come down with." She leaned over the seat and placed her hand on the girl's forehead. Hannah stirred, moaning slightly. "She's on fire, Otto."

He glanced over his shoulder. "Do you have anything to give her?"

She shook her head. "I didn't have time to pack any medicine."

"You've got some water. Soak something in it and put it on her forehead."

"It's more than just her fever that's worrying me. She's so weak she can't even sit up."

He nodded grimly. "I think she was just so upset at the way we had to drop everything and sneak out of the house. You can hardly blame her."

Eva took out her handkerchief and soaked it with water from the glass jug between her feet, then leaned into the back, placing the cloth on Hannah's forehead. The girl's eye's fluttered open.

"Thanks, Mutti," she murmured weakly.

"How do you feel?"

"Not very good. Are we almost there?"

"No, darling. We've only been on the road a couple of hours. Vati has to take these back roads so we won't run into any soldiers, and we have to keep our lights off, so it's very slow going." She wiped the perspiration from Hannah's brow. "You just try to get back to sleep. Vati's taking care of everything." Hannah gave her a wan smile and twisted in the cramped space, trying to get comfortable.

Eva settled back in her seat. "We'll have to get some help for her if she isn't better by morning. God knows what she might've come down with."

Von Kemp shook his head. "We can't stop. At the pace we're going, it'll take us several days to get to Reichenbach as it is. When I talked to Peter several days ago, he said the city hadn't been occupied yet, but they know the Russians are in Dresden—about seventy-five miles east of them. We simply can't stop, except for me to get a few hours sleep. I've got to pick up those papers before we join von Braun. Those're our ticket to freedom."

As the car bounced through the black night, his mind raced over the events of the past few weeks. What a nightmare he and his colleagues had been through! The frantic scuttling of hundreds of rocket parts; the burning of incriminating papers and the hiding of tons of other technical drawings and materiel; the distasteful effort to destroy hundreds of corpses; the constant fear of being shot by the SS so they wouldn't defect to the Allies with their secrets; and the cruel necessity of uprooting his beloved family in the middle of the night and subjecting them to this mad flight fraught with danger and uncertainty. And now Hannah so sick. Where would it all end?

Hopefully, in Oberjoch, where he and von Braun and the rest of their team were planning to surrender to the Americans as soon as they were all assembled there. But what kind of treatment could he reasonably expect from hostile, battle-weary soldiers? Would they shoot first and ask questions later? His secret contacts with the Allies over the past few years had only been known to a few, but would he have a chance to verify who he was before they arrested or shot him? He had to get to his brother's and get the documentation he was keeping for him, and he had to get in and out of there before the Russians took the city.

Why, oh why, had he waited so long before clearing out of the Central Works? If only he'd left a week earlier like some of the others had. If only! How many "if onlys" had there been in his life? Too many, that's for sure. But he couldn't have left any sooner. General Kammler, the new commandant, had been watching him like a hawk the last few weeks, fully expecting all the scientists to bolt at any moment. And, besides, his staying there had saved the lives of hundreds of inmates that Kammler wanted to execute. He'd been able to convince Kammler that it would go better for all of them if the Allies found the remaining inmates alive. They already had enough to answer for with the stacks of corpses in the tunnels—which Kammler hadn't had time to burn.

That's the other thing that worried him. How would he explain to the Americans his part in all that carnage? It certainly wasn't his doing, but he'd been there when these senseless deaths had occurred from the beatings and diseases and starvation. God knows he'd done his best to try to alleviate the conditions that brought this all about, but he had to admit—at least to himself—that his efforts had been mostly futile. And when the Allies looked for people to blame, he'd obviously be one of them. Maybe the help he'd given them would not offset this outrage in their minds.

Well, it was academic at this point. There was no undoing the things that had been done. Would he have done differently if he had it to do over again? He didn't see how. His whole life was science. Joining the Nazi Party had been mandatory for any German scientist who wanted a career in that field, and going where they sent you and doing what they told you were all part of the job.

He'd done nothing that hundreds of other German scientists hadn't done. Maybe some had had higher regard for Hitler than he, but that was their decision. He'd made his decision years ago when he'd decided to accommodate Hitler's scientific aspirations while rejecting his moral philosophy. He'd had to think about his family and future—and refusing the projects he'd been assigned would have doomed both of those. He'd have been left behind with all the incredible advances his colleagues had made in the course of their rocket research, and there would have been no place for him in the scientific world of a post-war Germany.

No, he'd squared things with his own conscience, and others would have to judge him according to theirs. He only prayed that he'd be given the opportunity to explain his actions before he was judged too harshly.

✝ ✝

It took them two terrifying days and nights to get to Reichenbach. They'd skirted the cities, keeping to backroads, sharing the driving and sleeping intermittently in the car under bridges and in dense forests. In some areas, especially the rural countryside, it was deceptively peaceful, but there was bombing damage in most of the areas they passed through. Whether it had been caused by the Americans or Russians—or the Germans—von Kemp didn't know.

It was early on the morning of the third day when they entered Reichenbach. Peter von Kemp lived on the outskirts of the small village. The doctor's house, a stone cottage with vines growing up the sides, was dark when they pulled up. Otto banged on the door, and in a few moments a light went on as his brother pulled the curtain aside and peered out. Peter quickly opened the door.

"Otto! My God, man! I expected you days ago. What took you so long? You look like hell!"

"That's where we've just come from," he said, embracing his brother.

"Are Eva and Hannah with you?" Peter asked, glancing at the car.

"Yes, but Hannah's very sick. Can you help me get her into the house?"

"Of course." He embraced Eva as she came forward, then he and Otto carried the delirious girl into the house and laid her on the sofa.

Peter knelt down beside her and felt her forehead, then looked up at Otto in alarm. "She's burning up. Do you have any idea what's wrong with her?"

"No. She's been vomiting off and on for the past week, but this high fever really started after we left the camp. We've been worried sick, but I felt it was best to try to get her to you as fast as we could."

"You did the right thing. Let me get my bag."

He disappeared into the bedroom, and when he reappeared, his wife, Natalia, was with him. She embraced Otto and Eva, then knelt beside Hannah and felt her forehead.

Peter moved her aside and sat on the edge of the sofa. He put his stethoscope around his neck, and began unbuttoning Hannah's fever-dampened blouse.

"Oh, my God!" he said, as he got a look at her chest. It was covered with red splotches. "Look at this, Otto."

Von Kemp knelt down beside his daughter and blanched at what he saw. "It looks like typhus."

"It is," Peter nodded grimly. "Have you had typhus at the camps?"

Otto nodded. "Hundreds of cases, but as far as I know, Hannah hasn't been anywhere near the camps or anyone who's had it. I don't know how she could have gotten it."

"Well, it's spread by infected fleas or lice or ticks, so if she's been in the woods, she might have picked it up there."

"The summerhouse!" said Eva. "I bet that's where she got it. She spent so much time out there."

"That could be it," Peter said. "Let me check her heart and pulse and then I've got some Tetracycline I can give her and some aspirin to get that fever down." He looked up at Otto. "She's not going anywhere for a couple of weeks, though. I hope you realize that."

"Peter!" exclaimed von Kemp. "We can't stay here that long. I've got to be in Oberjoch as soon as possible."

"Eva and Hannah will just have to stay here with us, then, and join you later," Peter said.

"We can't get separated," Eva cried. "How would we get to Oberjoch without Otto?"

"We could drive you," said Natalia. "It's only a couple of hundred miles."

"Yes," Peter said, "we'd be glad to do that."

"But you don't know whether whoever occupies this city will even allow anyone to leave," von Kemp protested. "They might get stuck here indefinitely." A sudden thought struck him. "And if it's the Russians, and they find out that Eva and Hannah are my family, they might try to hold them for ransom to get me to go to work for them." He shook his head. "I think it's too risky, Peter."

"What do you suggest then?" he asked.

Von Kemp sat down heavily in a chair and shook his head. "I don't know. I just don't know. I was only planning on staying here one night, but I guess I could stay a few days longer and see how Hannah does. Maybe she'll be able to travel sooner than we think. I don't know what else we can do."

"I'm going to make us some coffee," Natalia said, "then get some breakfast on. You folks must be starving if you've been on the road two days."

Eva got up. "I'll give you a hand."

Peter completed examining Hannah, then gave her a shot of Tetracycline with a mild sedative and some aspirin. Von Kemp carried her into one of the bedrooms and put her to bed.

After the two men had come back out into the living room, Otto explained to his brother the urgency of his getting to Oberjoch no later than April 20, a week away. "Everything's very uncertain right now with all of us who worked at the Central Works, but we feel it's critical for us to be together when we surrender to the Americans. We'll have more leverage that way. Besides, I've got some of the papers from the Central Works that we plan to use to bargain for better contracts, plus the ones you've been keeping for me that I personally need for my own safety. I simply can't stay here for more than two days, Peter, and I'll have to leave sooner than that if the Russians show up. Much as I hate to do so, if you feel Hannah isn't ready to be moved when it comes time for me to leave, I'll have to leave her and Eva here with you and trust you to look after them until I can get back to get them or you can get them to me. That's another thing I'm not even sure of—where the Americans will take us for interrogation—but I certainly hope they'll let me bring my family wherever it is."

"Then you really feel the war is lost? Isn't there any hope?"

Von Kemp gave his brother an incredulous look. "The war was lost months ago—hell, a *year* ago. Hitler's been the only German who wouldn't admit it. The Americans overran the Central Works the day we left. We just barely managed to sneak through and get out. Hitler's ordered his *Gauleiters* to burn everything in Germany: bridges, public buildings, power plants, factories, schools, even hospitals. The man is stark-raving mad. He's holed up in Berlin in his bunker below the Reichstag screaming out his final insane orders to those few idiots like Goebbels and Goering who are still sticking by him. They'll carry out his orders, too, even if it means leaving Germany a smoking ruin. Hitler doesn't care about Germany. He never did. All he wanted was to go down in history as the genius who put together a new Thousand-Year Reich."

Peter put his hands to his head. "What am I going to tell Natalia?"

"Tell her the truth for God's sake! Everything Hitler and his bunch have spouted for years is fantasy or outright lies. It's time every German opened his eyes and saw that. It's a little late—I know—but better late than never."

Peter pulled his robe up around him and gave the belt a nervous tug. "All we've gotten here in Reichenbach the past months have been rumors, but we were all under the impression that Hitler had some kind of secret weapon that would turn the tide for us. Is that wrong?"

"Peter," von Kemp said wearily, "Hitler's secret weapon is what *I've* been working on for the past four years, but I could've told you a year ago that it wouldn't change Germany's chances. It was too little, too late. We tried to make him see that, but you can't reason with a madman."

Peter slumped back on the sofa. "Then it really is over, huh?"

"It depends on what you mean by 'over.' Hitler's phase is over, but I'm not sure the Russians are going to be any better. Do you have any idea how close they are to here?"

"A week ago we heard they were in Dresden and headed this way, so they could be just a few days, or even a few hours away."

Von Kemp leaned forward in alarm. "We need to get out of here as soon as possible, then—you and Natalia with us. You can't be here when they arrive."

"I can't run off and leave my patients. I couldn't live with myself if I did. They'll need me now more than ever."

"Peter, I don't think you realize what it will be like living under the Russians. They're barbarians!"

"You don't think they're going to stay in Germany indefinitely, do you?"

"Are you kidding? They've been itching to get their hands on this country for centuries. I don't know what kind of long-term occupation plans the Allies have, but let me make a prophecy: the Russians will *never* give up any territory they occupy unless we take it from them forceably. I wish you'd reconsider staying here."

"I understand what you're saying, but Natalia and I have already talked about it and made our decision. She's Russian, as you know, so we feel we'll be given special treatment for that reason. Also, they'll need doctors, so I shouldn't fare too badly. I don't want you to worry about us, Otto. It's you I'm worried about."

Von Kemp nodded wearily. "With good reason, too, but the die is cast, so I'll just have to live with the consequences. I need to lie down now, Peter. I'm exhausted."

"Let's see if the women have that coffee ready yet."

Four days later, Hannah was no better, but the sounds of heavy cannons just a few miles to the east of the village made von Kemp realize he could wait no longer. He had to leave. At nine o'clock that evening he said a tearful goodbye to his family. He clutched Eva to him. "Be brave now, Liebchen," he whispered hoarsely. "I'll see you in just a few short weeks. As soon as I find out where I'll be sent, I'll get word to Peter, and he'll bring you. Look after our little girl for me. I'm so sorry to have to leave her like this—and you, too—but I know you both understand that I can't let the Russians take me."

Eva clung to him in desperation, trying to fight back her tears. "I know Peter will pull Hannah through this and get us to you, but, darling, please be careful. I couldn't stand it if anything happened to you."

"Nothing's going to happen to me," he said. "We'll be together soon. You just be brave for Hannah's sake."

She drew back and searched his beloved face for a long moment, then reached up and gently touched his cheek. "Nothing's ever going to be the same for us again, is it?"

A pained look stole across his face. "No, Liebchen, I'm afraid it isn't."

☩ ☩

Thankfully, it was another dark night. Peter had been able to get his brother some gasoline from his physician's ration, and had carefully marked his map, routing him in the opposite direction from where the Russians were most likely coming. His vital documents had been stuffed inside the spare tire in the trunk of his car, along with those papers he'd brought from the Central Works. A heavy rain had begun falling, making the road even more treacherous as he crept along with his headlights out.

He was about an hour out of Reichenbach when he saw bright lights ahead of him. He couldn't make out whether they were on the road coming toward him or from a building near the road, but as he drew closer, he saw it was the headlights of two army trucks straddling the road. He immediately pulled to the shoulder, but there was no place to get out of sight. He sat there in a panic, trying to decide what to do. Had they seen him? He couldn't be sure. After a few minutes he decided to try to turn the car around, but the shoulder was narrow and his wheels had sunk into the loose wet dirt, so it took several attempts and considerable gunning of the engine before he got turned around and back on the road.

He inched forward, still with the lights off, praying they hadn't seen him. He kept an eye on his rear-view mirror as he picked up speed, frantically searching his mind for what to do. Should he try to get back to Peter's, or was there another road he could take? He didn't dare turn on the overhead lights to look at the map.

The rain was coming down harder and the wipers could barely keep up with it. His breath came in short spurts as he leaned forward trying to see through the windshield. He glanced in his rearview mirror and saw the headlights rapidly bearing down on him. They'd seen him! A rush of adrenaline shot through him, and in that terrible frozen moment in time, he made a decision—a decision that would forever alter his life. He reached over and switched on the headlights, jamming his foot down on the accelerator at the same time. The car shot forward down the rain-slickened highway. The last thing he remembered before everything went black was the sensation of floating upward into bursts of iridescent color, then searing pain as his head hit the windshield and flames engulfed his body.

21

Reichenbach, Germany
June, 1945

A month had passed since Hannah's father had stolen away into the night leaving her and her mother feeling abandoned. The red splotches of typhus were gone, and the fever had finally subsided, but Hannah was still too weak to be up for any length of time. Her clothes hung loosely on her, and clumps of her golden hair had begun falling out, leaving her feeling ugly and desolate. She thought of Kristopher constantly, praying that he was safe—but thankful he couldn't see her like she was.

Russian soldiers had occupied the village the morning after her father left. Four days later they had come knocking at the door of her uncle's house and demanded to see everyone's papers. Fortunately, the name von Kemp didn't raise any recognition with these peasants. When Natalia had explained that Eva and Hannah were relatives who were visiting and had been forced to stay because the girl had typhus, the men wasted no time in leaving the cottage. In a parting shot, one of them warned that no one was to leave the village without permission, and the doctor was to make himself available to them at any time.

A constant worry to all of them was why they had not yet heard from Otto. Phone service was sporadic, but a month would have given him plenty of time to get to Oberjoch, even if he'd had to hole up along the way. Peter was especially anxious. What if he'd been arrested, or—the unthinkable—shot by marauding soldiers or civilians. Peter had heard about Himmler's "Werewolves"—the fanatical hordes of young Hitler Youths who had been turned loose in the last months to terrorize and murder any Germans who showed the slightest signs of not remaining loyal to the very end. They were known to stop travelers and demand to know their destinations, then shoot them on the spot if there was the slightest suspicion they might be trying to flee the country or surrender to the enemy. Suppose they'd discovered the stash of secret papers Otto had hidden in the trunk of his car? That, in itself, would doom him. But there was no way to know where Otto was until he contacted them, so that meant Eva and Hannah would just have to stay until word came.

They were all still reeling from the news on May 2nd that Hitler had committed suicide in Berlin with his bride, Eva Braun. Few Germans really understood the extent of the havoc he had wreaked on Germany. All they knew was that he had controlled every aspect of their lives for over twelve years, and now they had to take care of themselves with no idea how to do it in a shattered country under enemy control.

There were bitter tears of rage and relief in the little stone cottage on the outskirts of Reichenbach when a devastated Germany surrendered to the Allies on May 11. Like their lives, the dream of a European empire that would last a thousand years was shattered as they wept for the past and the uncertain future.

✛ ✛

Although Hannah's typhus had passed, she was slow in regaining her strength as the weeks went by. She still had regular bouts of nausea in the mornings, and this puzzled Peter. Could it be possible she was pregnant? No! She was just a child, herself. Could she have been raped and too afraid to tell her parents? He finally decided to confront her. They were alone in the cottage one afternoon, and Hannah was lying on the sofa trying to read when Peter pulled up a chair by her.

"Hannah, is there anything you want to tell me?" he asked kindly.

She laid the book on her chest and gave him a questioning look.

"About what?"

He cleared his throat nervously. "Well, I've been very concerned that you're still nauseated every morning, and I just wondered if there's something you haven't told us."

A look of fear came into Hannah's eyes. "I don't know what you mean. It's the typhus, isn't it?"

"No, darling, I don't think it is. It looks more to me like . . . like . . ." he took a deep breath, "like you might be pregnant. Is there any chance of that?"

She sat up on the sofa and a rush of tears filled her eyes. "Oh, Uncle Peter. I don't know. It just couldn't be, could it?"

He took her hand. "You'll have to tell me. Have you had . . . I mean, did someone take advantage of you?"

She pulled her hand from his and covered her eyes as her whole body began to shake with sobs. He waited a moment, then touched her arm. "What is it? Did someone rape you? You can tell me. I'll understand."

She continued sobbing, incapable of speaking.

He reached for her hands and drew them down from her face. Her head remained bowed, her eyes closed tightly as she wept in great sobbing gulps. She finally managed to speak, her voice barely audible. "No. I wasn't raped."

Peter felt an immediate sense of relief. "I'm certainly glad to hear that, but what is it that's upset you so, honey? Is it something you can tell me?"

She slowly lifted her tear-streaked face and looked at him. He'd never seen such sadness. Very softly, she murmured, "I wasn't raped, Uncle Peter. The boy I've loved all my life made *love* to me a few weeks before we left."

His face dropped. "Oh, Hannah!" he moaned. "Then I was right. You must be pregnant. Your mother and father will be devastated." He was silent for a moment, then said, "I'll have to do an abortion. That's all there is to it."

Her head snapped up, and she shook it adamantly. "Absolutely not!" she blurted at him. "I want this baby. I love Kristopher, and this baby is the only part of him I'll ever have. I won't let you take it away from me, Uncle Peter. I won't!"

"But, Hannah . . ."

"I love you very much," she said, "but I have to make this decision for my own life. Please try to understand."

"But what about your parents?"

She took a deep breath. "I know this will break their hearts, but we don't even know if Vati's still alive, and there's been so much death that I don't think Mutti would want to see one more thing die." She reached over and took her uncle's hand. "Please try to understand, Uncle Peter. Please!"

He looked into her earnest face and saw a half-woman, half-child. She had no idea what she was letting herself in for, but maybe this baby would be like a Phoenix rising out of the ashes of Hannah's shattered life. God knows, this seventeen-year-old girl would need something to hold on to in the months and years ahead. Maybe this child would be her salvation.

"I think I do," he nodded. "Now we'll just have to convince your mother."

Eva was shattered by the news. On top of her worry about Otto, she now had an unwed pregnant daughter to care for and no home of her own in which to do so. Peter was adamant that they not leave until they heard from Otto, and it had been nearly two months since he'd left. Hannah was in her third month of pregnancy, and they all decided that it was best for Eva and Hannah to stay until the baby was born, unless Otto sent for them.

Hannah wanted Kristopher listed as the father on the birth certificate, but her mother and Peter convinced her to pick a different name in light of the fact that the von Falkenhorst name had been badly sullied in Berlin because of the general's involvement in Hitler's assassination plot. There might be attempts at revenge against her and the child. The name they chose as the father was Ernst Kramer.

Hannah had already decided that if it was a boy she would name him Kristopher, but when she told her mother, Eva spent the whole day crying. "After what that boy did to you, how can you throw it in my face by naming that poor baby after him?" she'd said. "I'd never be able to call him by that name without thinking about how he was conceived."

As much as it pained Hannah to think he would not bear either Kristopher's first or last name, she finally agreed to name him Nikolaus if it was a boy, or Nichole if it was a girl.

In July, a Colonel Konov appeared at Peter's home and interrogated the von Kemps as to the whereabouts of the rocket scientist, Otto von Kemp, but they had been able to say truthfully that they had no idea where he was. Never-the-less, they now knew they had been identified as von Kemp's family, and that he must not have been captured by the Russians.

☦ ☦

The warm summer days of 1945 slowly faded into a brilliantly hued autumn in Reichenbach, and not even the oppressive Russian occupation could forestall the serene beauty of the changing seasons as the trees went from gold and yellow to bare. Few Germans, though, had the time or interest to enjoy the beauty that had always given them such pleasure. Their beloved forests now had a more functional use. With coal supplies non-existent, the trees were needed for fuel, and thousands of them were chopped down that winter to bring a little warmth into the homes of the freezing citizens. Medical supplies were almost non-existent, utilities were erratic—especially the telephones—homeless people huddled together in abandoned buildings and scavenged the countryside for food, and the citizens' movements were all restricted by the Russians.

As the time for Hannah's delivery grew closer, Eva brooded over what their next step should be. It had been her plan for them to try to get to their home in Berlin as soon as the baby was born. She was convinced that Otto would get there if he was still alive. He'd never come to Reichenbach, since it was inside the Russian zone, but she'd heard that Berlin was partly under American control and that the Americans were treating the Germans well. She had no idea whether their home was still standing, or—if it was—whether it was in the Russian or American part of the city, but they had many friends and relatives there that she was convinced would take them in while they waited for Otto to come to them.

If the growing mound in Hannah's belly had brought a beautiful bloom to her, all the events of the past months had taken their toll on Eva. She had been a beautiful woman with peaches and cream skin, her blond hair always beautifully coifed, her nails long and polished, and her clothing the latest fashion from well-known designers. All that had changed in the last seven months.

The others did what they could to cheer her up, but they were fighting their own depression. All except Hannah. As her delivery drew nearer, she bloomed. She was carrying Kristopher Falkenhorst's child; a part of him that no one could ever take from her. Day after day she plotted and schemed how she'd find him and they would marry and live happily ever after, just the three of them. The beautiful dream always brought a glow to her cheeks and a warm smile to her lips.

The child was born in the little cottage in Reichenbach on a snowy January 30, 1946. He had a head of curly blond hair and blue eyes, just like hers and Kristopher's, and was christened Nikolaus Kristopher Kramer. Hannah's joy was marred only by her disappointment that Kristopher and her father could not be there to see this beautiful offspring of theirs.

22

The Central Works
1946

The possibility of a grandchild was the furthest thing from Otto von Kemp's mind as he lay on his cot in the detention camp at Jena thinking back over the past seven months. His hand moved involuntarily to the ragged scars on his face and neck, and he winced in memory of the pain he'd endured for so many months after his capture.

He knew, now, how insane his attempt to outrun the Russians had been, but at the time it had seemed the only thing he could do in light of the incriminating papers he had with him. However, he would never forgive the brutality that had led them to shoot the tires out from under his car, nor would he ever be able to understand how he'd escaped death in the twisted, burned wreckage that had been his BMW.

But there were times, like tonight, when he wasn't sure he was glad he had survived. His coma had lasted for over a month, time for the broken nose and cheek bones to begin mending—but without medical attention, the cuts and burns had healed into crimson welts of gnarled flesh. His Russian captors had lost no sleep over his looks, however; they cared nothing for his vanity as long as his brain was still functioning and could be put to use for them. He'd already endured hundreds of hours of questioning about the partially burned papers they'd discovered in the trunk of his car, and they let him know that they knew exactly where his wife and daughter and brother were, and unless he cooperated willingly with them, their safety could not be assured.

That threat had been the final turning point in his decision to go to work for them. That, and the fact that numerous other German scientists were finding their way into the Russian sector, lured by the promise of lucrative salaries and unlimited research in well-equipped facilities. These men brought word with them that the Americans were eager to keep them in the American sector, but their occupation policy forbade any research that could be construed as having to do with military hardware. Only labs and research institutes that related directly to the protection of public health were allowed to remain functioning in the American zone; whereas the Russians were only too eager for the German scientists to continue with projects that could give them a military edge over their allies.

Most of these scientists would rather have worked for the Americans or British, but months of going through endless interrogations by the Western Allies, being promised contracts that never materialized and having to be separated from their families without any means to support them—and the fact that any scientists who had been Nazi Party members could only work at non-scientific jobs in the American zone—had led many of them to leave that sector in disgust.

Von Kemp had no options about where he would work, though. Not only was he a prisoner of the Russians in Jena, but they had not allowed him to get word to his family of where he was, obviously fearing an incident with the Allies if the manner in which they had captured him became known. It was fairly common practice in the first year after Germany's surrender for all four Allies to lure or kidnap scientists from each other's sectors, but as the months had gone by, a hardening of policy had developed among the four occupying powers, and major confrontations were now being had over incidents similar to what had happened to von Kemp.

Otto had no appetite for being caught in the middle of an international incident of that kind, especially since he'd been told of the American's attitude toward German scientists who had been members of the Nazi Party. At least the Russians weren't holding that against him. And since all his documentation about his previous secret correspondence with the Americans and the papers he'd brought from the Central Works had been burned or confiscated by the Russians, he had lost his leverage for being recruited by the Americans. Consequently, he had decided to go ahead and work for the Russians with their promise that they would contact his family at the first of the year and bring them to Jena.

☩ ☩

The first week in January of 1946, von Kemp was awakened by the sound of trucks pulling into the compound outside his barracks in Jena. He got up and stumbled sleepily to the window. In the early morning light he made out some large trucks with canvas coverings pulled over metal frames on the back. Others were now climbing out of their bunks, and one man, Arthur Dietrick, joined him at the window.

"What is it?" Dietrick asked.

"I don't know. Maybe they're bringing some more men in."

They turned abruptly as the barracks door opened and several armed Russian soldiers stormed into the long, dark room. "*Raus! Raus!*" they yelled. "Everybody up. *Schnell!*"

"What's going on?" von Kemp asked in alarm.

"You're being transferred," one of the soldiers snarled, jabbing the end of his rifle into the blanket of a man who had not yet awakened. "Come on, you lazy Kraut. Out of there! This isn't a rest home."

"Transferred where?" von Kemp asked.

"You'll find out in due time," the man answered. He yelled down the length of the room, "All of you Krauts, get your things together immediately. I want you in those trucks in ten minutes."

There was a frantic scurrying as the fifty or so scientists quickly dressed and gathered together their few possessions. They were herded out and loaded into the trucks, then driven off into the frosty morning fog.

Von Kemp was seated next to a very nervous Arthur Dietrick. "Do you suppose they're going to execute us?" Dietrick asked.

"I doubt it," von Kemp said. "They've gone to too much trouble to get all of us."

"But where do you think they're taking us?"

"Probably somewhere where they can put us to work." He looked around the truck. "You'll notice that most of the ones they've taken are the rocket men. They probably got tired of feeding us when there hasn't been anything for us to do."

Dietrick leaned toward him conspiratorially. "Do you think there's any chance we could escape when the truck stops? I speak fluent Russian."

"You can try if you want," von Kemp replied, then reached up and ran his hand across his face. "I got this for my trouble the last time I tried to get away from them. Anyway, I've got my family to think about. The Russians know where they are. What about your family?"

"My only relative was my mother in Cottbus, but she died a year ago. That's where the Russians got me. I'd been taking care of her for the last couple of years after I left the physics department at Berlin University."

"You're probably lucky, then. They won't have anything they can hold over your head to keep you working for them."

"Well . . . there was a little problem just before I left the University, but hopefully they won't find out about that."

"What kind of problem?"

Dietrick gave a nervous little laugh. "Oh, nothing, really. I just chose the wrong friends in Berlin. That's the main reason I left there. That, and my mother, of course."

"Of course," von Kemp said, then fell into silence as the truck rumbled along. He knew more about Arthur Dietrick than Dietrick thought he did. He'd heard rumors about his involvement with Ernst Roehm, the notorious head of the SA that Hitler had had executed. He also knew that Dietrick had been fired from the physics department of

Berlin University right after that. But none of that mattered particularly to von Kemp. A few at Jena had snubbed Dietrick, but he wasn't going to judge the man for his past life. If they got into that game, quite a few of them, including himself, wouldn't come away untainted. They were all in the same boat now, and Dietrick obviously was frightened and needed a friend.

After a long day's trip with no food and little water for the men, the trucks finally came to a halt. It was dark again and a stiff breeze was stirring up little whirlwinds of freshly fallen snow as the men pulled back the canvas flaps and staggered numbly out. Most of them immediately stepped to one side and relieved themselves. As von Kemp was fastening his pants, he glanced up at the snow-covered buildings in front of him. There was something vaguely familiar about them. He stepped around on the other side of the truck, and saw, to his utter shock, that these were his old buildings at the Central Works. He moved back in line next to Dietrick. "My God!" he whispered. "We're at the Central Works, where I used to work."

A stocky Russian colonel had just come out of the administration building and was headed toward the group of scientists who stood shivering in the cold wind, clutching their meager belongings. He greeted the men with a broad smile. "Good evening, gentlemen," he said grandly. "Welcome to the Central Works. I'm Colonel Vasily Kirin. I trust that your trip was not too uncomfortable. I apologize that we were not able to provide you with food and a more comfortable means of transport, but we don't have all our facilities back in order yet. But that's where you come in, gentlemen. We hope you'll be able to help us get things moving again. I think you'll be very pleased with your work here. You'll be receiving double rations of food and the highest wages in our zone, and we plan to have your families join you just as soon as we have quarters available for them." He smiled a toothy grin. "But, best of all, gentlemen, you'll get to do what you most like to do. You'll be working on rockets again." He turned to his aide. "Please take these men to their quarters now, will you? We want them to be well-fed and well-rested before we get to work tomorrow." He turned back to the men. "Good evening, gentlemen. I'll see all of you bright and early in the morning."

Von Kemp stumbled along to the comfortable quarters that had been prepared for them. He was dumbfounded by this turn of events. Of all things! To be back at the Central Works! What could be more ironic after all he'd done to try to destroy this place just a year earlier. Wait until Eva and Hannah heard about this.

Thinking about his family turned his thoughts to the letter he'd gotten from them a week earlier, the first letter he'd received since his capture. He hadn't even known that they knew where he was, but the letter told him that the Russians had notified them that they were going to join him. He was delirious at the thought of seeing them again, and beside himself with curiosity about Hannah's surprise. What could it be? Maybe just that she was her old self again, all recovered from the typhus. He hoped that was it. For the first time in many months, things were beginning to look brighter for him. Maybe it wouldn't be so bad working for the Russians after all. A good salary, plenty to eat, a place to live, his family with him, and best of all, working on the V-2 rockets again.

23

The Central Works
1946

It was nearly three months before dependent housing was ready for the scientists' families. Von Kemp had had several more letters from Eva, and she was ecstatic at the prospect of joining him. He'd told her that he'd been injured when the Russians had first captured him, but had purposely played down the severity of his injuries so as not to worry her. Now he was beginning to wonder whether he shouldn't have told her just how bad it was.

He'd gotten accustomed to seeing the ugly stranger staring back at him from the mirror, but it might be too much of a shock for Eva and Hannah without being prepared for it. The scarring was so bad that it was impossible to shave many parts of his face, so he had just let his beard grow where it would and trimmed it with scissors when it got out about an inch. Strangely, the flames had not touched his upper lip, so he was able to grow a mustache that gave a little more balance to his face. But his appearance was so changed that even his former colleagues failed to recognize him until they actually heard his voice. He hoped that, in time, he might be able to have surgery to remove the worst of the scars, but that couldn't be done before Eva and Hannah arrived.

The day of their arrival, von Kemp had picked some wildflowers and put them in a vase in the bedroom of the comfortable little bungalow they would be sharing with another family. As he'd walked in the woods, picking the flowers, his mind couldn't help but go back to just a year ago when there'd been such panic about getting out of there. He hadn't been able to bring himself to walk the half-mile to their old rented estate. There were still too many memories there for him to cope with. Maybe when Eva arrived.

He waited for Peter's car by the gate to the Central Works with a great deal of trepidation. So much had happened since he'd seen them. He'd certainly changed, and he imagined they'd changed, too. You couldn't go through what they'd all been through without it leaving scars. He touched his face and nodded grimly. Yes, he knew about scars. But they were all still young; he and Eva in their early forties, and sweet, innocent Hannah—what was she, now? Eighteen? Yes, Eighteen. She must be quite a grown-up young lady. There was so much ahead for her. For all of them—if they could only bring themselves to adapt to their new circumstances.

A broad smile broke out on his face as he saw Peter's car slowly approach the gate. It stopped, and the guard walked up to the window and motioned Peter to a parking area just west of the gate. Almost shyly, Otto took a step forward. There was Peter getting out, then Natalia, then—oh yes, his beloved Eva, as beautiful as ever—and Hannah! But what was that Hannah had in her arms? A baby?

He was too shocked to even wave at them as the guard let them through the gate. He tried to speak as they walked toward him, but no words came out. His eyes were flooding with tears when Peter glanced casually in his direction, then back at the others who were proceeding on toward the administration building. Peter's head suddenly jerked back to him. "Otto?" he exclaimed. "Is that you?" A light of recognition broke in his eyes. "My God! It *is* you. Eva! Hannah! Natalia! It's Otto!" he called.

The others looked back at von Kemp, their mouths opened in disbelief, then with a little cry, Eva ran to his arms. "Oh, Otto," she sobbed. "Oh, my poor darling. What did they do to you?" She pulled back and looked into his face. "Oh, Otto," was all she could say.

Hannah rushed to her father. "Vati!" she cried. "Why didn't you tell us something had happened to you? Are you okay?"

He gathered her and the baby into his arms, along with Eva. "Yes, I'm fine, now that I have my girls with me." He looked down at the baby. "But what's this we have here? Is this the surprise you had for me?"

Hannah shyly held the baby up, and he took it in his arms. "This is your grandson, Nikolaus. You finally have the boy you always wanted."

He held the baby up and looked at him. "Well, he's sure a cute little fella." He looked around. "Where's his father?"

Eva gave Hannah a quick glance, then said to Otto, "That's a long story, dear. We'll tell you all about it later, but we'd like to get moved in now."

Von Kemp handed the baby back to Hannah and hugged his brother and Natalia. The six of them proceeded to the bungalow, and while Otto showed them around, Hannah went into their bedroom to put the child down. Only then did she notice the vase of white trilliums interspersed with pink and blue crocuses sitting on the chest of drawers by the bed. Her mind flashed back to the countless hours she'd lain in the summerhouse looking out at the same fragile flowers, and, without meaning to, she felt tears begin to stream down her cheeks. She buried her face in the blanket of her sleeping child and wept softly.

✠ ✠

It was some time before Hannah could bring herself to walk to the summerhouse. She decided to avoid the main house, not knowing if it was occupied. Instead she went along the rim of the canyon. As she walked, she looked across the valley to the castle on the far hill, and a forlorn nostalgia overcame her. She smiled sadly, thinking of all the stories she and Kristopher had invented about the former residents of that castle.

She finally got the courage to go into the summerhouse. It, too, was as it had been. The weathered white lattice, the rough plank flooring, the wooden bench that circled the inside, even the chaise with its faded blue pad. She stepped inside and was flooded by such overwhelming emotions that she didn't notice the girl who had just come down the path to the summerhouse.

"Who are you?" the girl asked cheerily as she stepped into the gazebo.

Hannah looked up, startled. "I'm Hannah Kramer. Who . . . who are you?"

"Astrid Konig. I live here." She laughed. "Well, not here in the summerhouse. I live up in the mansion. Are you looking for something or someone?"

Hannah stood up, a little flustered. "No. I lived in your house during the war and used to paint here in the summerhouse. I just wanted to see if it was still here."

"Are all those paintings we found in the house yours?"

A little cry escaped from Hannah. "You found my paintings? I had no idea they'd still be here."

"Oh, yes! I love them! I have them all over my room. Why did you leave them?"

"We left quite suddenly and had no room for them in our car. I always wondered what happened to them."

"Would you like to have them back?"

"I couldn't ask you to do that. They really weren't that good." She hesitated a moment. "But there was one I especially liked. It was the best one I did of the summerhouse. It has a vase of white trilliums sitting on this table. Do you know that one?"

"Oh, yes. That's one of my favorites." She laughed. "I spend so much time out here that my mother always teases me that that painting has bewitched me. But you're certainly welcome to have it back." Her eyes suddenly brightened. "In fact, I'll go get it right now, if you like."

Hannah moved toward the railing eagerly. "That would be wonderful. I'd love to have it if you're sure you don't mind?"

"Not at all. Wait right here. I'll be back in a minute." With that, she ran up the winding path to the mansion.

Hannah sat back down on the chaise next to Nikolaus and picked him up, pointing to the castle across the valley. "See that magic castle?" she said to him. "Your daddy loved that castle, and someday he's going to come back and take us to live with him forever in our own special castle." She hugged him so fiercely that he let out a little cry, and she kissed him on his soft curls. "I'm sorry, sweetheart, but I was just thinking about your daddy. I don't know where he is, but you and I will find him even if we have to spend the rest of our lives looking for him. Won't we?"

She looked up as Astrid came running down the path smiling broadly, the painting held up in her hand. "Here it is. I told my mother about you, and she was delighted that you came back for your paintings. She said you're welcome to come to the summerhouse to paint any time you like."

Hannah set Nikolaus on the plank floor as Astrid stepped up into the summerhouse. "This is so kind of you," she said, taking the painting. "I really can't tell you how much this means to me. It brings back so many wonderful memories. I hope you'll have as many happy memories in this place as I have."

The girl knelt down by Nikolaus and tickled him. "Your baby is so cute," she said. "How old is he?"

"Eight months."

"I just love babies," she said wistfully, "but I guess I'm too young to think about having one. Besides, my boyfriend doesn't live here. He's in Dresden, where we used to live."

"How old are you?" asked Hannah.

"Almost seventeen."

Hannah smiled. "Seventeen, huh? I was seventeen when we lived here. I hope you enjoy the summerhouse as much as I did."

188

24

The Central Works
1946–1947

At forty-four, Arthur Dietrick was of medium build with thinning brown hair that encircled a good-humored face. His inquisitive gray eyes, accentuated by long thick lashes, gave him an effeminate look. Science was his profession, but photography was his obsession. He always had a camera in his hand, but over the months he had turned out to be more of a scientist than the dilettante everyone thought him to be. His background in physics and chemistry led him quite naturally into working with von Kemp, and they soon became good friends.

When one of the families that had been living in the bungalow with the von Kemps was transferred to another facility, Dietrick moved into their room, and the friendship with the von Kemps deepened. He brought out the motherly instincts in Eva, and she gradually took to including him in their evening meals.

He was very attached to all the von Kemps, but doted on Nikolaus. In the evenings after dinner, when Otto was poring over stacks of documents, Dietrick would be romping with the baby on the floor of the central living area. As the two tumbled over and over, Hannah thought it was such a shame that Dietrick had never married and had children of his own. She'd heard the rumors about him being a homosexual, but she couldn't believe it. He'd never done anything that suggested such a lifestyle. The only effeminate thing about him was the way he mothered Nikolaus—and all the rest of her family.

Summer had once again turned to autumn in the Hartz Mountains, and the changing colors of the trees and foliage of Mount Kohnstein were breathtaking. Hannah took many long walks in the woods. She often thought of Kristopher on those walks, but as time passed, a healing was taking place inside her. She no longer allowed herself the indulgence of mourning the past. She had Nikolaus's future to think about, after all.

Over the months, Hannah and Astrid Konig had become like sisters. She'd shared with her all her secrets of the summerhouse as they whiled away lazy summer afternoons under the latticework, Nikolaus crawling contentedly around its rough floor. She'd become very fond of Frau Konig, too, as the lady often provided the two girls and the baby with cookies and milk or other treats.

Frau Konig was a widow. She had lost her husband in one of the bombings of Dresden, but she was more fortunate than most citizens of that devastated city. Her husband had been a wealthy importer and had left her and Astrid well fixed, financially. She had bought the estate a year earlier to be near her brother—who owned one of the cotton mills in nearby Bleicherode—and was delighted with the house, and the fact that Astrid had found such a wonderful friend in Hannah.

Things were not so rosy for Otto von Kemp these days, however. His hope of one day working for the Americans and possibly emigrating to America had all but died when a colleague with whom he'd once worked was transferred to the Central Works. The man informed him that the Americans had him on a war crimes list stemming from the terrible things they'd discovered at the Central Works. He'd been depressed for weeks afterwards.

But there were more pressing issues that troubled von Kemp at the moment. Subtle changes were taking place at the Central Works; changes that alarmed him. He and his colleagues were still being treated well, and they were once again working on V-2s, but in the past month a number of Russian technicians had arrived at the Central Works and were taking an inventory of everything there. There could be no reason for this unless they were planning to move the operation to another location. That's what worried him. Where would the new location be? Surely not Russia. Nothing could induce him to move to Russia, not with Stalin still in charge there.

During the third week of October, von Kemp began to notice an unusually large number of Russian soldiers and secret police arriving at the Central Works. They were pleasant enough to the men and their families, but there was no reason that he could discern for their presence. There'd been no sabotage or attempts to escape on the part of any scientists. He spoke to Eva about it one evening.

"I don't like it one bit," Otto told her. "There've been too many rumors about men being kidnapped from some of the other facilities and not heard from again."

"Do you think they've been killed?" Eva asked.

"No, I think they've been taken to Russia."

Eva gave him a worried look. "Is that what they're planning for you and the others?"

"Well, if they are, this is one man who isn't going. It's one thing to work for them here, but there's no way I'm going to Russia."

"But, Otto, if they say you have to go, how can you get out of it? They'll force you to."

He lifted his hands and let them fall in a helpless gesture. "I don't know what I'll do, but I'm not going, Eva, and there's no way they can make me. I'd rather take my chances on sneaking out of here and trying to get to our place in Oberammergau. At least it's in the American sector."

"Do you know what you're saying? How could we get to Oberammergau—even if we could get out of here? We haven't got a car, and it must be over six hundred miles. And besides, you know they'd come after you, or inform the Americans that you were in their zone—and they'd arrest you."

He frowned. "I know, but if we can get to the American zone at Bad Sachsa, which is only about twenty miles from here, then we'd at least have a chance of getting to Oberammergau, and I doubt seriously if the Russians would risk an international incident by coming into the American zone after us. The whole thing would be risky, I grant you, especially getting from here to Bad Sachsa, but it would be better than being carted off to some god-forsaken place in Russia. Don't you agree?"

"I don't know what to think. It isn't just the two of us any more. We've got Hannah and the baby to think about. They could never make the trip to Oberammergau on foot."

"Not unless we had some help."

"Who'd help us? Nobody here would be willing to risk his neck for us."

"Arthur would. He's crazy about Hannah and Nikolaus. I'm sure he'd do it. Besides, I know he doesn't want to go to Russia, either."

Eva gave him a dubious look. "We could never ask him to do that. That would be asking too much."

"Let me talk to him tomorrow. I know I can trust him. If he says 'no,' then we'll just have to think of something else." He reached over and took her hands. "I'm sorry to have to put you through all this again, but I want you to start getting things together in case we have to get out of here in a hurry. I'll talk to Hannah and tell her the same thing."

The next day, von Kemp pulled Dietrick aside and broached the subject with him. Arthur was all for an escape, and he was overcome with emotion that they would want him to come with them.

"No one's ever been as nice to me as you and your family," he said, "and if there's anything I can ever do to help any of you, I'll be delighted to do it. Besides, I'll be helping myself at the same time. I don't want to go to Russia, either. There's nothing there for me." He grinned, "And I hate cold weather!"

Otto gave a little grunt. "Well, I hope you like hot water, because that's what we may be getting into."

Von Kemp had told Dietrick very little about his previous

experiences at the Central Works, and certainly had never mentioned that the Americans had him on their war crimes list. But, with the hard times ahead, he felt he must warn him about the danger—not just from the Russians, but also from the Americans. Dietrick listened to his story without a hint of condemnation, and, when von Kemp had finished, Dietrick gave him an inscrutable smile and told him not to worry about it. He'd take care of everything.

Arthur Dietrick had talents no one dreamed of. Within two days he'd produced identity papers for all the von Kemps and himself, complete with pictures that he'd snapped and developed in his chemistry lab. When von Kemp opened his document and looked at it, he was shocked to see his picture with the name, Arthur Dietrick, under it. He looked at Eva and Hannah's papers, and under Eva's picture was the name, Eva Dietrick. Under Hannah's was the name Hannah Kramer, and the baby's bore the name, Nikolaus Kramer.

"What's this all about?" von Kemp demanded.

"I told you I'd take care of the problem, didn't I? You see, if we're stopped by the Americans, nobody's going to be looking for Arthur Dietrick. I'm a nobody to them, so you can be Arthur Dietrick until we get where we're going, and then I can make us some new papers with whatever names we want on them. It's no problem."

"But what about *your* papers? What name have you got on them?"

Arthur whipped out his and showed them to Otto. Under his picture was the name Ernst Kramer. "Meet your new son-in-law," he grinned.

"You've got to be kidding! No one would believe that. You're old enough to be Hannah's father."

Arthur's eyes twinkled roguishly. "Can I help it if your daughter finds me to be a fascinating older man? After all, I'm not completely without a certain charm. There have been those who've found me attractive."

Von Kemp raised one brow. "I think we should leave that subject alone."

Dietrick let out a silly little laugh. "I guess you're right about that."

"But seriously, Arthur, what if the Russians stop us before we get to the American zone and see my picture with your name under it and your picture with a completely bogus name?"

"Nobody's going to recognize my name and face. You know that. They only took me because I could speak Russian, and they thought they could use me as an interpreter. What I've been doing for them is nothing compared to what you do. Besides, they're so tanked with vodka most of the time that they'll never spot the discrepancy. Take my word for it. We can pull it off."

Von Kemp was extremely skeptical. "I don't know. It seems awfully risky to me."

"Look," Dietrick said, "if the Russians stop us anywhere near the border, what our names are isn't going to matter much to them. I have a feeling they'll shoot first and ask questions later."

"You're probably right about that," von Kemp said. He slipped his arm around Dietrick's bony shoulders, and gave him a hug. "You know something, Arthur, you're a gutsy old fart."

Dietrick beamed at him. "That's the nicest thing anyone's ever said to me."

They both laughed.

When von Kemp had told Hannah of the possibility that they might have to leave, she was frantic with worry for the baby. Without a car they'd have to walk, and with the Russians chasing them, they'd be forced to hide in the woods. She confided her fears to Astrid that afternoon in the summerhouse.

"Look," Astrid said eagerly, "there's no reason for you to be worried. I have the perfect solution. You can all hide at my house in the wine cellar. You can stay down there for as long as you need to, and then when it's safe, my mother and uncle can drive you to Bad Sachsa. Uncle Eric owns a big factory there, and he's got all kinds of passes for getting across the border. I know he'd be happy to help you, and mother thinks of you like another daughter, and you know how crazy she is about

Nikolaus." She threw her arms excitedly around Hannah. "Oh, Hannah! Don't you see? It's the perfect solution."

"What I see is a precious friend who has more heart than brains. We could never put you and your mother and uncle in that kind of danger."

"But it isn't any danger. There's no way they would think to look for you at our place. And even if they did," she added quickly, "they'd never find you in the wine cellar. As you know, the door to it is part of the paneling in the library, and even Mutti can't find it when she wants a bottle of wine. She has to come and get me. Think about it, Hannah. Won't you please?"

"It's your mother who'll have to think about it. You'd better ask her before you make any more plans."

"I will! I will!" Astrid cried. "I'll go ask her right now. You wait here. I'll be right back."

In a few moments, Astrid returned with her mother.

"The Russians are all shameless barbarians as far as I'm concerned," Frau Konig told Hannah. "I'll do anything I can to help you and your family get away from them. You just show up at the house, any time, day or night." She leaned down and picked up Nikolaus who was tugging on her leg, trying to get her attention. "Your Tante Clare isn't going to let any old bad Russians get you," she cooed to him. "You just tell your mutti that I'll take care of you if they try to get you. Okay?" She gave him a squeeze, then handed him to Hannah. "You get back to your parents now, and tell them what I told you. You're all more than welcome to come to us if there's a need."

That need came sooner than any of them expected. Three nights later, October 21, as they slept, Russian soldiers surrounded the bungalows of the workers. At a given signal they broke in the doors of the buildings and roused the sleeping residents. They were told that at dawn the scientists, engineers, and technicians were being transferred to new facilities. Their families would be joining them later. This announcement brought a hysteric reaction, which the soldiers soon quelled. Von Kemp's plan had not taken into account that Eva and Hannah and Nikolaus might not be allowed to go with him. As soon as the soldiers left, he pulled Dietrick aside.

"What are we going to do, Arthur?"

"I have a plan," Dietrick said. "I'm going to slip out with my camera and begin taking pictures of this roundup. If anyone tries to stop me, I'll tell them that I've been commissioned by Colonel Kirin to record this momentous event. In all the confusion, I doubt that anyone will check with him, but if they do, I've noticed the way the dear old Colonel has eyed me in the past few months, so I think I can handle him if I have to. In any case, I'll do my best to distract them, and I want you to watch out the window. When you see their backs turned, all of you slip out and head to your friend's mansion. I'll join you there as soon as I can."

Von Kemp looked at him aghast. "You'll be committing suicide, Arthur. I'm not going to let you do that."

Dietrick had already slung the strap of his camera over his neck. He grasped von Kemp by both shoulders and looked him straight in the eyes. "I'm sorry, Otto, but you know how I hate to have anyone tell me what to do. My mother always said that was my greatest failing." His eyes misted momentarily. "Kiss your darling family for me, and tell them I'll never forget their love and kindness. It'll go with me to my grave." He turned and dashed out the door of the bungalow before von Kemp could stop him.

Von Kemp ran to the window and watched him saunter boldly up to a group of soldiers standing by a truck. He saw the pantomime of Dietrick motioning them to stand at attention, then saw him crouch down and the flash explode in the dim light as he snapped their picture. He began arranging them in groups of three, then had some climb into the back of the truck and wave to him as the flash popped over and over. Von Kemp's heart sank. Arthur didn't have a chance; but at least he was giving them one. He rushed into the bedroom and got Eva and Hannah and Nikolaus, motioning them to drop their suitcases. They'd have to go without them. He stuffed their papers and Eva's few pieces of valuable jewelry into his coat pocket, then pushed them in front of him to the door of the bungalow. Hannah suddenly gave a little cry and raced back into their room emerging with her painting of the summerhouse.

"I'm sorry, Vati, but I just couldn't leave without this."

Von Kemp frowned at the canvas. "Well, roll it up and stuff it inside your coat then. We can't wait another minute, and put your hand over Nik's mouth. He can't make a sound."

He opened the door a crack and saw that Arthur had lined the soldiers nearest them into a line with their backs to the bungalow. The flash was popping over and over as Arthur clicked away. Quickly, von Kemp pushed Eva and Hannah and the baby out, and in the covering darkness they raced for the woods behind their bungalow. The last Otto von Kemp ever saw of Arthur Dietrick was as a crazy man with a camera in one hand and his other arm slung around the shoulders of a stocky Russian soldier, their heads thrown back laughing raucously.

It was still dark when the von Kemps staggered exhausted up to the door of the estate. They banged on it, and in a few moments, Frau Konig appeared in a robe. She quickly pulled them inside and hurried them into the wine cellar where she had prepared some cots and blankets. She left them a moment, and presently she and Astrid returned with a tray loaded with food and drinks which they gratefully accepted.

"I don't want you to worry about a thing," she told them. "Astrid and I have planned everything. You'll stay in here until your friend arrives, then when it's safe, my brother will drive you to Bad Sachsa. He's the mayor of Bleicherode, so he has passes that can get him through any Russian roadblocks."

Three weeks later, Arthur Dietrick had still not shown up. They were convinced that he'd been caught and shot—or taken to Russia with the others. Grimly they made the decision that they had to go on without him. "I drew him a map of how to get to our place in Oberammergau," von Kemp told the others, "so if he can, he'll get there one way or another, but we've got to get out of here."

197

The next day, Frau Konig's brother drove them on a harrowing trip to the town of Bad Sachsa. As they'd expected, they were stopped at the border by Russian soldiers, but his official credentials and their fake papers got them through. The brother deposited them at a small inn in the town, insisting that they take a large sum of cash from him, then left.

Now the real challenge began: Getting to Oberammergau without being picked up by the Americans.

25

Oberammergau, 1947

Getting to Oberammergau turned out to be easier than they'd anticipated. In the three weeks they stayed at the inn, trying to plan their next steps, Hannah made friends with a young American sergeant who often ate in the dining room of the inn. He had become smitten with her, and after she told him a tale of how her young German husband had been killed by the Americans, he felt a strong responsibility for her and her baby.

The sergeant was the driver for an American Army colonel who had been flown to Garmisch a few days earlier. The prospect of keeping this beautiful *fraulein* near him made him willing to risk driving Hannah and her family to Garmisch—where he was to join the colonel—even though transporting civilians in an army vehicle was against military regulations. Von Kemp was hesitant about it, but since he was now going by the name of Arthur Dietrick, and looked nothing like any pictures of Otto von Kemp that the Americans might have, he felt the risk of his being arrested was minimal.

When they arrived in Garmisch, the sergeant detoured to Oberammergau and dropped them at their home tucked in an isolated, snow-covered mountain ravine about a mile outside the little city. He promised Hannah he'd come back the next day with food and other supplies they would need for the harsh winter that was upon them.

They still had money left from Frau Konig's brother, but von Kemp felt it best to lie low for a time and not show his face in Oberammergau until he knew what fate the Americans had in store for him. He knew he'd have to find work soon, but what he could do, given his background, was questionable. That, too, was settled for him much sooner than he'd anticipated.

They'd been in Oberammergau for about a month, and Christmas was only a week away. Nikolaus was nearly two years old, and this was going to be his first real Christmas, Hannah thought, as she sat with him in front of the warm fireplace watching him play with a stuffed toy that had been hers when she was a child in this same cottage. She wanted this to be a special Christmas for him, with presents and all the good memories she had.

Nikolaus toddled over to inspect the small tree that Hannah had cut from the forest and decorated with the antique Christmas ornaments they had always kept in the cottage. She looked over at her father sitting in the faded, overstuffed chair reading by the light of a lamp that burned on the table beside him. "Vati, do you think we could go into town and maybe buy some little presents to put under the tree for Nikolaus? I know you haven't wanted to go there since we got here, but don't you think it would be safe now? We've been here nearly a month, and no one has come looking for you. Besides, with that beard, you look more like Santa Claus than Otto von Kemp. No one's going to recognize you."

Von Kemp reached up and ran his hand over his beard. "I think it would safe, but it'll be a long, cold walk getting there and back. Maybe you could ask your sergeant friend to pick up some things for him."

"I don't want to do that," Hannah said. "He's already said he'd bring us a goose for Christmas if he can find one, and besides, I want to pick out some things for Nik myself. I want this to be a Christmas he'll always remember."

Von Kemp looked over fondly at his rambunctious grandson. He was such a delightful child, so full of life, so unaffected by all the trauma he'd been subjected to. He was, indeed, the "hope of a new Germany," as Hannah had so often said. When he'd first learned of the child's existence, he'd been furious at Kristopher Falkenhorst for taking advantage of his kindness by getting his daughter pregnant. But, as the months had gone by and the child had brought so much joy to all of them, he knew Nikolaus had been sent as a special gift from God to give hope that there was still a good future for them.

"If it isn't snowing tomorrow, maybe the two of us could go in in the morning," von Kemp said. "Mutti can watch our boy for us. Besides, I want to get her something special I've been thinking about, and I don't want her along spying on me."

The next morning the two of them bundled up in warm clothing, pulled ski caps down over their heads, and trudged over the snowy terrain into Oberammergau. The quaint stores in the little village were gaily decked with Christmas decoration, although the inventory in most of them was sparse. Von Kemp and Hannah meandered from shop to shop picking out a few things they could afford. Von Kemp was looking for one particular item: a pale blue sweater for Eva. Blue was her favorite color, and since they'd left all their clothes at the Central Works when they'd escaped, she had little to wear, other than the few things Frau Konig had given her, and the ski clothes they had always kept at the cottage.

Von Kemp finally spied what he was looking for on a shelf behind the counter. A pale blue, long-sleeved sweater with cable stitching down the front. He asked the clerk if he might see it. She handed it to him, and he held it up. "This is perfect," he exclaimed. "My wife will love this. How much is it?"

The clerk looked at the tag. "Twenty *Deutschmarks*."

He winced slightly. "Ooh! That's a little more than I was prepared to spend." He looked pensive for a moment, then handed her the sweater. "I'll take it anyway. Who knows what the next Christmas will be like for any of us. Can you please gift wrap it?"

While the clerk was wrapping the sweater, the man next to him said, "It's beautiful, isn't it? I just bought one for my wife in the same color." He held up the package for von Kemp to see.

Von Kemp turned and found himself looking into the eyes of Karl Guenther, a man he had worked with at Peenemunde. Before he could think, he blurted out, "Karl?"

The man cocked his head to one side and said, "I'm sorry. Do we know each other?"

"You're Karl Guenther, aren't you? From Peenemunde?"

The man looked around cautiously, then lowered his voice. "Yes, but I don't think I know you."

Von Kemp leaned toward him and whispered, "I'm Otto von Kemp. I worked with you at Peenemunde."

The man's face suddenly went quite pale as he gaped in shock at the bearded man standing in front of him. "My God! Is it really you, Otto? What happened to your face? I'd never have recognized you if you hadn't introduced yourself."

Von Kemp reached up and self-consciously touched his face. "A little present from the Russians when they got me."

"The Russians got you? What are you doing here?"

Von Kemp held his hand up to cover his mouth. "It's a long story, but we have a place up in the mountains where I've been hiding. Have you seen any Russians around here?"

"No, but the place is crawling with American recruiters. They've brought hundreds of us to Garmisch for interrogation." His face suddenly darkened, "But you must know they're looking for you, Otto. You're on their war crimes list because of what they found at the Central Works. My God, man! What happened there? All those bodies!"

"I had nothing to do with that. Hans Kammler was behind all of it."

Guenther scowled. "It was a black day for Germany when Himmler put him in charge of the work camps. You probably know he was the one that got von Braun arrested."

Von Kemp nodded.

"But his part in the slaughter at the Central Works should be fairly easy for you to establish," Karl went on. "The Americans have got him."

"They have? Wonderful!" von Kemp exclaimed, then his enthusiasm suddenly waned. "I don't think I can count on him to exonerate me, though. He'll do his best to put the blame on anyone *but* himself. I watched him at work for over six months. He's a butcher!"

"Look," Guenther said, "I've been working with an American recruiter, Major Tom Stover, who's interrogating with US Army Ordnance, and he's a nice guy; very fair, and very anxious to get as many of us as he can over to America. He could probably help you. He got Walther Riedel out of prison where they'd put him for allegedly inventing a bacterial bomb, and the Americans gave him a contract, so he could probably clear this all up for you. Do you want me to put him in contact with you?"

Von Kemp was hesitant. "I don't know. I'll have to think about it. Where can I reach you?"

"My wife and I are staying here in Oberammergau until the Americans make up their minds whether they want me or not. Who knows when that'll be? Some of us have been here for over a year while they drag their feet. They're so touchy about every little detail of our pasts, especially Party membership. But, I'm not going anywhere till they make a decision about me one way or the other. In the meantime, if you want to talk to Stover, don't wait too long. I don't know how long he's going to be here, and there're a lot of hard-nosed American recruiters you don't want to have to deal with. Stover's no push-over, but he's a real gem compared to most of them." Guenther took out a pen and piece of paper and wrote down his address. "I'll look forward to hearing from you," he said, "but don't let too much time go by. I don't know how much longer I'll be here."

"I won't," von Kemp said, then added, "but please don't mention to anyone else that you've seen me, Karl. I'll need to tell my story to the right people first, or I might not get to tell it at all. You understand, don't you?"

"Of course, but I do urge you to make a decision soon, at least while I'm still here to introduce you to Stover."

Von Kemp assured him that he'd be in touch within a few weeks.

In the first week of January, 1948, von Kemp had made up his mind. He contacted Guenther and arranged to meet Major Stover. The two men took an instant liking to each other, but Stover told von Kemp that it would be no easy matter to get him under contract. The US State Department was adamant about not letting anyone in who'd been put on the war crimes lists, especially when they'd also been Nazi Party members. It was hard enough getting the scientists who were relatively clean cleared for emigration to the States.

But Stover wanted von Kemp. He knew how valuable he was, and he wanted him badly. He had a great deal of personal latitude in cutting the ponderous red tape that had been placed on "head-hunters" such as he, and since von Kemp's papers identified him as being Arthur Dietrick, Stover suggested that he continue using Dietrick's name, and they would seek a contract for him under that identity. Stover checked and found that the real Arthur Dietrick had enough scientific expertise to justify recruiting him, and had no black marks against him as far as the Americans were concerned. Not even Party membership. And there was little chance that Dietrick would show up to claim his identity, since von Kemp assured him that Dietrick was most likely dead—or in Russia.

It would be risky trying to pass von Kemp off as Dietrick; no question about it, but Stover thought he could pull it off, and once he'd gotten von Kemp to the United States and the man proved his incredible worth to the space program, he could go back to calling himself von Kemp if he wanted to, though Stover strongly advised against it—both for his sake and von Kemp's.

Stover's one worry was that von Kemp might be recognized by some of the hundreds of German scientists who were gathered in

Garmisch and Oberammergau, even though Guenther had assured him that von Kemp's facial distortions and beard basically masked his identity. He decided the best thing to do was get the von Kemps out of Oberammergau to some place where there was less chance of someone recognizing him while he waited for his clearance to leave for the United States. Von Kemp suggested Berlin, since he had a home there—at least he *had* had a home there. Whether it was still standing or not, he didn't know. Stover thought about it for a few days, checked and found out that the von Kemps' home was still in one piece—and was in the American sector of Berlin. So, on a cold March morning in 1948, the von Kemps were once again back on the road; this time headed for Berlin in an American Army car.

Major Stover contacted a US Army surgical team that was operating on other wounded Germans, and two months after Otto von Kemp arrived in Berlin, he had a new face; not as handsome as the one God had given him, but one that would take him through the rest of his life as anyone he chose to be. The name he chose was Arthur Dietrick—the man who'd given him back his life on a cold October night in a forest in the heart of Germany; a man he'd come to love and admire as few men he had ever known.

PART THREE

Los Angeles, California
1954–1970

26

Los Angeles, California, 1954

Wild-eyed, Kris bolted upright in bed.

Laura turned over in disgust. "For crying-out-loud!" she fumed. "I wish you'd see a shrink so we can both get some sleep."

Kris sat there, trying to shake out the cobwebs of his recurring nightmare, but he could never get a handle on it once he was awake.

He didn't need a shrink to tell him why he was having nightmares, though. His subconscious was putting its own spin on what he'd gone through at the Central Works. No shrink could erase that. Nothing could.

He looked over at his wife—her auburn hair disheveled, her eyes puffy. "I think I'll look in on Lexi as long as I'm awake," he said. "Try to get back to sleep."

Laura grunted and turned away from him, pulling the covers up over her head.

Kris slipped into his flip-flops and went into Lexi's room. She had flung off her blanket, and he reached down into her crib to straighten it. At the touch of his hand, her eyes popped open, and she cooed softly as she recognized him.

He leaned down. "What's wrong, Princess? Can't you sleep, either?"

Her eyes fluttered excitedly at the sight of him and her arms shot up in his direction. He picked her up, feeling the dampness of her diaper.

"Uh oh! We'd better get this soggy thing off." He laid her on the changing table and deftly changed the diaper, dropping the wet one into the diaper pail.

He picked her up from the table, kissing the top of her head as her tiny hands reached out and patted his cheeks. "So, you're turning out to be a night owl like me, are you?" he said, carrying her over to the plate glass window that looked out over the dark turbulent ocean. He pointed to the sailboat pulled up on the sand in front of the cottage. "See that boat, Princess? Daddy's gonna teach you how to sail that as soon as you get big enough. Then we're gonna sail away to far-off lands, just the two of us." He looked into her bright blue eyes. "How's that sound to you? Okay?"

She wiggled excitedly in his arms.

"I better get you back to bed or your mother will wring both our necks," he said, turning back to the crib. He laid her down and pulled the blanket over her. "I love you, Princess," he whispered. "You're my whole life. You know that?"

As he climbed back into bed, Laura stirred beside him, but went on sleeping, her breathing loud and coarse. She'd probably have another hangover in the morning. He was going to have to get someone to come in every day to take care of Lexi if Laura didn't get her drinking under control. He was through caring what she did to herself, but he was not going to see his baby suffer because of her addiction.

He wadded the pillow under his head, punching at it several times, trying to get comfortable. Emotionally and physically, he was exhausted. The combination of his worrying about the baby, trying to keep up with his classes at USC, and coping with Laura's drinking was taking its toll on him.

He lay there, trying to figure out how he'd let himself get into such a predicament. He had first met Laura Gerard in 1947, just after his Uncle, Karl Falkenhorst, had found him in the displaced persons' camp and brought him to Los Angeles to live with him.

Karl was the senior partner in the law firm of Falk and Gerard and Laura was Sid Gerard's only child, a beautiful, auburn-haired girl of seventeen, spoiled and self-centered. She had developed a mad crush on Kris from the moment she saw him, and had pursued him obsessively for the next couple of years.

Kris's focus had been on trying to put his life back together and finish his schooling. There had been little time for girls those first years in Los Angeles, but his elusiveness had only spurred Laura on as their families were constantly thrown together. Eventually realizing that she was getting nowhere with Kris, Laura persuaded her father to send her to his sister's in Paris for a year, and when she returned—wiser and more sophisticated—she settled down in her father's Malibu beach house, spending her days in the sun, and her nights in different beds—including Kris's on more than one occasion.

So, Kris really had no one but himself to blame when Laura came to him during his last year at USC in 1954 and told him she was pregnant. There was no way he could prove it wasn't his, especially after she reminded him of the number of times they had slept together in the past few months, so he admitted he might be responsible, but made it clear that he had no intention of marrying her. But when she threatened to make trouble between her father and Karl if he didn't, he knew he couldn't let that happen after all Karl had done for him, so he reluctantly agreed to marry her. If it got too bad, he could always divorce her later.

The wedding had been a quick affair. Only their families and a few friends were present. As a wedding gift, Sid gave the couple his beach house north of Malibu. He also guaranteed them a monthly allowance of five hundred dollars until Kris could get into law school and then into practice in the firm. Sid told Karl he thought he'd gotten off pretty cheaply—all things considered.

When Lexi was born, Sid couldn't stop remarking at how healthy she seemed for being a seven-months baby. Karl had raised a skeptical brow, but kept his mouth shut.

When Kris first laid eyes on the tiny bundle of curly blond hair and big blue eyes, all doubts about her parentage evaporated. This was his baby. No question about it. She looked just like him. Everyone said so, and even if they hadn't, he knew. There was an instant sympatico between the two of them that could only be accounted for by blood.

Having put her back in the crib now, he went back to bed and lay there thinking. He was definitely going to get some live-in help to see that Lexi got the kind of care she needed. Laura spent most of her time running around in her Porsche Speedster with the baby in the bucket seat next to her, and Kris found his constant worry about it interfering with his studies. He simply could not concentrate, knowing she often had two or three glasses of wine at lunch with her girlfriends before trying to navigate the busy coast highway on the way home. Even sober that was a challenge.

The next morning, as he came into the kitchen, he broached the subject with Laura who was standing there in a sheer lavender robe pouring herself some black coffee. She looked at him through bleary eyes.

"I think it's a great idea if you can afford it," she said, sitting down at the oval kitchen table. "But I just don't know how we can work it out on the money Daddy gives us each month. I can hardly afford the things I need on that amount as it is." She took a drink of the coffee and reached for a cigarette.

Kris poured himself a cup and sat down across from her. He hated these confrontations. They always ended up the same way: him chiding her about her irresponsibility, and her accusing him of not loving her. The sad fact was that both accusations were true. He'd tried to make their marriage work, but he really felt like he had two children on his hands. Laura was simply incapable of functioning on an adult level.

They stared at each other with mounting hostility. Kris tried to keep his voice even as he spoke. "Maybe you could cut back a little on your spending. It isn't necessary for you to have lunch out every day now that you've got the baby. Is it?"

She bristled. "I'd go stir crazy around this place if I didn't have that to look forward to every day. You're never here, and even when you are, you've got your nose stuck in some stupid book."

Kris tried to keep his voice calm. "Lexi needs to be here at home where she can get into a regular routine of eating and sleeping. Can't you see that?"

"All I can see is that you're mad because you have to be at school all day and can't spend every minute with her. Don't you think I know she's the only reason you married me? I'm no fool, Kris. I may be a drunk, but I'm *not* a fool."

"I know you're not a fool, and I think you really do love her, but if you can't pull yourself together enough to take care of her properly, then I don't see any alternative but to hire someone to do the job for you, and that means we're both going to have to cut back on some of the things we like to do so we can afford it." He set his cup in the sink and started for the door. "I've gotta go. I'll be late, but I want you to call some agencies today and set up some interviews. Make them for an evening so I can be here. I want to personally pick out whoever we decide on." He slipped into Lexi's room and kissed her sleeping face, then went out to his white Ford parked in the driveway.

⊕ ⊕

"Yes, sir!" Laura snapped, saluting Kris's retreating figure as he drove out onto Pacific Coast Highway. She poured herself another cup of coffee, laced it with a shot of Irish whiskey, and went out onto the deck. A cool ocean breeze pulled at her silk robe as she leaned against the railing. She looked up, irritated, as she heard Lexi's crying from inside the house. "Hold your horses," she yelled. "I'll be in there in a minute."

A bronzed man jogging by on the sand slowed his pace and waved up at her as he jogged in place. "Hi, babe. How's it goin'?"

She leaned over the railing and yelled down at him. "Marriage and motherhood aren't all they're cracked up to be, I can tell you that." The breeze whipped open her robe, revealing her naked body underneath. She grabbed at it with a coquettish grin. "Sorry about that, Phil. My husband informs me this is private property now."

211

He gave a big guffaw. "It's a pity you can't spread the joy around like you used to, kiddo. We had some good times, didn't we?"

"Well, it may not all be over," she said. "If Kris doesn't get his act together pretty soon, I'm gonna give him something to think about. Just stay in touch, will you?"

"You got it," he laughed and blew her a kiss as he jogged on down the strand.

Lexi was screaming at the top of her lungs as Laura walked back into the house. "I'm coming," she yelled. "Will you knock it off?"

Laura went into Lexi's room and picked up the screaming child. As she placed Lexi on the changing table her sobbing subsided, and she began trying to reach up for the locket that hung from Laura's neck. She got her hand on it and put it in her mouth. Laura reached down to disentangle her fingers from it, and Lexi grabbed a strand of her long auburn hair with the other hand. Laura had to laugh, in spite of herself. All her friends were continually telling her how lucky she was to have such a beautiful child and such a sexy husband. If they only knew that he hadn't touched her in months. But, then, she hadn't gone to bed sober in a long time, either, so she supposed he felt very self-righteous in leaving her alone.

To be honest, she had to admit that he hadn't driven her to drink as she had so often accused him. She'd liked the booze even before she met him, but his nagging her all the time about being a bad mother hadn't helped the drinking. What could she expect, though? She knew he'd only married her because of Lexi, so she should've known what she was getting herself into.

Laura picked the baby up from the changing table and put her back in the crib, sticking a half-empty bottle of milk in her mouth. *If I'm going to have a live-in*, she told herself, *I'd better call Daddy and talk him into paying for it. I'm not giving up any of my allowance.*

She walked into the kitchen and dialed her father's office number. The secretary said he was with a client, but Laura demanded to be put through immediately.

Her father's voice was full of concern as he came on the line. "What is it, honey? Is something wrong with the baby?"

"Well, yes and no, Daddy," she said plaintively. "Kris thinks we need some live-in help with her. You know how she's always sick and never sleeps through the night. He doesn't want me to worry so much about her and thinks it would be best if we could have someone help out with her—just for a while, you understand—until I get fully back on my feet.

She paused, giving him a chance to digest that, then went on. "You know how hard it was on me having her, Daddy. Mother said she went through the same thing when I was born, and you insisted on having help for her, so I know you understand these things. Anyway, we really can't afford it by ourselves, and I was wondering if you and Mother could help us out, just until Kris gets out of school for the summer and can get a job. He'd never ask you himself. You know his stubborn German pride, but if you could slip me the extra money every month, I'd sure be grateful."

There was a long silence on the other end of the line, then a heavy sigh. Laura smiled to herself.

"Okay, Pumpkin, I know you kids are having a tough time of it with a new baby and all. Let me know how much you need and I'll get it to you."

"Not a word to Kris. Okay, Daddy?"

"Not a word," he said. "I've got to get back to my client now, so I'll talk to you later. By the way, we haven't seen much of you kids lately. When are you coming over?"

"We'll try to get by this weekend. I want you to see our little princess. She looks just like you. I'll talk to you later. Bye."

She hung up the phone and grabbed the directory. By noon she had the names of several women who would be coming by that evening for interviews. She went into her room and changed into a very brief bikini, examining her taut stomach for any signs of stretch marks. Satisfied that she had her trim figure back, she detoured by the bar on her way out to the deck and grabbed a cold beer. No sense getting dehydrated out there in the blazing sun.

Kris rejected the first two women they interviewed that evening. The first was too young and pretty—and by the jealous way Laura looked at her, he knew he didn't need that headache. Kris liked the second one, but never having had children of her own, he felt she lacked the experience he wanted. When Kate Mulhoney came in, her eyes twinkling merrily as she looked around the cluttered cottage, he felt a kindred spirit. Ignoring the messy house, she immediately asked to see the baby, and when he saw the way Lexi responded to her, he knew he had his nanny.

Kate moved in the next week, and to Kris's great relief immediately took charge, not only of the baby, but the entire household. For the first time in his brief marriage, there was a hot meal every night when he came home from school. The house was sparkling, with bouquets of flowers here and there, and even Laura seemed relieved and more agreeable. She was still drinking, but that, too, seemed more moderate. Kris actually began to believe they might be able to make their marriage work. For Lexi's sake, he hoped so.

27

Los Angeles, California
1955

Kris graduated from USC in 1955 and entered their law school in the fall. Kate Mulhoney was the definite salvation of his home life. At forty-five, she was on the plumpish side and wore her red hair piled helter-skelter on her head. She had lost her husband and son a few years before coming to America, but her lilting brogue and impish green eyes gave evidence that she had finally made peace with the hand she had been dealt. Kris would often sit on their deck, books piled high in front of him, and watch Kate and two-year-old Lexi romp in the surf or pick up shells on the beach. He was convinced that Lexi thought Kate was her mother.

On March 18, 1956, Kris's afternoon classes were canceled and he came home early. When he pulled into the driveway about two o'clock, he noticed Laura's car was gone. Kate told him that she had taken Lexi to lunch with some of her girlfriends in Beverly Hills.

Kris put on his trunks and spread out his books on the deck lounge. He read for a couple of hours, intermittently glancing at his watch, then decided to take a quick dip in the ocean while he waited for them.

He'd been in the water about twenty minutes when Kate came out onto the deck, frantically beckoning to him. He sprinted out of the water and raced across the stretch of sand, calling out to her, "What is it? Did Mrs. Falk call?"

Tears were streaming down Kate's stricken face. "No! It was a policeman. There's been a car accident."

Kris grabbed her by the shoulders. "Where? When? Are they okay?"

"I don't know. He gave me this number and said you were to call him immediately." She handed him a scrap of paper with the number on it.

Kris raced into the house, his heart pounding as he dialed the number on the paper. The phone rang numerous times before it was picked up.

"LAPD, Lieutenant Jensen here."

"This is Kris Falk. Did you just call my house about my wife and little girl being in a car accident on Pacific Coast Highway?"

"Does your wife drive a Porsche Speedster, Mr. Falk?"

Kris's voice faltered. "Yes."

"Then I'm afraid I have some very bad news for you, sir. Your wife's car went over the bank on the Pacific Coast Highway just north of Reeves Canyon about three o'clock this afternoon and both she and the child with her were killed. I'm sorry to have to break the news to you this way, but we thought you should know as soon as possible. Their bodies are still at Santa Monica Hospital. You probably should get down there as soon as you can to make arrangements for where you want them taken. One of my detectives, Bill Engels, is there, and you can talk to him. He'll explain what we think happened."

Kris slowly placed the phone on its cradle and began to moan softly.

"What did he say?" Kate cried. "They're okay, aren't they?"

He covered his face with his hands, unable to staunch the sobs that welled up. "No" he said, shaking his head. "They're both dead."

"Not my Lexi!" Kate cried. "Not my darlin' little girl! Oh please, God. Not Lexi!"

They wept in each other's arms for a few minutes, then Kris pulled back, the grief in his face mixed with confusion. "How could this have happened, Kate? Laura's driven that road since she was a teenager. She knows it like the back of her hand."

Kate hesitated a moment, then quietly said, "You don't suppose she'd been drinking, do you?"

Kris's face darkened. "Why would you say that? She hasn't had a drink in months." He paused, "Has she?"

Kate couldn't meet his gaze.

"Answer me, Kate. Has she been drinking again?"

She looked up. "I've smelled liquor in some glasses a few times recently. I didn't say anything about it, because it's nothin' like it used to be and I didn't want to worry you. I'm sorry I didn't tell you now."

Kris patted her shoulder. "You're not her keeper. I should've known better than to trust her." He started for his bedroom. "I've gotta get to the hospital," he said.

✠ ✠

After Kris had viewed Laura's and Lexi's battered bodies, the detective drew him aside. "Did your wife often drink and drive, Mr. Falk? Her blood alcohol level was over twice the legal limit."

Kris angrily brushed at his tears. "I thought she'd quit, but obviously she hadn't."

The detective gave him a sympathetic look. "I'm awful sorry for your loss, sir. I've got a little girl about that age myself."

Kris shook the man's hand, then left the hospital and drove toward home. As he came to the site of the accident, he pulled his car over to the side and parked. He could see the skid marks crossing the white line to the edge of the bluff.

He got out of the car, waited a few minutes for the traffic to thin, then dashed across the highway. The car had been towed, but pieces of it were scattered down onto the rocks. Something caught his eye, and he scrambled down the rocks to look at it. It was one of Laura's red shoes. He held it up and looked at it for a moment, then with a cry of rage, flung it as far as he could, his moans drowned out by the pounding surf.

After the funeral at Beverly Hills Mortuary, Kris was staggered to find out that Sid Gerard had kept in force a $250,000 life insurance policy on Laura, with Kris as beneficiary. At first he wanted nothing to do with it, but as he thought about it in the weeks following the accident, he decided the money would enable him to finish school and set up his practice with Sid and Karl. He could also keep Kate on at the beach house for as long as she wanted to stay with him. After all, she and Karl were the only family he had left.

✛ ✛

In the spring of 1958, Kris passed the bar and went into practice with his Uncle Karl and Sid Gerard as a junior partner specializing in International Criminal Law. Choosing this field had not been just a whim. There had hardly been a day since the Americans freed him from Juno that he had not dreamed of one day finding out what had happened to Otto von Kemp and seeing if he'd been brought to justice. Yet, somehow, in the three years since Laura and Lexi's deaths, he'd lost his motivation for even that. Occasionally some insignificant article in the newspaper about war crimes trials would bring memories flooding back, and he would be spurred to write another letter to the Berlin Document Center and the Office for the Investigation of War Crimes in Ludwigsburg, Germany, but the answer always came back the same: Otto von Kemp had been on preliminary war crimes lists, but his name was later removed, and no records existed on his whereabouts.

Kris was always discouraged when he got one of those letters, but he still felt—in the deepest part of his gut—that von Kemp was alive somewhere. Occasionally he thought about Hannah and wondered what her life had become. He hoped she had been able to make a life for herself somewhere. He certainly wished her no ill for what her father had done.

28

Los Angeles, California
1970

In the fourteen years since Lexi's death, Kris had found little joy in anything other than his work. He was considered one of the up-and-coming criminal lawyers in Los Angeles—and one of the most eligible bachelors—but when much of his pillow talk revolved around his lastest case, and the women wanted to talk about marriage, things usually went downhill quickly. He made it clear right from the beginning of any relationship that he did not want children, and few women seemed to want him on those terms, and that was okay with him. He had as much female companionship as he wanted, and he had his work and Kate, and his memories of Lexi.

Standing before the bathroom mirror, he ran his hand across the stubble on his chin and was surprised to see how much gray there was. "You're getting old," he said to the 43-year-old image that stared wistfully back at him.

He shot a soft white mound of shaving cream into his hand and began lathering his face. As he drew the razor carefully upward, he stared at the lathered face pensively, and for some morbid reason was reminded of the first time he'd ever used a razor. An American GI had loaned him one in the displaced person's camp he'd been sent to near Kassel after the Americans had liberated Juno. He remembered it vividly. Despite the thousands of other bedraggled half-alive refugees packed into the camp—and the uncertainty of his own immediate future—the very act of performing this ritual of manhood for the first time had given him hope that maybe he would survive and go on to some kind of normal life.

He'd been luckier than most of the millions of displaced persons who found themselves crisscrossing the ravaged cities and countrysides of Europe after the war, trying to pick up the pieces of their shattered lives. After all, he had an uncle who'd moved governmental mountains to find him and bring him to America.

He finished his shaving and bent over the sink to rinse his face, then grabbed the towel and patted it dry. His gaze fell on the scar above his right eye, and as he reached up and touched it, his mind flashed back to that day so many years ago when he'd fallen from his bike and the Jew had carried him home. Funny—he looked at the same face in the mirror every day, yet was never conscious of the scar, but for some reason today it seemed angry and ugly—a little like he was feeling.

He was patting on some aftershave when the phone rang. He waited, expecting Kate to pick it up, but when it had rung four times, he raced into his bedroom and grabbed it.

"Kris? This is Karl. Sorry to ring you so early on a Saturday, but I need you here at the office ASAP. Something *very* interesting has come up."

Kris groaned. "I've got a full day planned here. Kate and I are taking the boat out."

"It'll have to wait. This is a case you're not going to want to miss."

Kris was irked, but Karl had done so much for him, he hated to say no. "Well, can't you at least give me a clue what it's all about?" he asked.

"Let's just say this might be the break you've been waiting twenty-five years for. I just talked to a Nazi who's being held for extradition to Germany to stand trial for war crimes. He worked at the Central Works with your von Kemp, and says he knew him. Now will you get your butt down here?"

"I'm on my way," Kris said.

He stopped by the kitchen for a cup of coffee and told Kate they'd have to put off sailing until the next day, then raced for his car.

When he arrived at the building on Ocean Boulevard in Santa Monica, he bypassed the elevator and raced up the four flights to the office. He was breathing hard as he rushed past the vacant receptionist's desk and into Karl's well-appointed office. He plopped into a chair in front of the desk and paused to catch his breath.

"Okay. What's the deal?" he panted.

Karl waved a telephone pad at him. "Judy left this message on my desk last night to contact a Rudolph Kuntzler at the Federal Correctional Facility in San Pedro as soon as possible. I got hold of him this morning and that's when I found out he's being detained for extradition to West Germany to stand trial for war crimes and wants us to represent him. I told him we'd meet him there this afternoon"

"How did he get our name?"

"Someone told him we specialize in International Criminal Law and that you'd been interned at the Central Works where he worked, and I guess he felt you'd have more sympathy for his situation."

"You've got to be kidding! I wouldn't lift a finger to help anyone who'd worked at the Central Works. All those Nazis were guilty of something. It's only a matter of degree."

Karl held up his hands defensively. "Take it easy, pal. The only reason I agreed to see him is because he said he knew Otto von Kemp, and I knew you'd want to talk to anyone who knew von Kemp."

"That's for sure. I'll squeeze the little turd's neck and find out everything he knows about von Kemp."

Karl stood up. "Well, we'd better get going then. We've only got an hour and a half to get down there. We can talk in the car about the kind of questions we want to ask him."

☩ ☩

When Kuntzler was brought into the interrogation room, Kris felt immediate revulsion at the sight of him. He was short and balding and wore thick glasses in wire rims, but he swaggered in with an arrogance that made Kris despise him instantly.

Karl took out a legal pad and began questioning the man. He found out that Kuntzler and his family had come into the United States on Argentine passports in 1957, and he'd been working as a custodian for an elementary school in Long Beach, California, for the past thirteen years. A month before, the grandfather of a student in the school had recognized him at a school function and turned him in as a Nazi doctor in a concentration camp he'd been interned in. Subsequently, the man had been arrested and detained in the Federal facilities there in San Pedro awaiting arraignment. Kuntzler admitted he'd failed to report that he was a former German medical doctor and Nazi Party member when he sought American citizenship, but steadfastly denied that he had done any of the medical experiments on prisoners in Birkenau that this elderly janitor had accused him of.

As the day wore on, it also came out that the doctor had been caught in the Russian zone at the end of the war and had been sent by them to the Central Works to continue his study of the effects of pressurization on humans in manned missiles. When the Russians had abruptly transferred the Central Works rocket men to Leningrad in October of 1947, they had no more use for him and left him behind. He'd eventually made his way to the British zone, and from there had emigrated to Argentina.

When Kris probed him about von Kemp, he readily admitted knowing him while he was working for the Russians at the Central Works, but denied knowing anything about his movements after the Russians abandoned the project there. He had heard that von Kemp had escaped from the Russians, but no one knew for sure.

The one bit of evidence they'd gotten from him that excited Kris was that von Kemp's closest friend at the Central Works was a scientist named Arthur Dietrick. That name rang a bell in Kris's mind, and as he and Karl drove home from San Pedro late that afternoon, Kris struggled with where he'd heard it.

"I know that name from somewhere," he said to Karl. "This guy knows something he isn't telling us."

"I got the same feeling. I know you've already done it on von Kemp, but let's run Dietrick's name through Immigration and State when we get back to the office and see if they've got anything on him. If not, we'll check him out with the Berlin Document Center and the Ludwigsburg office. Somebody's got to know something about him."

"I want a full check on Kuntzler, too," Kris said.

Karl glanced over at Kris. "What's your gut feeling about him?"

"I think he's lying through his teeth. He's guilty of everything he's being accused of and more. He's a slimeball. I know the type, and I loathe them."

An enigmatic smile crept over Karl's face. "Sounds like you're not real excited about representing him."

"We don't want to get mixed up with his guy, Karl. We'd be opening ourselves up to years of trying to run down witnesses and check his story out. I don't have the stomach for it anymore. I really don't. Let's just leave him to the sharks."

"I don't think we'll get any more information out of him about von Kemp if we don't take his case."

Kris threw Karl a questioning look. "Would you really want to defend a scumbag like that?"

"Not particularly, but I'd sure like to pick his brain about a lot of things. Wouldn't you?"

"You don't want to know what I'd like to do with his brain. It's enough to get me disbarred."

29

Three days after his meeting with Kuntzler, Kris was in his office when Judy buzzed him. "I've got Immigration on line one, Mr. Falk."

"Good, I'll take it." Kris picked up the phone. "Hello. This is Kris Falk."

"Mr. Falk, this is Jim Avery at Immigration in Washington. We've checked out those names you gave us, and you were right. Arthur Dietrick is not only in the United States, he's one of NASA's top scientists in Houston. In fact, *Time* magazine did a big spread on NASA two years ago and there was a feature article about Dietrick. I'm surprised you didn't see it. But, as you'll see, if you get a copy of the article, Dietrick was a top German rocket man recruited by the OSS after the war. He came in with a bunch of other Germans scientists in that Project Paperclip venture sometime in 1947. He's clean as far as we're concerned. You might want to check with State, though, to see if they've got anything new on him. But I doubt it. He'd never have been cleared for entry if there'd been anything negative on his record."

"What issue of *Time* was that article in?" Kris asked.

"One of the June issues in 1968."

"Thanks. I'll get it, and I'll also get back in touch with State and NASA. Did you find anything new on von Kemp?"

"No," Avery said. "There's no record of his ever having entered the United States, even as a tourist. Check with State. They may have something."

"I did. A couple dozen times over the past twenty-five years, but they haven't got anything either."

"Well, it wouldn't hurt to check again. Things come up over the course of time. I'm sending you what we've got on Dietrick and a complete packet of info on Kuntzler. I hope you'll find some good pickings in there. I hate it when these guys slip through our fingers. Keep in touch with us about the Kuntzler case if you decide to take it. We'll want to update our records. Is there anything else I can do for you?"

"Not that I can think of right now, but I'll be in touch if we need you. Thanks again for all your help."

Kris hung up and swiveled his chair around, leaning back. He locked his hands thoughtfully behind his head and stared out at the Pacific Ocean. Catalina Island loomed on the horizon like a long, gray battleship. His mind was racing. What was the connection between Dietrick and von Kemp? If they'd been such great friends, as Kuntzler claimed, then it was a good bet that Dietrick knew what had happened to von Kemp, and maybe had kept in touch with him.

The first thing he needed was a copy of that *Time* article. Then he wanted a full, but very private, investigation of Arthur Dietrick. He knew just the man for that job: Bud Perry in Houston—an old law school buddy. He leaned forward and buzzed Judy.

"Judy, will you get me copies of all the June 1968 issues of *Time* magazine, ASAP, and then ask Karl to come in when he's through with his client. I'd also like you to get Bud Perry in Houston for me. His number's in the Rolodex. Thanks."

In a few minutes, Judy buzzed him. "Cynthia's on her way to the library to get the *Time* issues, and Mr. Perry's on line three. Mr. Falk said he'll be through in a couple minutes and will come in then."

"You're a doll, Judy."

"I know,' she said. "All the men tell me that."

Kris gave a snort. "Well, don't let it go to your head. I need a nice level-headed girl in your spot."

He pressed line three. "Bud? This is a voice out of your disreputable past."

"Kris Falk? The Avenger? Good grief! You *are* a voice out of the past. How are you, anyway? Did you ever get that German scientist you were looking for?"

Kris's voice took on a serious tone. "That's why I'm calling you. I've gotten a lead on a guy there in Houston who used to be one of von Kemp's old colleagues, and I need a very hush-hush investigation on him. Are you still into that?"

"Did God make little green apples?"

Kris let out a chuckle. "I guess that's my answer, huh?"

"What's the guy's name?" Bud asked.

"You've probably heard of him. It's Arthur Dietrick, at NASA."

"Dietrick? Of course I've heard of him. Hasn't everyone? He's one of the big wheels over there. What've you got on him?"

"Nothing on him personally, but according to a little Nazi weasel I've been interviewing at the Federal Correctional Facility in San Pedro, Dietrick was a colleague of von Kemp at the Central Works after the Russians took it over. Did you hear about Rudolph Kuntzler's arrest?"

"Yeah. I did. Are you on that case?"

"I haven't decided yet, but Karl and I spent a whole day debriefing him, and during the course of the interview I found out he worked with von Kemp and Dietrick at the Central Works after the war, and he's the one who told me that Dietrick and von Kemp had been big buddies there."

"Can you trust someone like Kuntzler? He may have some axe to grind."

"More than likely, he does," said Kris, "but I did find out from the State Department that Dietrick had been captured by the Russians after the war, then escaped and got the Americans to recruit him. Nobody knows for sure what happened to von Kemp, but what I want to know is whether Dietrick has kept in touch with von Kemp over the years, and that's why I need someone who can do some checking on Dietrick without alerting him that he's under surveillance."

"And that's where I come in, huh?"

"Yeah. I need as much background as you can get on Dietrick. His family life, his friends, what he does for NASA, where he goes on vacations, how he spends his free time, who he gets letters from, whether he's been back to Germany since the war. You know the sort of stuff I need. I don't have to tell you how to do your job. But this has got to be on the Q.T. in case he's still in contact with von Kemp. Do you think you can do it?"

"I can give it my best shot. It'll take me some time, though. When do you need this?"

"Yesterday."

"That figures, but just to be realistic, we'd better say two or three weeks. I'll have to pull in a lot of favors for this one since you don't want me talking to the guy directly, so I'd better stop jawing with you and get at it. Wish we had time for a good long visit. When I get back to you, maybe we can. Okay?"

Karl came in just as Kris was hanging up. "What's up?" Karl asked.

"Maybe something. Maybe nothing. It seems that Arthur Dietrick is one of NASA's top men. He came over in that OSS snatch of German scientists after the war. I knew I'd heard that name before. I just didn't connect it."

"Oh boy! That's going to be a touchy situation. Those were all Harry Truman's fair-haired boys."

"I know, but I've got Bud Perry in Houston working on it for us on the Q.T. He's going to snoop around and see if this Dietrick has kept up with any of his old pals, namely Otto von Kemp. Also, Avery, at Immigration, told me that *Time* did a big article on Dietrick and NASA a couple of years ago, and Cynthia's on her way to the library right now getting me a copy of the issue. I want to wave that thing under Kuntzler's nose and see what kind of reaction I get. Maybe it'll loosen his tongue up a bit."

"I think the only thing that'll loosen up his tongue is if we agree to represent him. Have you thought any more about that?"

"I want to stall for as long as we can until I hear from Bud, and then see what State's got on Dietrick and Kuntzler."

"When will that be?"

"I'm calling State today, and Bud hopes to take no more than a couple of weeks."

"Well, I told Kuntzler we'd see him again on Thursday. He's really starting to get antsy about whether we'll take his case or not."

"Let him stew for a while. He's in no position to be choosy."

"Fine with me," Karl said.

☩ ☩

The *Time* magazine article on Dietrick was what Kris might have expected. Dietrick was a genius with rocket propulsion fuels. He had been recruited by the Army in their Project Paperclip operation and worked with von Braun's Army team at Huntsville that had developed Explorer 1. When the Army was unwilling to support their projects any longer, all of von Braun's team transferred to the Marshal Space Flight Center in Huntsville where von Braun was director. In 1962, Dietrick was sent to Houston to the Johnson Space Center—later referred to as NASA—and had been there ever since. Several pictures of Dietrick showed him to be of average height, bearded, and rather unattractive with a full head of nearly snow-white hair.

Kris was disappointed. He'd hoped there would be something about Dietrick's past that might have mentioned his association with von Kemp, but that was really asking too much. The article wasn't much to use with Kuntzler, but he'd milk it for all it was worth. Seeing Dietrick's picture might trigger something in Kuntzler's memory.

☩ ☩

When Kris and Karl met with Kuntzler the following Thursday, Kris watched Kuntzler very carefully as he scanned the *Time* magazine article. It was obvious that something about the article was bothering him.

"Is there any comment you want to make about the article?" Kris asked.

Kuntzler looked at him with barely concealed contempt. "That depends," he said.

Kris felt himself begin to bristle. "Depends on what?"

"Whether you're planning to represent me or not."

Kris glowered at him with a menacing intensity. "Look, you little Nazi turd, you're in no position to negotiate with us. We're the only hope you've got, and you know it. Nobody else wants to touch you, and you'd better give us a good reason to. You tell us what you're hiding, and it'll make us a whole lot more interested in trying to save your hide."

Kuntzler looked back and forth at both hostile men, then shrugged. "Why not?" he said. "It's no skin off my nose." He pointed at one of the pictures of Dietrick. "That's not Arthur Dietrick."

"What do you mean?" Kris shot back.

"Just what I said. That's not the Arthur Dietrick I knew at the Central Works. Maybe it's someone else named Dietrick, but the Dietrick I knew didn't wear a beard, his nose wasn't crooked like this guy's, and he was losing his hair." He jabbed his finger at the face in the picture. "This is not the scientist I knew as Arthur Dietrick. That's all I can tell you."

"Do you recognize this man at all?" Karl asked.

Kuntzler shrugged. "Maybe."

"What do you mean, 'maybe'?" Kris snapped.

"Just that. Maybe."

Kris leaned menacingly toward him, and jabbed his finger at the picture of Dietrick. "Then who do you 'maybe' think this is?"

"What's in this for me?" Kuntzler asked.

"Maybe your freedom, mister, and maybe your life!"

A flicker of fear crossed Kuntzler's face.

"Well?" Kris demanded.

"It looks like Otto von Kemp to me," Kuntzler said.

Kris's brow wrinkled into a deep frown. "That's not Otto von Kemp. I knew him very well, and this isn't him. What're you trying to pull?"

"You asked me who I thought it was, and I told you. When I was at the Central Works with von Kemp, his face was a mess from an accident he'd had when the Russians captured him, but he had a full head of hair and a beard, just like this guy."

Kris pulled the magazine toward him and scrutinized the picture of Dietrick. "I don't know what you're trying to pull, but that's not Otto von Kemp. This guy's cheekbones aren't the same. His nose is too flat and von Kemp's ears stuck out." He shook his head. "That's not von Kemp."

"Have it your way," Kuntzler said. "You asked my opinion and I gave it to you. Maybe he had plastic surgery done. A lot of them did."

Kris flipped the page to the NASA article. He pointed to a picture of the NASA team. "What about the men in this picture? Do you know any of them?"

Kuntzler shoved his glasses up on his nose and looked down, pointing at each man. "This is von Braun, of course, and I don't know this man next to him. This one seated here is Ernst Stuhlinger. Behind him is Hermann Oberth, and this is Eberhard Rees. I don't know this next man, but this one on the far right is the man who calls himself Arthur Dietrick." He glanced up at Karl. "It's been over twenty years since I saw any of these men, you know. I'm sure they've all changed considerably."

"Maybe Dietrick has, too," Kris said.

Kuntzler again shook his head, this time emphatically. "This is definitely not the Arthur Dietrick that was at the Central Works when I was there. What more can I tell you?"

"Did you know, before I showed you this article, that this man was not the Arthur Dietrick you knew?"

Kuntzler shrugged. "Yes. I saw this same article myself when it first came out."

"And you didn't let anyone know of your doubts?"

"Why should I? I wasn't in any position to stick my neck out. Besides, it's none of my business if it's Arthur Dietrick or whoever. If NASA is using him, they must have checked his credentials and been satisfied with what they found." He gave Kris a questioning look. "Why are you so interested in Dietrick and von Kemp, anyway? They don't have anything to do with my situation."

"That's where you're wrong," Kris snapped. "They have everything to do with whether we're taking your case or not. We want to talk to everyone who knew you. Did all the men in this picture know you?"

"No. None of them were at the Central Works when I got there except Dietrick and von Kemp, but von Kemp is the only one who really knew me. The others I'd seen off and on during the war."

"Let's talk about von Kemp," Kris said. "You said his face was messed up in an accident. When was this accident?"

Kuntzler shook his head. "I don't know for sure, I never asked him, but I heard the Russians did it to him when they first got him. That had to be right after the war. That's all I know."

Kris frowned. "You said you'd heard rumors that he'd escaped from the Russians. Where and when did you hear these rumors?"

"A few weeks after the Russians moved most of the rocket men to Leningrad. They left a bunch of us behind, and that's when I heard von Kemp had escaped the night they took the others."

"When was this?"

Kuntzler thought for a moment. "The first part of October in 1947."

"And you never saw him again after that?"

"No."

"Did you see Dietrick again?"

"No. I told you. I'd heard he'd been shot."

"So you don't know for sure if either one might've escaped or were taken by the Russians or were shot."

"I've told you all I know. Now look, we made a deal. You said you'd take my case if I told you the truth, and I have. Will you represent me?"

Kris looked at Karl. "We've got some checking to do on your story, so we'll get back to you as soon as we've cleared some things up. You're not going anywhere, anyway. If you can't wait, try someone else. It won't hurt our feelings if you don't want us."

30

When Kris got back from seeing Kuntzler at the Federal Correction Facility, he went over all the information he'd gotten from NASA and the State Department on Dietrick. There was nothing there to suggest that Arthur Dietrick was not on the level, but there had to be some way to find out if this man was who he claimed to be. Kuntzler could have been lying about him not being the real Dietrick, but why lie about something that could be so easily verified. Or could it? If State and NASA believed him to be Arthur Dietrick, and the other Germans on the NASA team accepted him as Dietrick, how could he prove otherwise? And why bother, anyway? Kris wasn't after Dietrick. He wanted von Kemp.

But, try as he might to put this all in perspective as the next few weeks went by, what Kuntzler had said about Dietrick actually being von Kemp gnawed at him. If the man who called himself Arthur Dietrick wasn't Arthur Dietrick, but was someone who'd changed his identity and the others at NASA were all covering for him, then maybe von Kemp had done the same thing. He'd read somewhere that some of the German scientists who'd been brought over here after the war had had their Nazi pasts erased by the American recruiters who hired them, and some even had their looks changed, so why not von Kemp?

But if Dietrick wasn't von Kemp, how would he go about trying to find the real von Kemp? There was no way he could personally confront all the Germans working in the space program to see if one of them looked like von Kemp. Unless Bud Perry was able to come up with something that could point to him, there was only one other possibility of finding him—something he had vehemently sworn he would never do. He would have to go to Germany and try to retrace von Kemp's steps after the war. But that would be no easy matter since his last known days had been spent in the Russian sector of Germany. At least according to Kuntzler.

When the packet of information on Dietrick arrived from Bud Perry, Kris opened it eagerly. It reiterated much of what Kris already knew from the *Time* magazine article. What it did add was that Dietrick had lost his wife to cancer in 1961 and had one daughter and a grandson who lived in Houston.

Bud had included a newspaper picture of Dietrick standing next to a beautiful dark-haired woman in her late thirties or early forties. The caption identified the woman as Dietrick's daughter, Anne Kramer. Kris looked at every detail of the two faces, but this was not Otto von Kemp, and the woman bore only a passing resemblance to Hannah von Kemp whom he remembered as having been a blond. The picture had been taken two years earlier at the opening of a showing of Sixteenth-century German manuscripts at the Kramer Art Gallery in Houston.

Another news clipping caught his attention. It was a young man in an American Army uniform identified as Nikolaus Kramer, Anne Kramer's son. It noted that he had completed a tour of duty in Vietnam and was now doing graduate work at UCLA in Los Angeles, California. The thought suddenly struck Kris: Why not try to meet this boy and see if he could shed any light on his grandfather's friends?

He had Judy get him the UCLA Graduate Admissions office, and after identifying himself as an attorney working on a federal case, they reluctantly gave him Nikolaus Kramer's address and phone number. The boy lived in Pacific Palisades, a few miles down the coast from where Kris lived. Kris phoned Nikolaus, and after explaining that he was working on a case involving a detained German scientist that his grandfather might have some knowledge of, Nikolaus agreed to meet him for a drink that evening at Alice's Restaurant on the Malibu Pier.

When Kris entered the bar, Nik Kramer was already seated at a table with a drink. Kris stopped when he saw him. He was a lot like his picture: tall, well-muscled, and deeply tanned, with light brown wavy hair on the longish side. He looked to be about twenty-three or twenty-four years old. Nik glanced up as Kris came toward him with his hand out. "Nikolaus Kramer?" Kris asked.

The boy stood and gave Kris's hand a firm shake. "Yes, but my friends call me Nik."

Kris introduced himself and the two of them sat down. The waitress came and Kris ordered a beer. "So, you're doing graduate work at UCLA, huh?" Kris asked. "What field?"

"International Business."

Kris's brows went up. "Interesting field. What made you choose that?"

"I don't know, really. I've always been curious about Europe since that's where my roots are, and I know there's money to be made in companies willing to risk overseas ventures. I just sort of fell into it, I guess."

"You say your roots are in Europe. Where?" Kris asked.

"I was born in a town called Reichenbach in Germany. You probably never heard of it. It's in East Germany now."

"As a matter of fact, I have heard of it. I was born in Berlin, and I know of Reichenbach. It's in the mountains near the Czech border. A beautiful town, they tell me."

"That's what my mother says, but I was only a few months old when we left there, so I don't remember it."

Kris would have liked to pursue that, but he didn't want to probe too deeply and alarm the boy. "Well, tell me about your grandfather's work with NASA," he said.

"Are you familiar with what he does?" Nik asked.

"Some. I know he's been involved in important advances with rocket fuels, but I was more interested in how he was recruited by the

United States, the kind of work he did in Germany, the men he worked with there, and so forth. I know I could fly to Houston and interview him in person, but you have to get all kinds of official authorizations to talk to any of those scientists, so when I found out you were studying here I thought I might save myself the trouble by picking your brain about him. I hope that's all right with you. You don't feel uncomfortable talking about him, do you?"

"No. Not at all. I'm very proud of him, but I am interested in why you want information about him. Are you doing an article on him?"

The waitress set Kris's beer on the table.

"Not directly," Kris said. "As I mentioned on the phone, I'm an attorney, and I'm considering taking a case that involves a former Nazi doctor who's being held for extradition to West Germany to stand trial for war crimes. He claims he knew your grandfather, and I'm just trying to check out his story. I wondered if your grandfather ever talked about any of the men he worked with during and after the war. Did he ever mention a man named Otto von Kemp?"

Nik thought for a moment, then shook his head. "That doesn't ring a bell. I know some of the men he works with now were former colleagues, but I've never heard him speak of anyone named von Kemp. Is that the man you're representing?"

"No. His name is Rudolph Kuntzler."

"Oh, yeah. I read about him. He's accused of doing medical experiments on prisoners at Birkenau, isn't he?"

Kris nodded.

A look of alarm crossed Nik's face. "My grandfather wouldn't have had anything to do with someone like that! I hope you're not implying that he was mixed up with a Nazi war criminal."

Kris shook his head emphatically. "No! No! Not at all. It's just that Kuntzler named your grandfather and Otto von Kemp as men he'd worked with at some point, and I thought your grandfather might have mentioned Kuntzler's name."

Nik's manner had cooled. "That's something you'll have to ask him in person. I can't help you there."

Kris could see he'd upset the boy, so he decided to change his tack. "Tell me a little more about yourself. How did you end up in the States?"

"I came here with my mother and grandmother after the war."

"Are they still living?"

"My mother is. She owns an art gallery in Houston. The Kramer Gallery."

"Does she get back to Germany very often?"

Nik frowned. "No way! She won't go anywhere near that place after what she went through during the war."

"I know how she feels," Kris said. "When did you come over here?"

"Sometime in the early '50s. Opa was already here."

"You must have been pretty young," Kris said.

"I was. About two or three, I guess. I don't remember much about it. You said you're from Germany, too. How did you end up here?"

Kris shifted uncomfortably. "I lost all my family in the war, but I had an uncle who'd emigrated here before the war, and he brought me over."

"I lost my father, too," Nik said. "He was a German officer."

"That must've been hard on you and your mother," Kris said.

"My grandparents took care of us, but I know it was hard on Mom losing my father. She doesn't talk much about him, but I know that's why she's never remarried. I keep introducing her to guys, but she'll date them once or twice, then lose interest. I'm afraid she's a lost cause."

Kris gave a little laugh. "Marriage can be a complicated business. I know."

"You married?"

"I was, but I lost my wife and little girl in a car accident a few years ago. I'm still trying to get over that."

"That's rough," Nik said, then his eyes brightened. "Maybe I can introduce you to my mom."

Kris held up his palm to the boy and shook his head. "No thanks. Once is enough for me."

"That's what Mom says, too, but I keep trying."

They both laughed, then spent another half hour of pleasant conversation. Kris was very impressed with the boy. He didn't appear to be trying to hide anything about his grandfather. In fact, he confirmed all the things that Kris had heard about Dietrick. As they were getting up to leave, Kris said to Nik, "Why don't I give you my number in case you think of anything else about your grandfather that might help me? I'd really appreciate it. And I hope you won't mind if I think of any other questions and give you a call."

Nik took the napkin Kris had scribbled his number on and tucked it into his shirt pocket. "I don't know what more I can tell you, but I'm happy to take your number. If your investigation isn't classified, can I tell my mother that I met you and ask her if she knows anything about the men Opa worked with?"

"Sure. Maybe she's heard your grandfather mention von Kemp's or Kunstler's names."

"I'll ask her," Nik said.

They both headed for the door and paused to shake hands before Kris went to his car.

Nice kid, Kris thought as he drove home.

31

Houston, Texas
1970

At sixty-seven, Otto von Kemp should have retired. God knows, he could use the rest after nearly forty years of working, but with Eva gone, it would be too lonely rattling around all day by himself in his big house in the suburbs of Houston. The heart attack he'd had a year ago hadn't killed him, but the six months of recovery without Eva by his side nearly had. It had been nine years since he'd lost her, and yet the pain of her loss was as fresh to him today as it had been the day cancer took her. If it hadn't been for Hannah and Nikolaus, he didn't know how he'd have survived.

He was thinking about Eva one afternoon in early July when his secretary buzzed him. "I have a Major Thomas Stover on line three for you. Do you want to take it?"

A broad grin lit his face. "I certainly will." He pressed line three.

"Major Stover?" von Kemp asked. "Is that really you, Tom?"

"Yes, Art. It's me all right. How are you?"

"Fine. Fine. A little slower than I used to be, but I'm getting up there in years, so it's to be expected."

"I heard you'd had a heart attack last year. Is everything okay now?"

"Yes. I'm fine now. Really great. How about you?"

"Can't complain. Retirement agrees with me. I sit in the Florida sun every day and reminisce about those exciting days when we were young bucks. Remember?"

Von Kemp gave a tight little laugh. "I try to forget those days," he said, then his voice brightened. "But I can't get over hearing from you, Major. How long has it been? Twenty years?"

"Well, let's see. You came in in March of '48, so that's been almost twenty-two years. Can you believe it?"

"It doesn't seem possible, does it? So much has happened since then. Did you hear that I'd lost Eva in '61?"

"Yes, I did, and it really shook me up. I thought about getting in touch with you then, but I finally decided not to bother you at a time like that. I know that must have been an awful loss for you, but I've sure heard good things about Arthur Dietrick through the years."

"You know I'll be eternally grateful to you, Major. There wouldn't be an Arthur Dietrick without you."

"Don't say that. All I did was get the ball rolling. The rest was up to you, and you've certainly vindicated my trust in you. But that brings me to the reason I called. A couple of days ago I got a phone call from a Houston attorney—a guy named Bud Perry—and he was asking a lot of questions about you and about Otto von Kemp. Naturally I didn't tell him anything, but I thought you should know. Has he contacted you?"

Von Kemp was stunned. "No! No, he hasn't. What did he want to know?"

"He was mostly interested in Otto von Kemp. It seems that some Nazi that's being held in California said von Kemp had been a close friend of Arthur Dietrick, and somehow he found out that I'm the one who recruited you, and he wondered if I'd ever run across von Kemp. I told him I knew who he was, but, with his reputation, no American recruiter would ever have tried to sign him up—maybe the Russians had, but we didn't. That seemed to satisfy him, but it concerns me that he was even asking questions. I tried to find out why he wanted the information, but he said it was for a client and wouldn't give me his name."

239

"My God!" von Kemp exclaimed. "Not after all these years. Please, God!"

"I know how you feel, Art. It's a rotten break."

"What do you think I should do?"

"Well, first of all, I'd alert the top brass there at NASA so they won't inadvertently spill anything in case he contacts them. There's really no way he could verify anything even if he tried. All your records are in complete order. He might try to raise a stink, or even go to the papers with it, but I think it would backfire on him considering all the good you've done with the space program. Then I'd alert Anne in case he tries to contact her. Does Nik know anything?"

"No, we've never told him. There didn't seem to be any reason to."

"Good," Stover said, "so he'd run into a blind alley there. I don't think you need to be unduly worried. When he doesn't get anything, it'll probably all blow over. You're about to retire anyway, aren't you?"

"Not for a couple of years, I wasn't, but I've always known this day could come." He paused for a moment. "I'm not sorry I did it, though, Tom. Arthur Dietrick gave his life for me, so I'm glad I could give it back to him in this way."

"Well, I just want you to know I'll stand by you no matter what happens, and so will a lot of important people. You have every reason to be proud of yourself. Your contributions to this country's space program have been immeasurable, both with your help during the war and after you got here. Everyone who knows you, knows that. If some jerk wants to take a poke at you, I think he'll find he's bitten off more than he can chew."

"I really appreciate your saying those things, Tom. It makes me feel better. Will you let me know if you hear anything more from this guy?"

"I sure will, and you call me if he tries to contact you. I'll sic some of the big boys in the State Department on him. That'll shut him up quick."

"Thanks, Tom, and thanks again for sticking your neck out for me once again. I'll try not to let you down."

"You haven't, and you won't," Tom said. "Just hang in there. This'll all blow over."

"I will. Thanks for your call, and thanks for your faith in me."

Von Kemp slowly hung up and leaned back in his chair. He pressed his fingers to his temples and took a deep breath, then let out a long sigh. Had it all caught up with him? He'd always known there was that possibility, but every passing year had diminished the danger until he'd actually come to think of himself as Arthur Dietrick. And now it might all be coming to a head, and he didn't know exactly how he felt about it.

He didn't mind so much for himself, or even for Hannah—she was too well established with her career for it to taint her—but Nikolaus was another matter. He had no idea of his grandfather's questionable past, nor of the identity of his real father. All of this might lead to an exposure of that, and that weighed heavily on him.

He got up from his chair and went down the hall to the office of Acting NASA Administrator Ed Paine. The secretary informed him that Paine was free, so von Kemp went into his inner office.

Paine looked up as he came in. "Hi, Art."

"Do you have a few minutes, Ed? Something's come up that I think you should know about."

"Sure. Sit down. Is everything okay?"

Von Kemp sat down wearily in the chair. "I hope so, but I just got a very disturbing phone call from Major Tom Stover. You remember him? He's the one who initially recruited me."

"Sure, I remember Tom. I haven't seen him in years, though. I understand he's retired."

"Yes. He's down in Florida."

"What did he want?"

"He told me that a Houston attorney, a guy named Bud Perry, contacted him a couple of days ago asking questions about me and about Otto von Kemp. It upset Tom enough to call me."

Paine leaned forward in his chair. His alarm was evident. "What kind of questions was he asking?"

"It seems that some client of his is representing a former Nazi being held for extradition in California, and this guy claims he knew me and Arthur Dietrick at the Central Works. The attorney asked Stover if he'd ever heard of Otto von Kemp, and he said yes, but that he had no idea what had become of him. Maybe he'd gone to work for the Russians. He thinks it satisfied the attorney, but we're both concerned that anyone is asking questions at all. This attorney wouldn't tell Stover who his client was, but I'd sure like to know myself. I'd also like to know who this former Nazi is that they're holding in California."

"I can get that information for you. I'll also contact this Perry guy and find out what he's up to. I want to nip this thing in the bud right now."

Von Kemp gave him a worried look. "Wouldn't it be better to just let it rest and see what comes of it? If we start putting pressure on any of these people, they'll know something's up."

Paine thought for a moment. "Maybe you're right, but I can find out who the Nazi is that's being held in California, and we can work it backwards from there. We'll find out who he's talked to and then decide how much further we want to take it."

Von Kemp went back to his office and tried to finish up some papers he'd been working on, but couldn't concentrate. He left early and drove to the Kramer Gallery. He wanted to talk to Hannah as soon as possible. She needed to know the possible danger they were all in.

⊹ ⊹

Anne looked up with delight as her dad walked into her office. "Daddy! Hi. What are you doing here in the middle of the day?"

"I need to talk to you, honey. Something rather disturbing has come up."

She got up from her desk and led him to the sofa in her outer office. "Let's sit down here. Is your heart acting up?"

"No, I'm just tired. And a little worried."

"What's wrong?"

He proceeded to tell her about Stover's phone call and his talk with Ed Paine.

She was obviously shaken. For years she'd done her best to conceal her identity, going so far as to keep her blond hair dyed dark brown and using the name Anne Kramer. She'd even avoided any serious personal relationships out of fear of being found out. She'd built a good reputation as an art dealer and museum curator, and it frightened her now to think of being exposed.

"I need to get in touch with Nik as soon as possible," she said. "If someone's snooping around, they might try to contact him. I want him to be warned."

"What can you tell him without alarming him? He doesn't know anything, but if he thinks we're scared, he might start asking us questions that we can't give him answers to."

"We'll just tell him that someone's trying to smear you, and that'll at least put him on his guard. I have to call him, Dad, right now."

She went to her desk and dialed his number. The phone rang and rang, but no one picked it up, so she put it back in its cradle. "He isn't home, but I'll try him again tonight."

She sat back down by her father and took his hand. "Try not to worry, Daddy. You've got a lot of powerful friends, and no one's going to let you get hurt. Why don't you go on home and try to rest. This is going to be too hard on your heart if you stew about it. Would you like me to come over this evening?"

He squeezed her hand, then stood. "No, honey. Esmarelda will take good care of me. She loves fussing over me." He looked wistfully at his daughter. "I wish I had your mother tonight, though. She always knew how to see the bright side of everything."

"I miss her so much, too," Anne said as she hugged him.

He kissed her cheek and left.

Anne sat at her desk looking at the phone. What could she say to Nik? For twenty-four years she'd lied to him about everything, but how could you tell a little boy that he was illegitimate? Not that she had ever thought of him that way. She'd loved his father more than life itself. In fact, Kristopher Falkenhorst had been the only man she'd ever loved in all these years. It had not been easy raising a son by herself, but her father had always been there providing him the companionship and male role model he needed. Nik was devoted to his grandfather, and to her, but what would be his reaction if he knew the truth about both of them? Would he understand, or would he feel like he'd been cheated? She prayed to God it would never be necessary to tell him the whole truth.

That evening she fought with herself about whether to call Nik or not. He was so sharp that he'd spot her concern immediately. She finally decided not to call. If anyone started asking him questions, his innocence about the whole thing would be her father's greatest protection.

☩ ☩

A few days later, while Anne was conducting a tour through her gallery, an assistant handed her a note. Nik had called and left a message for her to call him. As soon as she finished with the group, she went to her office and called him.

"Nik? It's Mom. Is something wrong?"

"Does something have to be wrong for me to call my mother?"

She found herself relaxing slightly. "Well, no, but you don't usually call me in the daytime."

"I know, but I couldn't let this pass. I met a very interesting man last week that I think might be just the one for you. He's German, a widower, an attorney, and very good-looking. You haven't found a man since I last talked to you, have you?"

Anne laughed. "No, dear. I'm still your old widowed mother, too busy trying to make money so she can keep her destitute son in school. Is this some aging grad student who's looking for a rich widow to take care of him?"

"No. He's a bigshot attorney here in L.A."

"How did you meet someone like that? You aren't in any kind of trouble are you?"

Nik laughed. "No, Mom. He's representing some Nazi they've caught out here who said he knew Opa back in Germany, so this attorney found out Opa was my grandfather from that *Houston Chronicle* story about all of us a couple of years ago, and he called and asked if he could buy me a drink and ask me some questions about the scientists Opa works with. I couldn't tell him much, but I liked the guy a lot, and I think you would too."

Anne's heart nearly stopped. Someone *had* contacted Nik about her father. She tried to keep her voice light. "Did he give you the names of any of the scientists he was asking about?"

He paused to think. "The only name I can remember is someone named von Kemp, but I told him I'd never heard of anyone by that name."

When Anne didn't respond immediately, he asked, "Are you still there, Mom?"

"Yes, of course."

"I thought I'd lost you there for a minute."

"No, no. I'm still here."

"How's Opa doing? Is his heart okay?"

"He's under a lot of stress right now."

"Why?"

She paused, trying to decide how to phrase her response. "Well, it seems like someone's out to smear him, and they're asking a lot of questions about his past, and he's a little uncomfortable about it."

"Why should he be uncomfortable about that? He hasn't got anything to hide." He hesitated. "Does he?"

"Of course not! It's just that people like to associate all the German scientists with what went on during the war. He has nothing to hide personally, but he's always sensitive about things some of his former colleagues did. It reflects on all of them." She paused a moment. "What kind of questions did this man ask you about this von Kemp?"

"Nothing specific. He was mostly interested in whether I'd ever heard Opa mention his name or the names of any other men he'd worked with in Germany, but I told him the only ones I've ever heard him say anything about are those he works with now. Are you sure nothing's wrong, Mom? You really sound funny."

"No. I just thought I'd warn you to be careful about what you say to anyone about Opa."

"You're starting to scare me. What could I possibly say that could hurt him?"

"Nothing, so don't worry about it. This will probably all blow over in a few weeks. People are always taking shots at men in Opa's position. Not everybody supports the space program, especially since the deaths of those three astronauts. The Review Board has been trying to lay the blame on the men who developed the Apollo, and they might be behind this."

"For crying out loud! They can't pin that on Opa. That was an electrical failure, not a booster failure."

"I know that, but they're looking at everything and everyone."

"Well, they'd better keep their hands off Opa, or they'll have to answer to me."

Anne gave a little laugh. "I don't think you'll have to go to battle for him, but just be careful what you say to anyone who asks you questions about his work now, or in the past. Okay?"

"Okay. When are you coming out here?" he asked.

"I can't get away for a month at least. I've got a big shipment of paintings coming in from Europe, and I never feel like I can leave that to others. Why don't you come home next weekend? I know Opa would love to see you."

"Will you float me a ticket?"

"Don't I always?"

Nik laughed. "Okay, I'll see when I can get free and call you."

It suddenly occurred to her that Nik had not told her the name of the attorney. "Hey, Nik," she said. "Before you hang up, what's the name of the attorney you spoke to? I want to let Opa know who's asking questions about him."

"His name is Kris Falk, but I checked him out myself when he asked to meet me. He's part of a big firm in L.A. that practices international law. A company named Falk and Gerard."

Anne could barely breathe as she hung up. "Kris Falk" was obviously Kristopher Falkenhorst, and he was about to destroy the world she had so carefully built around herself and her father—and Nik.

32

Houston, Texas

Anne sat staring at the phone, then asked long distance to get her the law offices of Falk and Gerard in Los Angeles. Twenty minutes later she knew who Kris Falk was and called her father.

A half hour later, von Kemp rushed into Anne's gallery, the worry on his face evident. She led him to her second-floor office, closed and locked the door behind them, and burst into tears in his arms.

He held her for a few moments, then pulled her down on the sofa beside him. "What is it, Liebchen? You wouldn't tell me on the phone."

"It's all caught up with us, Vati. Kristopher Falkenhorst has found us."

"What do you mean, 'found us'? You mean he's here in Houston?"

"No, but he soon will be. Somehow he found Nik, and knows that he's Arthur Dietrick's grandson, and it's only a matter of time before he finds out that you're not Arthur Dietrick."

"I've been Arthur Dietrick for more than twenty years, and no one here will dispute that."

"I know, but Kristopher's an expert in international law, and he'll dig out the truth. I'm sure he still blames you for his parents' deaths, and he won't let go of this until he's destroyed you. What are we going to do?"

"Well, first of all, we're not going to panic. I talked to Ed Paine last week when I found out that a Houston attorney was asking questions about me, and he assured me that they'll protect me."

248

"Yes, but what about Nik? If Kristopher finds out your true identity, he'll put two and two together and realize that Nik is his son."

"I don't see how," Dietrick said. "He didn't know you were pregnant when we left the Central Works. You didn't even know it yourself, so Nik could be anyone's child as far as he knows." He reached over and patted her hand. "We have to put this in God's hands, Hannah. We gave this whole thing to Him many years ago, so let's not take it back now. It's much more than we can handle by ourselves."

She reached up and wiped at her tears. "I know you're right, but I just don't want you and Nik to get hurt."

"We're big boys, so don't worry about us."

"Of course I'm going to worry. You two are all I've got, and if anyone wants to touch either one of you, they'll have to take me on first."

Her father gave a little chuckle and pulled her into his arms. "I wouldn't want to be in Kristopher's shoes if he gets in your way."

Anne pulled back, her face resolute. "As much as I've loved him all these years, I won't let him destroy us."

"Neither will I. If he shows up here, I'll direct him to Ed Paine, and he'll set him straight."

"And if that doesn't satisfy him?"

"Then we'll just wait and see what he does. We've always known there was the possibility that my real identity might be uncovered and I might have to stand trial or be deported, but I don't think they could touch you and Nik. All this has come up now because there've been several cases lately of former Nazis being extradited for trial in different countries. Rudolph Kuntzler's case has got everyone stirred up again."

"Did you know him, Dad?"

"Only slightly. He was working on some medical research related to weightlessness in space, but we certainly weren't friends. I'd heard of his experiments on prisoners at Birkenau, and was disgusted by it. I'm glad they caught him."

Anne gave him a grim look. "If they hadn't, you wouldn't be in the spot you're in now."

"We don't know that. There was always the possibility I would be exposed. I've known that, and I don't bear Kristopher any malice for trying to vindicate his parent's deaths. The Falkenhorsts were a wonderful family, and truthfully, I'm glad to know Kristopher survived."

"Even if it means your exposure?"

He nodded wearily. "Reverend Falkenhorst used to preach that we reap what we sow, and this is just an example of that truth."

"As I recall, he also preached forgiveness," Anne said, with a trace of bitterness, "but it's obvious his son didn't learn that lesson."

"Hannah! Hannah! Don't let this make you bitter. I've had a very full life, and with this old ticker of mine like it is, I don't have all that much time left anyway, so let's not waste the rest of our lives regretting what we can't change. It may well be that Kristopher won't come up with a thing on me. Major Stover did a very thorough job of erasing my past, so let's just wait and see what comes of it. But, in the meantime, we have to tell Nik the truth before he finds out some other way."

She gave him a look of alarm. "You want me to tell him about Kristopher being his father?"

"That's up to you. Whatever you want to tell him about *that*, I'll support you, but I want to make a clean breast of everything about me before some reporter gets hold of this and Nik reads it in the newspaper."

Anne got up and moved over to the large picture window and stood looking out at the moss-covered oaks. She was silent for several minutes, then turned back to him. "We'll tell him about you, Vati, but not about Kristopher being his father. I'm not ready to deal with that yet."

"If that's what you think is best," he said, "but whatever we do, we need to do it right away."

Her eyes began filling with tears. "I can't believe I found him after all these years, and I still can't have him. It's so darned unfair."

"We both know life isn't always fair, Liebchen, but it's better than the alternative. Isn't it?"

She snuffed back her tears and nodded.

Anne called Nik that night and told him that Opa had something very serious that he needed to talk to him about, and he wanted to see him right away. The fact that his mother refused to tell him what was so urgent made Nik sure that it must be Opa's heart, and he probably had only a few days to live.

Nik immediately booked a flight and got into Houston the next afternoon. He took a taxi straight to his grandfather's house. His mother and grandfather were seated at the table in the breakfast room when he barged in. He tossed his overnight bag on the floor and hurried over to his grandfather. "Opa! Are you okay? Mom said something had happened to you. Is it your heart?"

"Not this time," he said.

Anne threw her arms around Nik, and he hugged her, then gave his grandfather a questioning look. "What's going on then?"

"Sit down, Nik," von Kemp said. "We hated to get you down here under false pretenses, but your mother and I need to tell you something before you read about it in the papers."

Nik shot him a cautious look. "Read about what?"

"It's about that attorney who talked with you about Rudolph Kuntzler."

"You mean Kris Falk?"

Von Kemp nodded. "Yes, but his name isn't Kris Falk, it's Kristopher Falkenhorst. He's someone we knew many years ago in Germany. His father was the minister of the church we attended in Berlin, and your mother was a good friend of his."

Nik gave him an incredulous look. "You mean you both know him?"

"Yes," von Kemp said, "and we knew his parents, too. They were arrested for giving refuge to Jews in their church, and were sent to Juno where I was in charge of the rocket program. I didn't even know they were there for many months, and when I finally found out, Frau Falkenhorst was so ill that she soon died. I tried my best to get

Reverend Falkenhorst and Kristopher released, but the SS wouldn't even consider it, then Reverend Falkenhorst ended up being injured when the Americans bombed the camp, and when he couldn't get back to work right away, he was sent to Auschwitz, where we presume he died."

Anne cut in quickly. "But Kristopher survived because Opa put him to work as a gardener on our estate so he wouldn't have to go into the tunnels. He saved Kristopher's life."

Nik leaned back in his chair as relief spread across his face. "You mean this is the big reason you had to get me down here? To tell me this? I think Kris will be delighted to find out who you are."

Anne shook her head. "No, he won't. There's more to the story. Let Opa finish."

Nik's brow wrinkled. "What do you mean?"

"Kristopher blames me for his parents' deaths," von Kemp said. "He expected me to get them out of the camp, and I swear I did everything I could to try to get them released, but Himmler had it in for Reverend Falkenhorst's brother, General Falkenhorst, and for that reason he refused to give the family any special consideration."

"Wait a minute!" Nik said, holding up a hand. "You say Kris blames *you* for his family's deaths? He told me that a German scientist named Otto von Kemp was responsible. What's that got to do with you?"

Von Kemp suddenly looked very weary. "That's my real name, Nik. I'm Otto von Kemp."

"What?" Nik exploded. He gaped at his mother. "What's he saying? That he's not Arthur Dietrick?"

"He isn't, honey. Opa's real name is Otto von Kemp, and mine is Hannah von Kemp."

Nik jumped up, his hands punctuating the air as he confronted them. "Wait! Wait! Wait!" he blurted. "What's going on here?"

"Sit down. Please," von Kemp said. "I'll tell you the whole story, and as God is my witness, every word I tell you will be the truth."

Nik sat spellbound as his grandfather told him everything. When he'd finished, it took Nik a moment to find his words. "How did you end up with Dietrick's name, then?"

"When we first talked about trying to escape from the Russians, Arthur made all of us false identity papers with *his* name under my picture, and I used that."

"Why didn't you use your own name?"

Von Kemp hesitated a moment, then said, "Because the Americans had mistakenly put my name on their war crimes list, and I knew if they caught me, I'd be imprisoned for things I hadn't done."

"What things?" Nik challenged.

"A lot of people died at the Central Works, but I swear to you that I never killed a single person, nor did I ever order anyone's death. I knew the SS was doing terrible things to the prisoners, but if I had tried to stop them, Oma and your mother and I would have been killed."

Nik could no longer hold back his mounting anger. "You mean you just stood by and did nothing?"

"Certainly not!" his mother put in sharply. "Opa was secretly giving information about Germany's space program to the Allies all during the war, so he couldn't dare bring attention to himself."

"So how did you talk the Americans into hiring you?" Nik challenged.

"After we escaped from the Russians, I made contact with an American Army recruiter who was signing up other German scientists for the US space program, and I told him the whole story, and he's the one who advised me to keep using Dietrick's name until I could talk it over with the people at NASA, so that's what I did."

Nik glared at his grandfather. "So, you've been living a lie all these years? Are there any other lies I should know about?"

"Oh, Nik!" his mother said. "You wouldn't even be here if it hadn't been for Opa's courage. He could have gone to Russia and helped develop their space program, but if he had, you'd be slaving away in some Russian factory right now, or in the Russian army. I think you owe Opa an apology and a 'thank you' for saving your ungrateful hide."

Nik turned to the distraught old man. "I don't mean to sit in judgment on you, Opa. I'm sure you did what you thought you had to, but it's just such a shock. How many people know about all this?"

Von Kemp looked up and met his grandson's accusing gaze. "A few in the State Department and Immigration, most of my colleagues, and all of the top brass at NASA."

"And now you're worried that Kris Falk is going to find out and expose you. Right?"

Von Kemp nodded. "He blames me for what happened to his family, and there's no telling what kind of ruckus he'll raise if he finds out who I really am."

33

1970

Kris had tried for years to get information about von Kemp from the Berlin Document Center and the War Crimes office in Ludwigsburg, but nothing he got from either of those centers had ever amounted to much, so he'd finally come to the conclusion that if he was ever going to get the information he needed about Dietrick and von Kemp, and now Kuntzler, he'd have to arm himself with court orders from the US government and take them personally to the right people in Germany.

It was not something he'd looked forward to, and as it turned out, his search was mostly fruitless, anyway, as he spent a week combing through boxes of old documents in the two information centers and finding huge gaps in the movement of the three men after the war. Whether Dietrick and von Kemp had somehow exchanged identities, or von Kemp had been killed by the Russians and his wife had later married Arthur Dietrick, as the Ludwigsburg Center alleged, Kris couldn't say. But, if he wanted absolute certainty of Dietrick's real identity, he could see that he would have to dedicate the rest of his life to tracking down the few leads he had gotten, and that wasn't something he was willing to do. Twenty years ago he would have been, but now the fire was going out of his belly, and he just wanted this all over with.

The one thing from his Berlin visit that did arouse his interest, though, was the allegation that Eva von Kemp had married Arthur

Dietrick after von Kemp's reported death. If that was true, then Nik Kramer's mother might be Hannah von Kemp, and that was something worth looking into.

In the week after his return from Germany, Kris hashed over every aspect of what he'd learned with Karl and Sid, and they all agreed that they needed to take one final stab at trying to determine if Arthur Dietrick was genuine. It would be impossible to get official permission to interview any of the NASA scientists about their war-time activities, but there was nothing to stop Kris from going to Houston and confronting Anne Kramer. He'd know in a minute whether she was Hannah von Kemp. Where it would all go from there depended on who she was.

☩ ☩

It was close to midnight when he pulled his rented Corvette up to the Houston Sheraton a week later. He was in no shape to confront Nik's mother until he'd had a chance to get a few hours sleep. What he was facing would require having all his wits about him.

He checked in, grabbed a quick shower, and fell in bed exhausted. He woke about six a.m., showered again and shaved. He put on a white shirt, slipped into khaki pants and loafers, and went down to the hotel coffee shop for breakfast.

When he'd finished, he went out to his Corvette. It was still too early for the gallery to be open, so he drove around the city for a while, past mansions hidden behind moss-covered oaks in the exclusive River Oaks area, around the expressway that belted the city, and into the heart of downtown, through streets hemmed on both sides with tall gleaming skyscrapers. He could see why Bud Perry liked Houston. There was mega-money here.

Around ten in the morning he headed for DeSoto Street and spotted the gallery right away. It resembled an antebellum plantation house with six white columns adorning the front. Kris pulled his car into the parking area beside it. There were several cars and a school bus already parked there.

He sat in his car for a few minutes, trying to formulate a plan of exactly how to approach the situation. He had no idea how this woman would react when she saw him. If she was Hannah von Kemp, she'd probably recognize him and panic, so he had to be ready for a scene. But, scene or not, he had no intention of leaving until he got the answers he'd come for.

Kris could not put a name to his feelings as he approached the door of the gallery. Part of him wanted it to be Hannah, and part of him didn't. A uniformed guard smiled at him as he entered the lobby. Kris wondered if he'd still be smiling when he left.

From the lobby, several hallways led into different rooms, which in turn opened into still more galleries. He began wandering through the corridors looking at the impressive array of paintings. He'd gone through several of the galleries when he heard children's laughter in the room ahead of him. He peeked his head around the corner and saw a group of school children laughing at a woman who was pointing to the picture on the wall in front of them. This was definitely the woman he'd seen in the pictures Bud had sent him, but from where he stood, he could not tell if it was Hannah von Kemp. The children giggled again at something she said, and Kris felt a knot tighten in his stomach as the woman threw back her head and laughed. She led the group on to another painting, and Kris followed along, feeling a little foolish as he attempted to stay out of sight.

As the woman and the children reached the final gallery before the end of their tour, she looked up just as Kris slipped into the room. She gave him a questioning look, and when she finally turned back to the children, her gaze darted back to him several times. When she'd finished, she herded the children and their teacher toward the lobby. Kris loomed in the doorway of the room watching her.

The children finally left, and the tour guide came back to him, politely extending her hand. "I'm Anne Kramer, the director of the gallery. Is there something I can show you?"

He took her hand, his eyes wary as he scrutinized her face. This could definitely be Hannah von Kemp, but the hair color was wrong. "I'm Kristopher Falkenhorst," he said.

She forced a little smile, but he could see that behind the smile there was real fear. "Do we know each other?" she asked.

"I think we do," he said, "but it's been twenty-four years since we last saw each other. That was just a few days before you and your father, Otto von Kemp, sneaked out of the Central Works to avoid capture by the Americans."

A smudge of pink colored her cheeks, but she kept her composure. "I think you must have me confused with someone else. My father's name is Arthur Dietrick. Now if you'll excuse me, I have other patrons to see to." She turned to leave.

He raised his voice after her. "Just a minute, Mrs. Kramer. I think it might be a good idea if we talked about this."

She stopped and turned back to him, her anger barely under control. "I don't believe we have anything further to talk about."

Several people heard Kris's raised voice and stopped to observe the scene with interest.

"I intend to talk with you about this, whether here or in a courtroom," Kris said firmly. "Now, if you want your patrons to hear what I have to say, that's fine with me. But we *are* going to talk."

She looked at the people who had turned in their direction, and stepped back toward him. Her voice was tight. "If you insist on this rude behavior we can go up to my office, but I'll have to call my assistant to cover for me." She went to the phone at the entry desk and dialed a number. When she'd spoken to her assistant, she went back to Kris and asked him to follow her.

Kris looked behind him, fully expecting that her phone call would bring a handful of armed guards to escort him out, but none came. He followed her up the marble steps to the second floor.

Anne Kramer's office had a comfortable waiting area with a sofa and two chairs. She motioned for Kris to sit down on the sofa, and took a chair opposite him.

"Now," she said curtly, "what is it you want with me? I have no idea what you're talking about, but I can certainly tell you that I don't appreciate your making a scene in my gallery."

A sadness came into his eyes as he scrutinized her face, almost certain now that she was Hannah von Kemp. "Look, Hannah . . . Mrs. Kramer—or whatever your name is—I don't have any desire to hurt you or your son, but I don't want to play any more games, either. I've always had a gut feeling that your father survived the war, and it was only a matter of time before I found him. There's no need for you to pretend any longer."

Anne refused to be rattled. "I don't know what you're hoping to accomplish by these absurd accusations, but whatever you're after, I want you out of this building before I call a guard."

The phone in her inner office rang.

Kris stood, his voice cutting as he glowered down at her. "I'm doing this because your father *is* Otto von Kemp. It's written all over your face, so there's no use denying it."

Anne was seething. "This conversation is over!" she announced coldly, putting her hand on the doorknob to her inner office. "If you'll excuse me, I have business to take care of. You can find your own way out, and don't come back. You're not welcome here." She went into her inner office and closed the door.

Kris was livid. She was lying, and they both knew it.

He grabbed the doorknob and shoved her office door open. Anne was sitting behind her desk, huge tears swimming in her eyes as she looked up at him. Kris was about to say something when his gaze went to a small painting on the wall directly above her head. He stared intently for a moment, suddenly feeling as if his breath had been driven out of him. Anne stood abruptly, trying to cover the painting with her body.

"How dare you come in here?" she demanded, reaching for the phone. "I'm calling a guard!"

Kris moved behind the desk and shoved her out of the way, his

259

heart pounding against his chest. He wet his lips and tried to conceal his excitement as his eyes took in the scene on the beautifully framed canvas. It was a white, lattice, summerhouse set in a dense green forest. He looked at the brass plate on the bottom of the frame. "The Summerhouse," it read. His eyes moved to the signature in the lower right-hand corner. Scrawled in youthful script were the words, "Hannah von Kemp", and beside it the date, "1944."

He stepped slowly back and looked at Anne, her eyes wide now with terror. "You painted this. Didn't you?"

"I . . . I . . ." She tried to answer, but no words came.

He grabbed her roughly by the shoulders. "It's the summerhouse, isn't it? At the Central Works!"

Tears began to run down her cheeks as she looked up at him, shaking convulsively. "Yes!" she blurted. "Yes, it is!"

He dropped his hands from her shoulders and stared at her, his mouth gaping in astonishment. "Then you *are* Hannah von Kemp, aren't you?"

"Yes, I am," she said, "but there's so much you don't know, Kristopher. So much."

He sat down heavily in the chair, nodding his head. "So I was right after all," he said thinly. "I finally found the butcher."

Anne came around the desk and stood in front of his chair, pleading. "Kristopher, please! Before you do anything you'll be sorry for, I must tell you some things you couldn't possibly know. Some things I'm sure will change your mind about my father."

He looked up coldly. "I know all I need to know about him. He's to blame for my parents' deaths, and that's all I care about."

"But he *wasn't* to blame. That's what I'm trying to tell you."

"Save your breath. You forget I saw with my own eyes the things he did. Do you think I'd ever forget that?"

"Listen to me, please! What I have to tell you is so classified that I don't know whether I'm doing the right thing in telling you or not, but since you've found out who my father really is, I have to trust you with this information. It could mean the end of his career, and possible deportation, if it was ever revealed."

He gave her a look of astonishment. "And you think I care? Deportation should be the least of his worries. There are a lot of people, like myself, who'd be glad to save the government the trouble of deporting him. The fact that he succeeded in fooling our government doesn't change what he did."

Anne leaned toward him, her voice urgent. "But that's just it, he didn't fool this government. He was working with them all during the war, and they're the ones who changed his identity and brought him over here."

Kris curled his lip in disbelief. "What kind of fool do you take me for?"

"It's the truth. I swear! My father supplied secrets to the Allies all during the war, and he planned to come here to work for the Americans, but as he was trying to get to the American sector, the Russians captured him and made him go to work for them back at the Central Works."

"And where were you and your mother all that time?"

"We'd been at my uncle's in Reichenbach until the Russians let us join Vati at the Central Works for a few months, but when they decided to send all the rocket men to Russia, we had to escape, and an American Army recruiter arranged for Vati to exchange identities with a friend of ours, Arthur Dietrick, because the Americans had mistakenly put Dad on their war crimes list."

Kris gave her an incredulous look. "And you expect me to believe this?"

The level of her voice came down. "I'll have you talk to the head of NASA, and he'll confirm what I've told you."

"Okay. We'll play your little game. What's his name, and how can I get in to see him?"

Anne sat back on the corner of her desk, breathing a little easier. "His name is Ed Paine. I'll call Dad right now and tell him what's happened and ask him to have Ed meet us at his office as soon as possible."

"How do I know you won't just tip your father off so he can disappear before I get my hands on him?"

"You can talk to him yourself and warn him what you'll do if he doesn't do as you ask."

Kris was silent for a moment. "Okay," he snapped. "Get your father on the line and tell him an old acquaintance wants to talk to him, but don't tell him who it is. I'd like to save that little surprise for myself."

Anne picked up the phone and dialed her father. "Dad? I hope I'm not taking you away from something important."

"No, Liebchen. I've always got time for you. Is something wrong?"

"There's someone here who wants to speak to you. I'll put him on." She handed Kris the phone.

"Von Kemp? This is Kristopher Falkenhorst."

There was a prolonged pause on the other end. The voice that finally answered sounded uncertain. "Is this some kind of joke?"

"It's no joke. Hannah and I have just been sitting here reminiscing about the good old days at the Central Works. Remember those, von Kemp? I've never forgotten them. Believe me. Not one day of my life since I left there."

"I don't know what you're talking about. You obviously have me confused with someone else. Who is this, really?"

"I told you who it was. Kristopher Falkenhorst. Don't you remember the Falkenhorsts? You were so fond of my father, Paul Falkenhorst. He was your spiritual leader. Remember?"

Kris heard a sharp intake of breath. "Let me talk to my daughter."

"She's admitted everything, so don't bother to lie. She made up some cock-and-bull story about you working for the Allies during the war. I don't believe a word of it, but I told her I'd listen to you before I go to the authorities, so if you've got someone there that can verify your story, I strongly suggest you and he meet me in your office in one hour, and if you won't, I'll be there myself with some FBI agents."

He handed the phone back to Anne.

"Dad? Oh, Dad, I'm so sorry. Somehow Kristopher found out about you, and I had to tell him the truth to keep him from rushing out of here and doing something crazy. Can you and Ed meet us right away in your office?"

There was a pause on the other end, and Anne could hear her father gasping.

"Dad!" she cried. "Dad, are you okay?"

"What's wrong?" Kris asked.

"Something's happened to him!"

"What do you mean?" He grabbed the phone and shouted into it. "Von Kemp? Dietrick?"

There was no answer, only the rasping sounds of someone's labored breathing near the receiver.

"Either he's faking, or he's in trouble," Kris said.

Anne grabbed the phone. "Are you okay, Dad? Dad?"

When she got no answer, she jammed the receiver down. "I've got to get over there immediately. Something's happened to him."

"I'll follow you," Kris said.

Anne gave him a look of raw hate. "Don't you come anywhere near him," she hurled at him. "If he dies, I'll never forgive you. Never!"

34

They had just loaded von Kemp's gurney into an ambulance when Anne and Kris drove up to the NASA headquarters. Anne jumped out and had a few quick words with one of the ambulance drivers, then climbed back into her car and began following the ambulance with Kris close behind.

When they arrived at Houston General, Anne left her car with an attendant and raced into the emergency room behind her father's gurney. Kris drove into the lot and gave his car to another attendant, then went into the emergency waiting room. He asked the nurse if he could go into the emergency room, but was told he couldn't unless he was family, so he sat there for about two hours until the desk nurse finally told him that von Kemp had been taken for some tests and would most likely be admitted.

Kris went back and sat down just as Anne came into the waiting room, her face drawn and red from crying. She refused to even acknowledge his presence as she took a seat across the room from him. Somehow, as he watched her anguish, it seemed like a hollow victory to think of von Kemp possibly dying just a few feet from where he sat. He thought about what she'd told him about her father's collaboration with the Allies during the war, and of their having brought him here under another name, and it troubled him. What if she were telling the truth? What if von Kemp really had been working for the Allies? How else could he have gotten here if he hadn't had some kind of leverage?

He searched his mind to see if there was any way he could have been wrong in his judgment of the man, and was forced to recall some of the more humane things he'd done: getting his parents to the infirmary when they had first gotten so ill, visiting them there almost daily, getting his father an easier job after he'd gotten out of the infirmary, and then letting Kris work on the grounds of the estate in order to keep him out of the tunnels. But then, in his mind's eye, he saw von Kemp standing on that train platform while his father was being herded into that boxcar, and it wiped out any good he may have done for Kristopher's family.

He kept glancing over at Anne, but she never once looked at him. Her gaze remained rigidly fixed on her folded hands in her lap. He wanted to say something, but she was making it abundantly clear that she wanted nothing to do with him.

He finally stood and was about to leave when two men came rushing in. With a little cry, Anne jumped up and threw her arms around the younger of the two, a well-built, good-looking man of about forty-five, with prematurely gray hair. He held her tightly in his arms, and all the tears she had bottled up came rushing out against his chest.

"There, there," he soothed, patting her on the back. "Everything's going to be okay. Art's a tough old bird, and he's pulled through this before. You just gotta have faith, Annie."

Her tears finally subsided, and the man gave her his handkerchief. She wiped her face with it, then handed it back. The other man spotted Kris, and assuming that he was with Anne, stuck out his hand.

"I'm Zeke Anders," he said. "Are you a friend of Anne's?"

Kris took the man's hand. "I'm Kris Falk."

The man who had been holding Anne also came over to him and shook his hand. "I'm Jack Hendren. Sure glad Annie's had someone with her." He turned back to Anne. "We just heard about it, or we'd have been here sooner. Have you heard anything yet?"

Anne sniffled back her tears. "No. The nurse said it would be several hours before they know how bad it is."

"Does anyone know what happened?"

265

Anne nodded toward Kris. "He does. Why don't you ask him?"

Zeke gave Anne a puzzled look, then turned to Kris. "What's going on? What happened?"

Kris gave Anne a questioning look. "Do you want me to tell these men everything?"

"Go ahead. They both know the truth."

A frown creased Hendren's brow. "The truth about what? What are you two talking about?"

"Mr. Falk was in one of the labor camps Dad administered during the war, and he blames him for the deaths of his family. Somehow he found out about Dad being at NASA and came down to my gallery and made all kinds of wild accusations, then made me get Dad on the phone and threatened him." The tears started again. "And Dad's heart simply couldn't take it."

Both men turned on Kris. "But didn't you tell him the whole story?" Anders asked.

"Yes, but he wouldn't believe me."

"Wait a minute," Kris said, the hackles beginning to rise on the back of his neck. "Wait just a damn minute! I don't know whether von Kemp was working for you guys during the war, or not, but I know some things about his activities at the Central Works that I'm sure you don't know."

"Like what?" Anders challenged.

Kris bristled. "Where do you think all those bodies came from that were stacked in the tunnels when you Americans got there? He was responsible for much of that. He may not have killed them himself, but he was in charge when they were being beaten and shot and starved to death, and he didn't do a thing to stop it. And he worked the prisoners until they dropped dead, only giving them enough food to keep them barely alive. But as far as I'm personally concerned, I hold him responsible for not getting my family released when my father was the minister of the church he'd gone to for years, and he knew we had no business being in that camp. Is that enough, or do you want me to go on?"

"Mr. Falk," Hendren said coldly, "Otto von Kemp—or Arthur Dietrick as we prefer to call him—worked as an informant for the Allies all during the war. His efforts on our behalf cut down Germany's war capabilities—especially with the V-2 rocket—by at least six months, and saved thousands of lives. It was information from him that enabled us to bomb Peenemunde in August of 1943, and even before we entered the war he gave the British consul in Oslo some of Germany's top secrets regarding their missile research."

Anders cut in, "Those Oslo papers were the first inkling we had about what Hitler was up to with his aerial weapons, and even though von Kemp was pretty sure the Nazis had begun to suspect him in the fall of 1944, he continued to feed us information about the V-1s and the V-2s. Our government intended for him to come to America when the war ended, but the Russians captured him before he could get to us. After he escaped from them, and the decision was made to change his identity, it was to protect him from the Nazis and Russians—and people like you."

Kris felt the blood begin to drain from his face.

"As for von Kemp not helping your family get out of Juno," Hendren added, "that's unfortunate, but SS General Kammler was sent to the Central Works with the express purpose of trying to catch him doing something wrong, and I'm sure he must've felt that demanding your release would have jeopardized his position there. As harsh as it may sound to you, his work for us was more important than the lives of one family."

"And as for the other crimes you've accused him of," Anders put in, "I'm sure there were things he was forced to do to avoid blowing his cover, but in the final scheme of things, the good he did us—then and now—more than mitigates that. As far as we're concerned, Arthur Dietrick is a respected member of our team with a long list of proven credentials, and there's no way we're going to let someone like you bring him down. Do I make myself perfectly clear?"

Kris took note of the threat as his gaze moved frostily from one man to the other. "I get the message," he said.

"I thought you would," Hendren replied testily, "but just so we understand each other, let me make it crystal clear. If you intend to stir things up about this, all you're going to do is make a whole lot of trouble for yourself, and there's no way you can win. I guarantee you that."

Kris gave him a stony glare. "You should be careful when you're threatening an attorney, especially when you're defending someone like von Kemp. It may come back to haunt you."

"I'm not worried about that," Hendren replied. "Dietrick's work speaks for itself, but as an attorney myself, I think you've forgotten that there are none of us alive who didn't do things we wish we hadn't when we were younger, but we don't judge a man's worth by an isolated period of his life over which he had no control. We judge him for the whole gambit, and—believe me—Dietrick has more than made up for anything he may have done under pressure in a time of war."

Anne had been glaring at Kris, and now she said accusingly, "If I recall, Kristopher, you have some things in your own past that you shouldn't be too proud of. Didn't you used to beat up on defenseless old Jews and destroy their property and strut around bragging that Hitler was Germany's savior? Before you start throwing stones at others, you'd better take a good look at your own past."

He whipped his head in her direction. "I've more than paid for my mistakes, believe me."

"And so has my father!"

Kris shrugged dismissively, "Well, I'm not going to stand here and defend myself to you. I'm not the one on trial here. Your father is."

"Only because you've decided to be his judge and jury," she retorted icily. "I wonder what your mother and father would feel about how you've turned out. I think they'd be ashamed of you. I only hope you can live with what a bitter human being you've turned in to. It makes me sick to my stomach."

He regarded her soberly. "I don't expect you to understand, but I am sorry for the pain this has caused you personally. I know you aren't responsible for what your father did."

They looked at each other, hard and fast, then Kris turned to Hendren and Anders. "I intend to check all this out with your superiors, but I assure you men that what you've told me will remain in strictest confidence until then. Now, if you'll all excuse me, I think it's time for me to leave."

He started for the door, but turned back to Anne. "Whatever happened to the real Arthur Dietrick?"

"He gave his life to save ours."

Kris let out a caustic little laugh. "Sounds like what my father used to say about Jesus."

⊞ ⊞

Kris got into his car and started driving, not knowing where he was headed, until he suddenly saw that he was entering the Port of Galveston. He drove his Corvette down to a deserted strip of beach, parked it, and got out. He took off his loafers and socks and put them in the seat, then rolled up his pantlegs. The feel of sand under his feet, and the smell of the sea suddenly made him homesick.

As he walked, he thought back over the years of bitterness and rage toward von Kemp, and now, apparently, it had all been for nothing. The man he'd spent all that negative emotion on had just been a man trying to walk a thin line between his conscience and his career, and Kris and his family had gotten caught in the middle.

He kicked at a small piece of driftwood, and it went skittering across the wet sand. Hannah was right. How could he honestly judge what was in another man's heart when his own was so full of bitterness?

A cool breeze tugged at him as he walked along, and he found himself thinking about his father, and it brought the sting of tears to his eyes. Oh, how he wished he were still alive. He always had some wise insight that others didn't have. But even as Kris thought about him now, he knew what his father would be telling him: "If you want forgiveness, you need to be willing to give it."

He stooped and picked up a small stone and ran his fingers over its smooth surface, then angrily flung it far out into the surf and started back toward his car. Hannah's scathing accusations and then the revelations about von Kemp's work for the Allies had made him take a good look at himself, and he didn't like what he saw. He had spent years blaming von Kemp for all the things that had gone wrong in his life, when the man had obviously had nothing to do with it, and now he saw that his father had been right all along when he told him that if he ever wanted any inner peace, he would have to let go of his rage toward von Kemp and forgive him.

It had been years since he'd tried to pray, and he wasn't sure if God would even listen to him, but a sudden rush of tears came to his eyes, and he found himself on his knees in the sand, pouring out his pain to God and asking His forgiveness, not only for the hate he'd had for von Kemp, but for all the years he'd gone his own way and done his own thing with little thought for God and what He might want from him.

He didn't know how long he knelt there, but he was emotionally spent when he finally stood and headed for his car. Something had just happened to him, and he wasn't sure what it was, but after years of being so weighed down with bitterness, he suddenly felt light-hearted and clean. Maybe God hadn't given up on him after all!

35

By the time Kris got to his hotel, he knew that a weight had truly been lifted from him. Regardless of whether von Kemp had wittingly or unwittingly caused much of Kris's grief, the man had suffered for what he'd done, and there was no more need to exact any payment from him. It was time to let it go and get on with his life.

He began by calling the hospital to see how von Kemp was. They told him he was holding his own, and the prognosis looked good. He ordered some flowers to be sent to his room with a note that read, "Please forgive me, if you can. Kristopher Falkenhorst."

He called Bud Perry and told him he'd been wrong about von Kemp and Dietrick and asked him to forget the whole thing. He said he was satisfied that Dietrick was not von Kemp, apologized for acting like a crazy lunatic, thanked him profusely for all the time and help he'd put into this for him, and hung up feeling somewhat better.

All that was left was making amends with Hannah, but he honestly didn't know what to do. She was so angry at him that he felt it might be too difficult right now to try and contact her. He'd wait a few days and see how von Kemp did, then he'd write and ask her forgiveness. He could only hope that she'd give it.

It was nine p.m. and he realized he hadn't eaten since breakfast. He went down to the hotel restaurant and ordered a steak. As he sat there in the dim light of the plush Diamond Jim Brady Room, looking around at all the couples enjoying each other's company, he was suddenly conscious of how alone he really was. He missed not having someone special to love. He knew he had no one to blame but himself, but that didn't make it any easier. He ate slowly, then sat nursing a cognac, listening to the music from a harpist in a corner of the room. At around ten thirty he went back up to his room and turned the TV on. He was about a half hour into a rerun of an old western, when his phone rang. He was startled to hear Hannah's voice when he picked up the receiver.

"Hannah! How did you know I was staying here?"

"I called several hotels."

His pulse quickened. "Is your father okay?"

"Yes. He's doing much better, and the doctors say he's going to pull through."

He let out a sigh of relief. "I'm really glad to hear that. I honestly am. I hope you believe me."

There was a pause on the other end, then she said, "I do, but Opa asked me to see if you'd come by the hospital before you leave town. He has something he needs to tell you. Would you be willing to stop by in the morning?"

Kris was taken aback. "Well, yes, if you don't think it would upset him too much."

"It won't. Would ten o'clock be okay?"

"Sure," he said, then added tentatively, "I'd like to see you, too, Hannah. Will you be there?"

She didn't answer immediately, and he thought she had hung up, until she said softly, "Do you have a few minutes right now?"

"Well, sure," he said, a little surprised. "Do you want to come over here? I'm in room 503."

"I'm downstairs in the lobby. I can come right up."

"Fine," he said, then stood looking at the silent receiver as she hung up. What was so urgent that she needed to see him immediately? Now that his business with von Kemp was settled, he wasn't sure how much more he wanted to involve himself with this family, but it was too late now, so he quickly straightened up the room and sat down to wait.

When she knocked, he found himself a little apprehensive as he went to the door. Seeing her standing there in a long ivory jacket and matching pants tucked into brown lizard boots, her dark hair pulled back severely into a ponytail, he thought he had never seen anyone so lovely.

"Come in, please," he said, stepping back.

"Hello, Kristopher," she replied, her voice devoid of the bitterness that had been there when he'd seen her at the hospital.

"Would you like me to order something to drink?"

She shook her head. "No, thanks. I won't be here that long."

He motioned her to the sofa. "I'm glad you came over," he said. "All evening I've wanted to call you, but I wasn't sure you wanted to hear from me. I'm just glad you've given me this chance to tell you in person that I believe what you and your NASA friends have told me about your father, and I have no intention of pursuing this thing any further. As far as I'm concerned, your father did what he thought he had to to protect himself and you and your mother. I'm just glad that we can put it all behind us now and get on with our lives."

Anne stared down at her clasped hands. "I'm afraid we can't do that yet," she said.

Kris felt his throat tighten. "Why?"

She was quiet for a moment, then seemed to find her courage as she looked up at him. "There isn't an easy way to tell you this, Kristopher, so I might as well just come out with it. I got pregnant that night we made love in the summerhouse, but I didn't know it until after we left the Central Works. You're Nik's father. His real father."

Kris looked like he'd just been kicked in the stomach. "I don't believe it!"

"I'd never lie about something like this. You should know me well enough to know that."

He lowered himself next to her on the sofa and took her hands in his. "Oh, Hannah! What did I do to you? Dear God, what did I do?"

"You gave me the most wonderful son any woman could ever have, and I've never regretted it for one moment."

"Does Nik know?"

She shook her head. "I told him about Dad, but I didn't have the courage to tell him about you. He still thinks his father was a German officer. I've wanted to tell him the truth for years, but now that he knows Dad's going to be okay—and you're not out to destroy him anymore—I think it'll be easier for him to accept you." She paused, then plunged ahead with the question she'd been dreading, "Do you want him to know that you're his father?"

Kris was silent for a moment, then stood up and looked down at her. "I don't know. This will change all our lives. Are we all ready for that?"

Anne stood up beside him. "I've had twenty-five years to think about it, but I know it comes as a shock to you. If you're not ready to take this on, we can just let things go on as they are. Nik is happy—especially now that he knows Opa's going to be okay. It's up to you. Are you ready to be a father to a twenty-four-year-old man who didn't even know you existed until a month ago?"

Kris tried to speak, but a rush came to his eyes, and he could barely find his voice. "I had a little girl, once, who was my whole life, but she was killed when she was barely three. I never thought I'd ever have another child of my own, but this scares me to death. I don't know if I'm ready to give my love to Nik or not. I'm going to have to do a lot of thinking about this."

Anne put her hand on his arm. "Regardless of what you decide, I hope we can renew our friendship."

He reached out and wiped away a single tear that had escaped down her cheek. "I think I'd like that, Hannah, but I just need a little time to digest all this."

She looked down, hoping the rest of her tears would not break loose. "There's never been a day in the past twenty-four years that I haven't thought of you." she said. "Nik's a constant reminder of that boy I fell in love with so many years ago."

"How could you have loved me, as screwed up as I was?"

She met his eyes boldly, as if she'd prepared for a long time to tell him this. "I told you once that I would always love you, and I've never loved anyone else."

He started to speak, but she reached up and gently touched his lips with her finger. "I'll see you in the morning," she said, then turned and went out before he could say anything more.

36

As Kris walked down the long, white corridor to von Kemp's hospital room the next morning, he was filled with trepidation. What was it going to be like to finally see this man after all these years, especially now that everything had changed so drastically? Would von Kemp really forgive him, and could he forgive von Kemp? He wouldn't know till he saw him face to face.

He knocked softly on the door and Anne opened it. "Is it okay to come in?" he asked.

"Yes. Dad's expecting you."

Kris stepped into the room, and the fragrance of numerous bouquets assaulted him. He saw von Kemp in the bed, his eyes closed, and gave Anne a questioning glance, but she motioned for him to go over to the bed. Kris went to the old man's side and looked down at him. It was a shock to finally face this man who'd haunted so many of his nightmares, and even though the changes in his looks would have made it impossible to recognize him, it was a relief to see him for what he really was: a sick old man, white-haired, shriveled, and no longer a threat to anyone.

"Dad?" Anne said, shaking him gently. "Are you awake?"

He opened his eyes and looked up at her and then at Kris. "Yes. I was only praying for a few moments." His hand reached up toward Kris.

"Doctor," Kris said, taking the old man's frail hand, "I don't know how to tell you how sorry I am for what I've done to you. I wouldn't blame you if you never forgave me."

"I couldn't withhold my forgiveness even if I wanted to, Kristopher. Your father is the one who taught me to forgive."

"My father was a very wise man," Kris said. "I'm just sorry it took me so long to realize it."

"All these years, one of my great regrets is that I couldn't free all of you, but your father and I had talked about it more than once, and he understood the precarious position I was in."

"You don't have to explain it, sir. I know now that you would've helped if you could have."

The old man squeezed Kris's hand tightly, and shook his head. "No. I know your father would want me to tell you. When I first found out that all of you were in Juno, I went to Himmler and pleaded for your release, but he was in a rage over your uncle's participation in Hitler's assassination plot. As soon as I could, I told your father about my involvement with the Allies, and he prayed with me that God would keep me from being discovered, and I know those prayers were part of what saved my life."

He began to cough, and Kris and Anne both leaned over him anxiously. "You don't have to go on," Kris said. "I understand."

He waved his hand weakly at them. "No. It's been on my heart too long. I tried to save your mother, but she was too far gone by the time I discovered you were in the camp. Later, when Kammler was rounding up prisoners to ship to Auschwitz, both you and your father were earmarked to go, and I pleaded with him to spare both of you, but he refused me, then came back the next day and told me that for the right price, he'd save one of you. I told your father that I had to make a choice, and he insisted that he be the one to go."

Tears began to trickle down von Kemp's cheeks. "Your father was a beacon of light in all that darkness, and I know it was his prayers that brought my family through it. We all owe him our lives."

"Even in death, my father's life has rebuked me," Kris said. "What a disappointment I must've been to him."

Von Kemp raised his head up a few inches from the pillow, and grasped Kris's hand tightly. "Never!" he said. "He was the most forgiving man I ever knew, and what he'd want is for you to forgive yourself, Kristopher. Give him that one last gift."

☩ ☩

After leaving the hospital, Anne and Kris went to her house for lunch, and then spent the afternoon talking about their lives since they'd last seen each other. Kris told her about his failed marriage and the heartache of losing his precious little girl, and how he'd thrown himself into his law practice trying to dull the ache of losing everyone he'd ever loved.

Anne told him about the years after her family left the Central Works and how her father was captured by the Russians, and she and her mother didn't know whether he was dead or alive; then the joy of finding out that she was pregnant, and the adventure of reuniting with her father and coming to the United States.

They were both close to tears on more than one occasion. As the day wore on, Kris made the decision that he did want Nik to know he was his father, so Anne suggested that Kris should stay over another day, and she would ask Nik to fly down so they could tell him together. She offered him her guestroom for the night, but he declined. By this time, so much emotion had been stirred up in him, he wasn't sure he could trust himself, so he went back to his hotel.

The next day, Kris was filled with more than a little trepidation as he and Anne went to the airport to pick up Nik. This boy was his son, a young man he'd liked very much that one time he'd met him, but would Nik understand about the way he'd been conceived? Would he accept Kris as his father and let him become a part of his life? Did Kris even want the responsibility of being part of his life?

Kris had no answers to any of these questions. He'd just have to take things one step at a time, but there was no getting away from the fact that things would never be the same for any of them once the news was out. All their lives had become inextricably woven together, and the ramifications of that had Kris feeling very unsure of himself—something that was new to him.

They spotted Nik standing in front of the Delta terminal and Kris pulled Anne's car over to the curb. Nik started toward the car, then paused when he saw Kris Falk get out of it, followed by his mother. Kris stuck his hand out to the young man, and Nik tentatively shook it, then gave his mom a quick hug and whispered, "What's he doing here? What's going on?"

"I asked him to come," she said, turning back to Kris.

"You didn't tell me you knew him when I told you about my interview with him. Why?"

"I didn't know then that the Kris Falk you talked to was Kristopher Falkenhorst, a boy I'd grown up with in Berlin. I didn't find that out till Kris came down here a few days ago to interview Opa, but then Opa ended up in the hospital, and that's where Kris and I saw each other and recognized that we were old friends from our Berlin days."

Nik gave his mother a questioning look. "Does he know about Opa?"

Anne nodded. "Yes, they had a wonderful talk at the hospital yesterday."

Nik turned to Kris. "So you're cool with Opa now? He wasn't the guy you were looking for?"

"I'm cool with him," Kris said. "And, no, he wasn't the guy I was looking for. We didn't get to do much talking yesterday, but there'll be plenty of time for us to get reacquainted in the future. I have a feeling I'll be spending a lot more time in Houston."

Nik gave him a quizzical look. "Any particular reason why?"

Kris let out a little laugh. "Well, I've got friends here now, and . . . I love this climate."

Nik cocked his head to one side and his brows went up. "Now I know there's something fishy going on. Nobody loves this climate."

They tossed Nik's backpack into the trunk of Anne's car, and headed toward the hospital. Von Kemp was out of the room undergoing some tests when they got there. "I've got lunch set up at my house," Anne said, "so why don't we go there, and we'll come back this evening? Opa's so excited that you'd come down again so soon, Nik." She grinned at him. "I think he faked the heart attack just to get you here."

✠ ✠

The maid had set up their lunch on the back patio overlooking the swimming pool. Three yellow ceramic plates were piled high with a chicken salad, and a basket of hot biscuits sat next to a centerpiece of yellow and white tulips. The Casablanca fan above the table made a soft whooshing sound as it stirred the muggy air.

During the meal, Kris told Nik the whole story about his years in the camp. He told him how he'd blamed von Kemp for everything that had happened to him and his family, and how he'd just learned yesterday from von Kemp about his secret work for the Allies during the war and his part in keeping Kris from being shipped to Auschwitz. The talk was hard on all of them, and there were more than a few tears.

When they'd finished eating, and the maid had cleared the table, they settled back in their chairs, emotionally drained. Anne and Kris had decided that Anne would take the lead in breaking the news to Nik that Kris was his father, so she leaned over and took Nik's hand in hers. "There's one very important thing that we left out of our story," she said, glancing anxiously at Kris. "Perhaps the hardest part."

Nik gave her a puzzled look. "What?"

"Kristopher and I made love just before the Americans liberated the camp, and …" Her voice began to falter, "and I got pregnant. Kristopher didn't know it until I told him yesterday." She took a deep breath and plunged on. "Kristopher is your father, Nik."

He jerked his hand from hers. "What?" he exclaimed. He glared over at Kris then back to his mother. "I don't believe you! You've always told me my father was a German soldier who was killed during the war. Was that a lie?"

280

"I had to make that up to protect us both," she said. "You don't know how it was back then."

Seeing tears begin to fill her eyes, the anger went out of Nik, and he reached over and took her hand again. "Don't cry, Mutti. I never really believed in my phantom father anyway. Opa is all the father I ever needed—or wanted."

Kris had sat there uneasily, not sure where to jump into this, then leaned over and clamped his hand on Nik's shoulder. "Well, like it or not, it looks like you're stuck with one more father," he told Nik, "but let's just take things one step at a time and see how it sits with all of us. Okay?" He glanced over at Anne with a little shrug. "Who knows? My father would probably have said this is the way things were supposed to work out. He tended to see God's hand in everything."

"Your father was a very wise man," Anne replied.

ABOUT THE AUTHOR

Jan Houghton Lindsey

Jan Lindsey's interest in World War II started shortly after the war ended in 1945, and she was given the name of a young German girl who was looking for an American pen pal. That correspondence began her lifelong interest in the war.

Jan grew up on the Yakima Indian Reservation in central Washington State, and was very active at White Swan High School with sports, cheerleading, choir, school plays, newspaper and the National Honor Society. In her senior year, she was selected to represent her high school at Girls' State where she was elected Governor and chosen to represent Washington State at Girls' Nation in Washington, D.C.

After graduating from Yakima Valley Junior College and Whitworth College in Spokane, Washington, she taught history and English for a few years, then joined the staff of Campus Crusade, an international organization offering spiritual counseling to college students around the world. Her assignments took her to Oklahoma University, Southern Methodist University, UCLA, and Smith College.

In 1960, she married Hal Lindsey and they continued their work with Campus Crusade, then left the staff and began writing books. Hal's first book, *The Late Great Planet Earth*, became an international bestseller, followed by additional bestsellers over the next few years. Jan collaborated with him on several of his books.

She eventually went back to teaching in Southern California and spent the next thirty-five years writing the book about World War II that you hold in your hand.

CPSIA information can be obtained at www.ICGtesting.com
Printed in the USA
BVOW010821130313

315417BV00010B/152/P